bright

BETHANY FRENETTE

HYPERION
NEW YORK

First Edition

1 3 5 7 9 10 8 6 4 2

Printed in the United States of America

G475-5664-5-13349

This book is set in Garamond Premier Pro.

Library of Congress Cataloging-in-Publication Data
Frenette, Bethany.
Burn bright : a Dark star novel / Bethany Frenette.—First edition.
    pages cm
Summary: "Drawn into the battle against the Harrowers, Audrey Whitticomb
    must find the Remnant, a Kin girl with enough power to unleash the
demons that were trapped Beneath. But discovering the girl's identity may
    be a task Audrey's not ready to face"—Provided by publisher.
ISBN 978-1-4231-4666-7
[1. Supernatural—Fiction.   2. Psychic ability—Fiction.   3. Demonology—Fiction.
    4. Mothers and daughters—Fiction.   5. Superheroes—Fiction.]   I. Title.
PZ7.F889345Bur 2013
    [Fic]—dc23   2013001576

Reinforced binding

Visit www.un-requiredreading.com

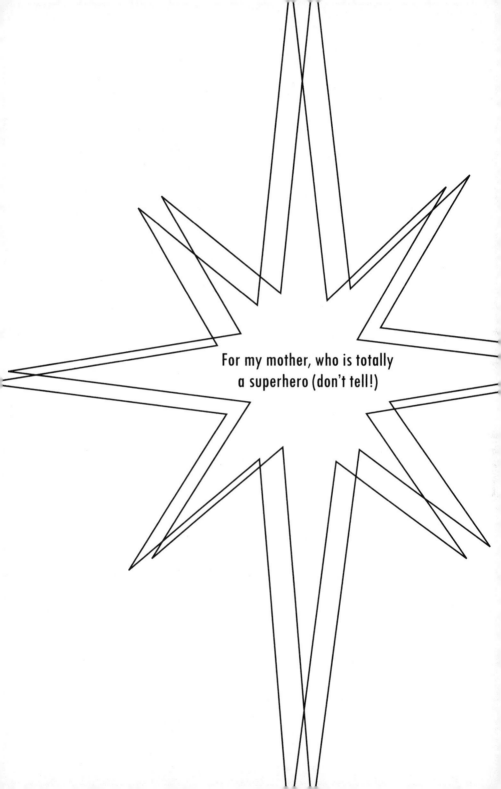

For my mother, who is totally
a superhero (don't tell!)

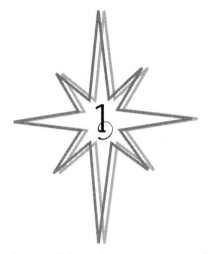

The girl in the golden dress was a demon.

She didn't look like one. Not at first glance. She looked human, with long red hair that spilled down her shoulders, the curve of a smile upon her face, the dark ink of a tattoo circling one wrist. Her eyes were closed. She danced alone. Her movements were slow, languid, not in time to the music, but that wasn't what gave her away, either. Watching her, I simply Knew.

I shouldn't have been surprised. I was aware that there were neutral demons living within the Cities—Harrowers who coexisted with humans, more interested in minding their own business than in raining destruction upon the land. I just didn't encounter them often.

But, really, if I'd wanted to avoid demons, it probably would've been a good idea to steer clear of the Drought and Deluge, the club downtown that happened to be owned by one.

Not that I'd been given much choice in the matter of my attendance. My friend Tink had spent the past two days badgering me into accompanying her to the Drought and Deluge, countering every argument I came up with.

"That was *months* ago," she'd said earlier, after I'd pointed out that we'd both had less than pleasant run-ins with demons in the alley behind the club.

"And my mom specifically forbade me from going there," I'd added.

"New year, new rules," Tink had declared. "It's a parenting law. Look it up."

"She said, 'Not until the earth collides with Mars.'"

"She did not."

"She may as well have," I'd replied. "She had a very serious look."

"Unless she started shooting lasers from her eyeballs, I am unimpressed."

It was a rare person who could out-stubborn Tink. I usually just gave in. And that particular afternoon, she'd had extra leverage. For the first time in her life—after leaving a steady stream of crushed hopes and trampled hearts in her wake—Tink had been dumped.

"For a *freshman*," she'd moaned, as though this were the worst offense in the history of the planet, if not the universe. "He dumped me for a freshman!"

Instead of bringing up the fact that we'd been freshmen

ourselves a mere two years ago, I'd found myself agreeing to spend the weekend helping Tink prove that she didn't actually care that she'd been—in her words—tossed aside for a younger woman. Which was how I ended up at the Drought and Deluge that night, seated at a table with my best friend, Gideon, while Tink demonstrated her lack of concern by dancing to every song.

We'd been at the club maybe an hour when I noticed the demon. At the far edge of the dance floor, a glimmer of light touched her dress. She tilted her head as she swayed. Red curls slid along the slope of her shoulders. The space around her seemed to shiver, and a jolt of Knowing shot through me.

Harrower.

I went still. Uneasiness welled up within me, even as I told myself there was no cause for panic. After all, the Harrower wasn't threatening anyone. She wasn't attacking. No one spoke to her; no one approached her or brushed against her as she danced. For the most part, she ignored her surroundings. She was likely neutral.

But then again: she might not be.

I bit my lip, considering my options. My best bet was probably to locate Shane, the owner of the Drought and Deluge. He must know other Harrowers in the Cities. Maybe this girl was a friend of his. Maybe she came here all the time. Maybe they had parties where all the neutral demons got together and discussed how much they didn't want to bring about the utter annihilation of the Kin, and all of that *left behind in a realm of endless torment and despair* stuff was just water under the bridge.

At the very least, maybe Shane knew if she was dangerous.

But I hadn't seen him in the club that evening, and I didn't want to draw attention to myself by seeking him out.

I thought of calling Leon, my Guardian and sort-of boyfriend. He'd know how to handle the situation. Unfortunately, the number one problem with dating your mother's sidekick? It meant you were dating your mother's sidekick. At that moment, Leon was somewhere out in the night, patrolling, performing daring deeds—or so I assumed—and doing everything he could to keep the Cities safe. With Mom. And if I called to ask whether or not the demon in the slinky gold dress was likely to start slaughtering people all over the dance floor, he'd *tell* Mom. When it came to matters of safety, Leon was Guardian first and sort-of boyfriend second. The seriousness with which he took his responsibilities landed somewhere in the middle of *annoying* and *endearing*—and also ruled him out.

Since calling my grandmother to ask for her opinion of the situation would have been an even worse idea, and my cousin Elspeth was out of the country, that left—me. My own sense and intuition and Knowing. I'd have to decide on my own whether or not this girl was a threat.

I turned toward the Harrower, studying her. She was swaying, hugging her arms against her. There was no hint of what lay beneath the human skin she wore. Beyond the certain, insistent knowledge that she *was* a demon, I couldn't get any sense from her, at all.

Frustrated, I elbowed Gideon to get his attention. He grumbled a complaint, but dutifully turned to me. I gestured to the dance floor.

He gave me a curious look. "Do we know her? Who is she?"

"Not who. What." I lowered my voice. *"Demon."*

He twisted around, gazing across the length of the room. The girl's back was to us now. In the semidark, she was nothing but a slender form, a dress and a shadow and the fall of red hair. Human. Harmless.

Gideon's brow wrinkled. "Should we do something?"

"Like what? She's probably neutral. I mean, she's not hurting anyone. She's just..."

"Dancing creepily to music only she can hear?"

"If awkward dancing was an indication of evil, we'd be surrounded by serial killers."

"Can we at least relocate Operation Pity Party?" Gideon asked. He dropped his voice to a whisper. "Neutral or not, I'd sort of like to keep my evening demon-free."

"Agreed." That was for the best, I thought. While some Harrowers might attack without discretion, most didn't concern themselves with normal humans. It was the Kin that they hated, the Kin that they hunted. If anyone in the club was in danger, it was Tink or me. I hopped to my feet. "I'll fetch Tink."

To my surprise, she didn't put up a fight about leaving. She only shrugged, claimed she was bored anyway, and headed to our table.

"Greg isn't even here with his freshman," she lamented.

"I thought you didn't care about that," Gideon said.

"I don't. But what's the point in not caring if he's not here to see it?" She whirled about and hurried toward the door.

"I will never understand that girl," Gideon said, shaking his head.

I patted his shoulder. "I'd worry if you did."

We moved to follow her, slipping past crowded tables and harassed-looking waiters. When we reached the door, I swung back, giving the room one final search, in case Shane had appeared. My gaze swept over the dance floor, then to the booths and the bar. Beyond the restrooms, a hallway curved back toward the alley. On one wall, beneath the club's name, a mural was painted: the Minneapolis skyline, outlined in white, red stars burning all around it. I didn't see Shane.

But something else caught my attention. On the dance floor, the girl had stopped swaying. She stood perfectly still, her hands clasped, her eyes closed. Smiling.

Unnerved, I turned away.

Outside, a crisp wind was blowing. It was the middle of February, and though the afternoon had been warm enough for rain, the evening proved much colder. The temperature had dropped significantly in the past hour, coating everything with a thin layer of ice. Sidewalks and streetlamps glistened. Snow flurries turned gold in the lights of downtown traffic.

Tink announced a need for fresh air, so we didn't bother taking the skyway. Instead, we hurried the several blocks between the club and the parking ramp where we'd left Gideon's car, our breath fogging before us. We made good time, in spite of the fact that Gideon—who hated competing for parking—always chose the farthest ramp possible. He shouldn't have worried; traffic was sparse for a Friday night, and the ramp was all but deserted.

"If the car is frozen shut again," Tink said as we reached the elevators, "someone else is in charge of getting it open, because I am not crawling in through the trunk in this dress. I don't care what you bribe me with."

Since Tink was barely five feet tall and the approximate width of a Q-tip, she was the natural choice for trunk duty. Last time, Gideon had bribed her with the money remaining on a Target gift card—but Tink had been wearing jeans and a sweater then, not a black dress so short we saw her underwear every time she bent over. And her coat and gloves offered little in the way of protection. Her legs were completely bare. Considering how cold it was, I wondered how she hadn't yet transformed into a human icicle.

"I guess we'll just have to chisel our way in like normal people," Gideon said.

"Or we could blackmail her," I suggested.

Tink rolled her eyes. "Like you could. You have nothing good on me, and Gideon doesn't scare me."

"Hey," he said, sounding wounded.

I laughed. Gideon was cursed with kindness. He had no

temper to speak of and could hold a grudge about as long as he could hold his breath. Scary he wasn't. "That's what you get for being so nice all the time," I told him.

"No," Tink countered. "That's what he gets for having no backbone. He can't blackmail me, because he knows I'd tell Brooke about how he spends all of History imagining her naked."

This was an old argument between them. Tink thought Gideon should try asking out his longtime crush, Brooke Oliver, instead of fleeing in the opposite direction whenever she approached. He wasn't normally shy, so I couldn't understand it—but I'd also learned that Brooke was the one topic able to bring about his rare moments of ire.

He didn't respond to Tink. His nose and cheeks had already been reddened by the wind, and now the rest of his face followed suit. Giving her a disgusted glare, he stepped out of the elevator and headed for the car.

I turned to Tink. "You are diabolical."

She beamed. "I know."

We hurried after Gideon, who had jogged halfway to the car. Around us, the parking ramp was quiet, nearly empty. The few nearby cars were dark, their windshields glistening with frost. A truck with a flat tire and a rusty bumper drove toward the exit. Ahead, Gideon halted, standing beside his car with one hand on the door.

"Is it really frozen shut?" I called, quickening my pace.

Gideon lifted his other hand, waving me away. I felt a prickle of alarm, but it wasn't until I'd almost reached him that I understood why. Two steps from the car, I stopped short.

We weren't alone.

The Harrowers had been waiting for us.

"Oh, God," Tink breathed, skidding to a halt beside me. She clutched at my arm, her grip painfully tight. We stared, frozen where we stood. In the abrupt silence, my heartbeat was loud in my ears.

The demons had been hidden from view by the ramp's concrete pillars, but I saw them now. There were four of them. The first appeared to be a boy about our age, standing with arms crossed, one foot propped against the bumper of Gideon's car. He was as tall and skinny as Leon, with black hair and dark brown skin. A tattoo snaked around his left wrist. He wore only a thin blue T-shirt and a pair of jeans with a hole in one knee. I couldn't see his face.

The other three were on motorcycles: a scrawny blond guy with a leather jacket and a pierced lip, and two burly white men who looked like escapees from a prison film. Or maybe just from prison, period.

Except that these weren't men. I didn't need a Knowing to tell me that. Their human forms were imperfect. Beneath their blank eyes, wide grins revealed teeth that were jagged and red.

Gideon took a short step backward, releasing his grip on the car door. "Can I help you?" he asked. His voice was calm, polite, but his hands were clenched at his sides, and his face had gone very pale. He flicked a glance at Tink and me. "We don't want any trouble."

One of the demons on the motorcycles let out a gasp of laughter.

"Won't be trouble," another said. His voice was gruff, abrasive. "Not much, anyway."

Tink continued tugging at my arm. "This is bad. We can't fight four of them."

"I don't want to fight *any* of them," I whispered back. I'd been in martial arts since I was eight, and for the past two months Leon had been training me in the specific ways Guardians fought demons—but without Guardian powers, my abilities were limited. While I might be able to hold my own against one demon, four was out of the question. And Gideon and Tink had no training at all.

"We have to do *something*," Tink said. She released my arm and stepped forward, calling out, "You really want to mess with Morning Star's daughter? Isn't that sort of like wearing a giant neon sign that says *Come kick my ass?*"

That earned us more laughter—not a particularly reassuring sound.

I yanked her back to my side. "Uh, Tink? How about we don't provoke the freaky demonic biker gang?"

"I'm trying to scare them off!" she hissed. "You have a better idea?"

Actually, I did. I pulled off my gloves and fumbled in my coat pocket for my phone.

Immediately, the Harrower nearest to Gideon's car turned to face me.

"You," he said.

I paused. My gaze locked with his.

"I want to see your hands," he told me. Though his words were soft, the sound carried. His voice was rich, melodic, not what I expected to hear from a Harrower. And, unlike the others, he looked entirely human. There was no ripple of scales to betray him. Brown eyes watched me, narrowed and intent. When he spoke, I saw the gleam of neat white teeth. "Show them to me."

"Do I really look like I'm armed?" I retorted.

"Now."

I didn't move. I didn't get the chance. Knowing jolted through me once more. I felt a sensation like a cool breath on the back of my neck. Sudden dread crawled up my skin. I heard the loud, echoing tap-tap of heels on concrete.

And then, from behind me, another voice spoke. "Can't have you calling Mommy."

I spun about.

The demon approached leisurely, a slow smile spreading across her face. The gold of her dress was dulled by shadow. Her long hair was tousled by the wind.

"Hands, if you please," she said, raising her own in front of her, showing the tattoo at her wrist. "We value our privacy."

I glanced around me. The ramp felt bare, nothing but dark spaces and empty cars and a thin dusting of snow. Not that it mattered, I supposed; humans couldn't help us. And Harrowers had the ability to cloud the senses. Someone might drive right past us without even seeing.

Taking a shaky breath, I withdrew my hands from my pockets and held them before me. "Okay?"

The girl halted her advance, tapping a finger against her lips, a glimmer of gold on red. Her nail polish matched her dress. For a long moment, she stared at me, not speaking. Then, faster than I would have thought possible, she was beside me. She reached into my pocket and pulled out my phone. Before I could react, she threw it to the ground and kicked it beneath Gideon's car.

Then she retreated a few steps and set her hands on her hips. "That's better. I dislike interruptions."

"That was sort of expensive," I said.

"Not your biggest problem."

Or yours, I thought. I hadn't been planning to call Mom; I'd been planning to call Leon. And I didn't necessarily need a phone to do that. Leon was my Guardian. He could sense when I was in danger. This was usually the part where he'd teleport in out of nowhere to save the day. As much as I disliked playing the role of helpless damsel, I was feeling fairly distressed.

But even as I thought that, I felt a rush of panic. My chest tightened. Leon was a Guardian, but he wasn't invincible—and he would be severely outnumbered. He'd been hurt protecting me before; he could be hurt again.

With effort, I shoved the thought aside and concentrated on my current predicament. I wasn't going to just stand around waiting to be rescued. I moved to Gideon's side, Tink following me. My gaze flicked past the demons as I scanned the ramp once more. The three Harrowers on motorcycles blocked the way forward, and the other two demons could easily prevent us from reaching the exit. Cautiously, I reached behind me, pressing my fingers to the cool metal of the car door. I groped for the handle and tested it gently. The car was locked.

Gideon leaned in close. "What do you think they want?" he whispered.

"I can't tell." I frowned. If they simply wanted us dead, they would have attacked already. But they were keeping their distance. Waiting. And I couldn't get much of a sense from them—no hint of intent, only the barest trace of the hatred I'd felt from other Harrowers.

Ahead of us, the girl was humming softly as she strolled to the demon in the T-shirt. She wrapped her arms around his waist, pressing herself against him as she leaned her head on his arm.

"You were right, Daniel," she crooned. "Gave her a little scare, and she came right to us."

Her words sent a chill through me. I recalled her dancing in the Drought and Deluge, the deliberate way she moved, how everyone had avoided her.

She'd wanted me to see her.

She hadn't followed us here. She'd sent us here.

Beside me, Tink began to tremble. Gideon grabbed my hand, squeezing it painfully. Straightening my shoulders, I lifted my head and looked directly at the girl. "I wasn't scared," I told her.

Her lips curved upward once more. She let go of the demon she'd called Daniel, then took several short, unhurried steps, until she stood before me. Up close, I saw that her eyes were pale blue and not the unbroken white of the other Harrowers'—but there was a quality to them that was not quite human, either. A certain emptiness. Something ancient; something cold. Like I was staring into the Beneath.

She reached forward, lightly touching my face with the ends of her nails. "Are you scared now?"

I tried not to flinch. "A little," I admitted.

"Good girl. I can't abide liars." Then she shrugged, withdrawing her hand and turning away. "But you have nothing to fear. I'm not here to hurt you. I simply wanted to see you for myself."

"You're neutral, then?" I asked. She wasn't. I understood that now. I heard the menace in her tone, saw the sneer beneath her smile. Whatever her purpose was, it wasn't benign. But I had to stall. I needed to think. We couldn't fight, so we'd have to run—but unless we wanted to fling ourselves to our deaths off the side of the parking ramp, we had nowhere to go. And even if we had enough time to unlock the car and climb into it, I doubted we'd be able to keep the Harrowers out.

The girl's laughter—a harsh, jarring sound from deep in her throat—shook me from my thoughts. "Neutral?" she said, swinging back toward me. "Don't let them fool you. There's no such thing."

I opened my mouth to respond, but no sound came out. I thought of Shane. He'd rescued Tink the night she'd been attacked; he had come to my own aid twice. He'd traveled Beneath so that Leon could find me, and he had even killed other Harrowers.

"The beast within them sleeps," the girl continued. "But it will wake. They always do. One day they simply . . . rise, and remember their hate." She stepped close once more, tilting her head as she looked at me. Her tone was soft, sweet. "They yearn to see the Kin bleeding before them. They hunger for the kill. Just like the rest of us."

I swallowed thickly.

"Don't believe me?" Her voice went hard. "Wait and see."

My gaze dropped to her neck. *Go for the throat,* my mother had told me. Harrowers were stronger than normal humans, faster and more resilient, but they weren't invulnerable. If I landed a direct blow, I might disorient the girl long enough for us to run.

But before I could act, she drew back. She began to move away, and then paused, turning her head toward Gideon. For just a second, something flickered in her vacant blue eyes. "Now, this is interesting. Who are *you*?"

Gideon sucked in a breath. "Why?"

"Simple curiosity." She smiled again, showing her teeth. "But where are my manners? How about this—we'll have an exchange. I'll give you my name if you give me yours."

He hesitated a moment, glancing at me, then back at the demon. "Gideon."

Her smile widened. "And I am Susannah. There. Now we're friends."

"He's not Kin," I interjected, moving toward her and stepping between them. "He's no threat to you."

"Dear to you, is he? Isn't that sweet."

"What do you want from us?" Tink whispered.

Susannah didn't even glance at her. "We heard all about you, you know," she told me. "The dark star. The girl who hid a fire inside her. I must say, you're a bit of a disappointment." Clicking her tongue, she walked to Daniel and twined her hand in his. Their wrists touched, their tattoos blending together like a pair of inky handcuffs. "We can't use her," she told him.

"Not yet," he said. But he didn't look at her; he was looking at me. "It's time to go."

The girl nodded, turning her head. Over her shoulder, she called, "Leave the little darlings." She paused. Once more the smile appeared. This time her teeth were red. "Kill the Guardian."

My first thought was Leon. He must have finally appeared. I turned, searching, seeking his tall, familiar form in the half-light around us. Though I craved the sight of him, my stomach knotted as fear shot through me. The demon's words echoed in my ears, a dark, insistent chant set to the violent drumming of my heart. *Kill the Guardian. Kill the Guardian.*

But I didn't see Leon, and I had no time to process anything else.

Ahead of me, Susannah and Daniel vanished. For a fleeting instant, I caught the image of a world gone gray, a red light shining—and beyond that a void, cold and dark and silent. They'd gone Beneath.

The remaining Harrowers left their motorcycles, throwing off their human disguises. They stepped toward us, scaled and silver, their fingers turning to talons, their red grins widening. Gideon spun about, jamming the key into the lock.

Then the Guardian appeared.

At first, I caught only a glimpse of him: a thin body in a flurry of motion; wheat-colored hair drawn back into a short ponytail; the flare of colors shining from his left hand. I didn't recognize him—but at that moment, I didn't care who he was. He charged the demons from behind, his movements swift and agile. The Harrowers turned, but turned too late. The Guardian's fingers found purchase around one scaled neck, tightened, squeezed. The demon in his grip lashed out. It struggled and clawed, emitting an eerie, high-pitched wail.

My vision swam. My knees buckled. Knowing pulsed through me in a sudden rush, a sensation of rage so intense that it nearly knocked me from my feet. I clutched at Gideon's shoulder, leaning against the car to steady myself. I tried to shut out the fury that flooded my senses. Gideon said my name, asking if I was all right, asking what we should do, but I barely heard him over the pounding of blood in my ears.

It was Tink's scream that finally cut through my daze.

I turned, still fighting for balance. Ahead of us, a short distance from the car, the battle continued. One of the motorcycles lay on its side. The blond Guardian was grappling with two of the Harrowers, the scene a confusion of silver and red, talons slashing downward, warm glowing lights beneath skin. He'd steered the demons toward the corner of the ramp, widening the gap between us.

But the third Harrower was free. He was headed in our direction. And he had nearly reached the car.

"Oh, my God," Tink gasped out. She looked at me, her eyes huge.

Go for the throat, I thought. Then I was in motion.

I hurtled toward the demon. Distantly, I recalled my training: Mom's early instructions, Leon coaching me, sparring with me, showing me how a demon would think, how it would behave. How it would kill. All other thoughts vanished. Knowing subsided; rage ebbed away. Instinct took over. My body moved on its own.

I took the Harrower by surprise and delivered a blow to its throat. It lurched backward with short, staggering steps, and I followed it. But my advantage was brief. The demon recovered rapidly and swung toward me. Its talons flashed, aiming for my eyes.

Then Tink was beside me. She launched herself at the demon, her slim form colliding with it and throwing it momentarily off balance. It swiped savagely, claws arcing toward her neck. The attack only grazed her, but a thin line of blood began to bead along her throat, bright scarlet against pale skin. Horror bubbled up inside me. I grabbed Tink by the shoulder and didn't let go, using one hand to pull her out of the way while I struck the demon with my free arm.

For one terrible second, the demon caught Tink. Its claws sank into her coat, rending fabric, shredding cotton, seeking the vulnerable flesh beneath. But as I attacked again, my hit was solid and unexpectedly strong. Sudden heat surged through me, burning beneath the skin of my hand as my strike connected. The demon was flung back by the force of the blow. It lay stunned on the concrete, rasping.

Tink lost her footing. She landed badly, scraping her knee and tearing her dress. I didn't pause to think. I hauled her up and dragged her the few short steps to the car. Gideon had opened the driver's side doors and was motioning for us to get inside.

But something stopped me. I turned, glancing over my shoulder to where the Harrower that had attacked us lay. Slowly, it began to struggle to its feet.

It never got the chance to rise.

The blond Guardian had reached it. His arm whipped out, catching the demon by the neck and lifting it into the air.

I still couldn't see the Guardian clearly. I couldn't see his face, or say how old he was, or determine where he'd come from. But while I didn't know who he was, I knew who he *wasn't*: he wasn't any of the Kin I'd met. He didn't fight the way other Guardians did. His movements weren't careful and controlled. There was no precision to his attacks, no design. There was a wildness in him, a ferocity that radiated outward. With a start, I realized that the raw anger I'd sensed, the rage so great it seemed to burn before me in the air, hadn't come from the Harrowers. It had come from him.

The demon writhed in his grip. I expected the Guardian to pierce its throat, to snap its neck, but he didn't bother seeking weak points. He didn't go for the easy end. Instead, he ripped the Harrower open, from one shoulder all the way down to the groin.

I'd never seen Harrower blood before, at least not that I'd been conscious of; the fights I'd witnessed had been clean kills. I saw blood now, oozing into the darkness around us. Thick red. A dark pool that spread and spread. Its scent filled the air.

My stomach churned. I recoiled and turned away.

The other two demons lay dead nearby. For a moment, they remained on the concrete, ruined flesh with no semblance of pretended humanity, reeking of decay. Then the Beneath swallowed them, dragging them back into the void. Only a circle of crimson remained in the melting snow.

"Jesus," Gideon breathed.

The Guardian turned to face us, panting as he wiped the sweat from his brow. His hand left a smear of blood on his skin.

"You don't want to be here," he whispered hoarsely. As he spoke I caught a brief image, a Knowing quickly overpowered by the force of his anger: the memory of black hair; a woman's slim shoulders and bare, dark skin; a low, musical laugh; a sudden gasp. Then it was gone. "You should go," the Guardian said.

We went.

The snow was falling harder as we left the ramp, heavy flakes that turned to slush in the roads. Clouds hugged close overhead, hiding the stars. I let out a long breath and tried to slow the slamming of my heart. A siren blared in the distance. I looked down at my hands, holding the mangled remains of my phone in my lap. There was blood on my jeans, I didn't know whose.

"Are we going to talk about what just happened?" Gideon asked, turning a corner as we headed out of downtown, toward my house. His voice was steady, but he was clutching the steering wheel tightly, his knuckles white.

"I vote no," Tink said from the back of the car. She hadn't bothered with a seat belt. She was bent double, her head between her knees.

"Then can I make a suggestion? Let's never go downtown again."

My answer was automatic. "That won't really help. Esther says Harrowers don't always stay close to the center of the Astral Circle. The stronger ones branch out to other areas." I glanced toward Gideon. His expression was pained. "Oh. You didn't actually want to know that, did you?"

He shook his head mutely.

I bit my lip. This wasn't Gideon's first encounter with Harrowers. Two months ago, my cousin Iris had used demons to hold Gideon hostage atop Harlow Tower. The experience had changed him. He'd had nightmares for weeks afterward, and though he didn't like to talk about it, I knew he still had trouble sleeping. His parents had been concerned enough to make an appointment with a therapist, but it wasn't like he could explain the situation.

He'd seen the psychologist once and hadn't gone back. I had no idea how to help.

"So much for our demon-free evening," I said, sighing.

Gideon let out a short burst of laughter. "I've sort of been hoping for a demon-free *life*."

"Are you guys seriously joking about this?" Tink asked, lifting her head and leaning forward from the backseat.

"It's either that or throw up," I said. "Though I might do that, anyway."

"Do you need me to pull over?"

"No!" Tink and I said in unison.

"Let's just get home," I added.

"And can we *please* not talk about this anymore?" Tink turned toward me, furrowing her brow. "You might be used to this sort of thing, but I'm not."

"You think I'm used to being ambushed by demons in parking ramps? Because that was a first for me, too."

"You know what I mean. I am just way too freaked out right now."

I looked at her. Her coat was ripped where Harrower talons had sliced through the fabric, tufts of cotton stuffing spilling out. There was a smear of red where she'd scratched her knee, and I saw the shine of tears on her face. Noticing my gaze, she crossed her arms and turned toward the window.

We were quiet the rest of the way home. The lights of downtown dwindled to a faint, glowing outline behind us. I watched

the vehicles that passed beside us, the haze of exhaust, the blur of headlights. The air inside the car was cool. The only sound was the drone of the engine and the occasional hiccup from the heating system. The heat was acting up again, and what scant warmth it provided made the car smell like wet cardboard. Frost had painted little stars on the outsides of the windows. I lifted one hand, tracing my finger along the glass.

My mind was spinning. Everything had happened so quickly I couldn't seem to process it all. Stray sounds echoed in my ears. Colors formed a picture: the red of teeth and blood and hair; the gold of falling snow and Susannah's glittering dress; the blue-black of corners and shadows in the parking ramp.

I looked down at my hands. I wasn't a Guardian; I didn't have their powers—but as I'd fought the Harrower, I had felt a burn beneath my skin. And the demon had been thrown back by the strength of my blow.

I thought of the demon girl's words.

The dark star. The girl who hid a fire inside her.

The light of the Astral Circle, she'd meant. The Astral Circle was the barrier that protected us from the Beneath, preventing Harrowers from crossing over into our world.

Until two months ago, I'd held a portion of the Circle's power within me—and even now a link remained, a faint connection that I didn't fully understand, only felt now and then at the edge of my consciousness. But that connection didn't explain what had happened in the parking ramp.

I didn't have time to dwell on the matter. Gideon had pulled in to my driveway. Feeling a rush of relief, I hurried out of the car and up the porch steps. Within, the house was dark and still. No one was home, but I flicked on the hallway light and called into the quiet, anyway. Only the ticking of the hall clock answered. I shrugged out of my coat, locking the door once Tink and Gideon had followed me inside.

"We should take a look at your cuts," I told Tink, but she waved me away and hurried up the stairs ahead of Gideon and me.

"I can do it," she tossed over her shoulder. I watched her go, feeling a twinge of concern. The house was stocked with first-aid kits—something of a necessity when you have a mother who spends half the night prowling the city in search of demons to vanquish and evildoers to punish—but, knowing Tink, I worried she'd just slap on a Band-Aid and call it done.

"Make sure you wash out the wounds!" I shouted up the stairs.

We hadn't eaten at the Drought and Deluge, so Gideon and I wandered into the kitchen to heat up a frozen pizza and see what else we could dig up. I was busy trying to decide how long the leftover spaghetti had been in the fridge when Gideon asked, "So who was that guy? He was a Guardian, right? Do you know him?"

"I've never seen him before. He's not any of the Kin I've met. And, believe me, I'd remember." I lifted the cover of the spaghetti bowl and smelled it. "Seems okay," I said, sliding it into the microwave.

Gideon gave me a dubious look. "I'm not eating that."

"We'll feed it to Tink. She'll never know."

That earned me another look, but instead of commenting, he asked, "Where do you think he came from?"

"Outer space?" I suggested. I'd wondered about that, too, but I had more pressing concerns. Like why the demons had taken the trouble to seek us out in the first place.

And why Leon had never appeared.

Every other time I'd been in danger, Leon had known. He'd known when trouble was near, or when I was hurt; he'd known how to find me in the deep dark of the Beneath. He knew when I needed him. It was part of the Guardian programming, whether or not either of us wanted that connection.

Except that tonight he *hadn't* known.

I thought over what I knew of the calling, trying to figure out what might have changed. Guardians were only called to watch over a specific charge when there was a particular gift, or a particular danger. By myself, I didn't have any abilities that were unique among the Kin. It was the Astral Circle's power that had been my gift, my danger; I'd assumed that was why Leon had been called to protect me. Now it occurred to me that maybe it had never actually been *me* that Leon was guarding. Maybe it had only been the power I'd carried—the lost light of the Circle, that fire that had burned out of me into the snowy night atop Harlow Tower.

And maybe that meant he was no longer my Guardian.

I wasn't certain how to feel about that idea. I shook the thought away, turning back to Gideon. "I don't care where he came from. I'm just glad he showed up."

"What do you think the demons wanted?"

"Does it matter?" Tink asked, stepping into the kitchen. She was wearing a pair of pajamas she must have fished out of my dresser, which I took to mean she was intending to spend the night. "They were demons, and they're dead."

"Not all of them," Gideon said quietly.

Tink lifted her hand. "If you're going to have this discussion, have it without me. My plan tonight is to hide under the covers, go to sleep, and pretend none of this ever happened."

"That's healthy," I said.

"Exactly. *Health.* The thing I would like to keep by having as little to do with demons as possible, okay?"

I was too weary to argue with her. I shrugged and looked away, gazing into the icy darkness beyond the window while Tink moved on to safer topics. Once our food was done, we retreated to the living room to watch a movie, which effectively ended all argument.

But late that night, as I lay awake listening to Tink snore, the conversation echoed through me.

They were demons, and they're dead.

And—

Not all of them.

Behind my eyes, I saw Susannah's face.

My dreams were tinted gold and red. At first there was no sense to them, no pattern. Most of the images were only fragments—visions that slipped through my subconscious, fleeting and quickly forgotten. But others remained, flashes that burned in my memory. The last flare of the setting sun. Red stars rising. The sheen of a wedding band. For an instant, I saw my friends: Tink was glitter and flame; Gideon was wreathed in light, drenched in blood.

Then I was Beneath.

Susannah appeared in front of me. She smiled a crooked smile, turned away.

Beside her, the Harrower named Daniel met my eyes. He took a step forward, then another, and another, until he reached me. I stood frozen, wanting to flee but unable to. His hand slid into mine.

I'm sorry, he mouthed, and cold dread enveloped me.

I woke with a start, sweating. Feeling anxious and confused, I tried to pull the covers up over my head, but the sunlight streaming in through the window was too bright for me to ignore. I lifted myself onto my elbows, blinking away my dream until my panic faded.

Tink was already awake. She was seated at my desk, tapping away at my computer. She twisted in her chair as soon as she heard me move. "Erica says Greg and his freshman were at some party last night. I did the world a great service by teaching that boy not to slobber when he kisses, and this is how I'm repaid."

I groaned, rolling over and hiding my face in a pillow. "Are we back on this already? If I hear the word *freshman* one more time, I swear to God I'm going to smother myself."

"What are you mumbling about?"

"Never mind." With a sigh, I stretched and crawled out of bed, heading for the shower.

I padded toward the bathroom, stepping past my mother's door as quietly as possible. She was already asleep, and I didn't want to wake her. I wasn't certain what I was going to tell her about my encounter with the Harrowers. Or *if* I was going to tell her. Mom wasn't going to be thrilled about the fact that I'd been at the Drought and Deluge again. She tended to overreact, and I didn't relish the idea of spending the next month under house arrest.

By the time I'd finished my shower, Tink had changed back

into her dress from the night before, along with her coat and gloves. Gideon had promised to give her a ride home and had texted to let her know he was on his way.

"Though I don't know why we bother driving anywhere," Tink said, marching down the steps to the entryway, "when you're going out with a free transit service."

I laughed, following her downstairs. "The same reason I keep telling you we can't spend every weekend in the Bahamas."

Leon had the ability to teleport, and even though he felt at perfect liberty to scare years off my life with his unannounced appearances around the house, he was very strict when it came to what he termed the *abuse of abilities*. But even if he'd wanted to use his powers frivolously, he still faced restrictions. From what I understood, he wasn't able to teleport more than one person at a time, and his range was limited to somewhere around forty miles.

Tink waved a hand. "Yeah, yeah, I've heard it," she said. Though her back was to me, I was certain she was wrinkling her nose. "All I'm saying is, if I had a boyfriend who could teleport, you can believe we wouldn't be spending our time in the Cities. Especially in winter."

I rolled my eyes. "That would require you to date within the Kin, which—"

"Which I will never do," she finished for me, turning to give me a quick grin. Gideon honked his car horn. With another wave, Tink darted outside.

After she was gone, I made my way to the kitchen. I carved

out a piece of the egg bake Mom had left on the counter, poured myself a glass of orange juice, and seated myself at the table, but I didn't eat.

My mind drifted to Susannah and Daniel. They'd gone Beneath, but they wouldn't remain there. They were strong enough to breach the Circle, and they had come here for a reason. The void wouldn't hold them. Sooner or later, they would emerge, intent on whatever purpose had drawn them here.

I thought of my dream. I'd had more than a few nightmares since learning about the existence of demons—images of blood and fire, of shapes that twisted out of shadows. I'd woken recalling the tap and scrape of claws, the feel of teeth against me. But this hadn't felt like a nightmare.

It had felt like a warning.

"You know you're meant to eat that, right?"

I looked up.

Leon was standing in the doorway. His dark hair was damp, curling slightly at the ends, and he stood with his hands in his pockets. He tilted his head as he looked at me, a little smile curving his lips.

"I'm not convinced it's edible," I said, setting my fork aside as Leon strode into the room. "Mom made it." Cooking was usually left to me—at least, it had been ever since Gram's death. Mom worked nights, didn't have the time, and definitely didn't have the skill. Pancakes were about the only thing she could handle with any measure of success. Without me, she'd probably have lived entirely on mac and cheese and cans of SpaghettiOs. "She told me she's planning a pot roast next. Do you think she might be having a midlife crisis?"

"I hope you didn't ask her that."

"What, and piss off the woman who can bench-press an elephant? Give me a *little* credit." My eyes met his. My face felt suddenly hot. Even though it had been two months since our first kiss, I couldn't seem to stop grinning like an idiot whenever I saw him.

Not that I'd had much of a chance to adjust to the idea of us as a couple. I wasn't even sure we *were* one. We existed in a strange sort of limbo that had already lasted longer than most of Tink's relationships. Leon and I hadn't even been on an official first date yet, unless you counted making out in his hospital bed a date, which I really didn't. He said he wanted to move slowly, to give us time to think things through and figure out our feelings. Since I'd had a crush on him from the moment I met him—much as I'd fought and denied it—I didn't really need to figure out my feelings. But I supposed Leon, who was a worrier by nature, did.

I just hadn't realized that when he said *slowly*, what he meant was *glacially*. As far as I was concerned, he was doing way too much thinking and not nearly enough kissing.

But when I'd told him that, the familiar wrinkle in his brow had appeared. *This is important, Audrey*, he'd said. *Because whatever happens—or doesn't happen—between us, I'm still your Guardian. That doesn't go away. Ever.*

Unless it *had* gone away, I thought.

I shifted uneasily. I wanted to know why he hadn't appeared the previous night, but I didn't want to ask him. Now that it had occurred to me that he might no longer be my Guardian, the thought wouldn't leave. And I still didn't know how to feel about it. I didn't exactly hate that Leon protected me—at least when he wasn't being overbearing about it—but I hated that I *needed* protection. I hated knowing that, when it came to Harrowers, I was always outmatched. And I was bothered by what his protection meant. Defending me involved risking his own life. I doubted I'd ever forget the night he'd taken a blow intended for me. The feel of his body going slack. The way he'd slid from my arms, into the snow. How his blood had stained both of us.

I didn't want to think about that. I rose from my seat and stood looking up at him. Leon might have been a Guardian and my mother's sidekick, but he didn't much resemble a crime-fighter. Though his shoulders were broad, he was too skinny—at least, according to comic books, which always seemed to contain heroes who tore shirts simply by flexing—and his choice of costume consisted of dress pants, ironed shirts, and neckties. He looked so tidy all the time I couldn't resist the urge to rumple him. Standing on my toes, I reached toward him and ran my hands through his damp hair, making it stand straight up.

"Much better," I declared.

He smoothed his hair back down. "Did you still want to train today? You didn't answer your phone."

I looked away. "Oh. Yeah, I sort of, uh, dropped it."

"Isn't that the third one you've broken?"

"It's the second, and this wasn't my fault." I hesitated. "How were things in the Cities last night? Break up any brawls? Come across any demons to smite?"

He must have heard the uncertainty in my tone. He gave me a curious look. "It was quiet. It's *been* quiet. Why?"

"No reason."

Leon wasn't fooled. His expression went from curious to suspicious.

"I had a dream," I said with a shrug.

"A Knowing?"

"Maybe. There was a Harrower. A girl." I paused, seeing Susannah's wide smile, remembering her words. *Kill the Guardian.* I hugged my arms. "Maybe it was just a dream."

"We didn't see anyone," Leon said, but he was still watching me intently.

"It's probably nothing." Before he could question me further, I grabbed my plate and brought it to the counter, then turned to give him what I hoped was a sunny smile. "Let's go train."

Leon and I headed to the basement, where Mom's office and workout room doubled as our training space. The room was large but rather bare, containing a closet full of Mom's Morning Star hoodies, a desk with her H&H Security files, a few pieces of exercise equipment, and a large number of spiders I couldn't seem to eradicate. Though Mom assured me the spiders weren't radioactive, I did my best to avoid them.

I watched Leon as I followed him into the room. He moved easily, with the air of calm confidence he always had. I tried to ignore my lingering feelings of uncertainty and chose to concentrate on training. We went through warm-up exercises, then Leon moved to the center of the exercise mat, giving me his best serious instructor expression.

Over the past two months, Leon's initial reluctance to teach me about demons had transformed into a sort of grim determination to do so. But my own enthusiasm had begun to wane. I was growing frustrated. I was Kin, but I wasn't a Guardian, and I didn't have a Guardian's abilities. It was the calling that gave Guardians the increased strength, speed, and resilience that allowed them to fight Harrowers—which meant that, unless I was called, there were limitations to what Leon could teach me. We couldn't work on Guardian powers, or how to control them. Our sessions were mostly an extension of my martial arts training.

At least, that had been the case been until last week. Then Leon had decided that instead of focusing on powers I didn't have, we should focus on those I did. Physically, I wasn't on the same level as Harrowers; I couldn't be faster or stronger than they were, so I needed to be smarter. If I could anticipate their movements, I might gain the advantage. Leon thought I should use my Knowing.

We'd discussed the subject briefly during our last session. I was hesitant. My Knowing had strengthened over the past couple of months, but I wasn't certain it had much actual combat value; it generally involved concentration, not reaction. But Leon had spoken to my grandmother Esther about the issue, and she thought it was worth an attempt. Now he told me he wanted us to put the idea into practice.

"How?" I asked, setting a hand on my hip. "Are we taking a field trip Beneath, or do you have a demon tied up in the closet?"

The serious instructor expression slipped. He gave me a grin that was a little too mischievous for me to trust. "Attack me."

Sparring was part of our training, but I had the feeling that, this time, Leon wasn't going to play fair. I narrowed my eyes. "You're just going to teleport."

"That's right. Try to anticipate where I'll be. Use your Knowing."

I gave him a little salute. "Whatever you say, Obi-Wan."

I didn't move immediately. I waited, watching him. I'd never had an easy time reading Leon. What Knowings I'd had of him were few and fleeting, small glimpses, nothing concrete. But maybe that didn't matter. We'd been training together at least twice a week for the past two months; I had some sense of his style, of his movements and reactions. Since he was a Guardian and I wasn't, he was forced to hold back, to control his strength and speed—but I knew the way he fought.

"I'm waiting," he said.

I feinted, rushing toward him as if to strike, waiting for him to teleport.

He didn't.

Annoyed, I checked my movement and stepped back. I circled him.

He vanished without warning. I swiveled, but before I could block, he'd reappeared behind me and caught me in a firm grip.

"You told *me* to attack!" I protested, breaking free of his hold and elbowing him in the ribs. Hard.

He grunted. "You're overthinking it. You need to react, to—"

I aimed a blow at his stomach. He deflected, and I pushed the attack, striking and parrying while I looked for an opening. He teleported before I could get him in a hold.

"Are you sure this isn't just an excuse for you to show off?" I asked, after he evaded me once more. "Because this exercise seems like a lot more fun for you than it is for me."

"It isn't about fun. It's about preparation."

I took advantage of his pause. Before he could teleport away again, I tried to deliver a roundhouse kick to his side—but he was too fast. He caught my leg. I had a split second to consider my predicament, and then I was on the ground.

Leon gazed down at me. "You're a little off your game today."

"I knew this wasn't going to work," I muttered.

"You're still overthinking," he said. "Just trust your instincts."

"My instincts are telling me to kick your ass."

"From the floor?"

"You are so asking for it." I hopped to my feet. "What do I get if I win?"

"This isn't a competition."

"But what do I get? Humor me."

He considered for a moment. "What do you want?"

"A first date," I said. "One that doesn't include hospitals. Or Harrowers."

He raised an eyebrow. "And what if you lose?"

"Then it's a good thing this isn't a competition," I said. Without waiting for a response, I attacked. Leon vanished.

We sparred for the next fifteen minutes. Each time he reappeared, my timing was off just slightly. It was guesswork, not Knowing, but I held my own, blocking his blows and once or twice getting a decent hit in. Still, I wasn't anticipating his movements so much as countering them.

Finally, my moment came. Leon teleported. I half turned, then thought better of it. It might have been Knowing, it might have been instinct, it might have been pure exasperation—but this time, when Leon reappeared, I was ready. My kick connected. He was caught off guard long enough to provide me an opening, and I hurried to take it. I grabbed him by the collar and swept his foot from beneath him. He fell backward. I didn't trust him not to teleport, so I held on, following him to the floor.

I sat on his chest, feeling smugly triumphant. "Now who's off their game?"

Instead of shoving me aside, he shook his head, a smile tugging at his lips. "I assume you're not planning to sit there all day. What next?"

It was the smile that did it.

Suddenly, I was very aware of our positions. I gazed down at him. His hair was a mess, his face flushed. We were both sweating. My hand was at his collar, and I felt his pulse against my fingers. I felt the hurried rise and fall of his chest beneath me. He spoke again, but I didn't hear his words. Leaning down, I pressed my lips to his.

I meant it to be a gentle kiss. I meant it to be long and slow and sweet. I meant to take my time with it, to linger, to savor.

Mostly, I meant for him to participate.

Unfortunately, Leon didn't have the intended reaction. He didn't wrap his arms around me and pull me close. He didn't slide his hand through my hair. Instead, his face twitched and he started laughing.

Mortified, I scrambled off him, punching him in the shoulder as I went. "You were supposed to kiss me *back*, you big jerk!" I started to jump to my feet, but Leon sat up, catching my wrist and hauling me back down to the exercise mat.

"Wait, Audrey—"

"You're going to give me a complex if you laugh every time I kiss you," I grumbled, struggling to break free of his grip.

"It's not that." His laughter had stopped, but his blue eyes were bright. He was smiling at me in a way that made my knees feel watery. "I was just thinking I hope that's not how you plan to defend yourself against demons."

I hit him again.

"I suppose I should make amends," he said. He slipped an arm around me and attempted to draw me against him.

"It's too late," I said, wriggling away. "You completely ruined the mood."

He rolled over me, pinning me to the ground beneath him. "Really?" he asked, and then his mouth came down on mine.

His kiss wasn't sweet, and it wasn't slow. It was rough, urgent, all hunger and heat. I felt it instantly, all the way through me. And I responded eagerly, any thought of resistance forgotten. I dragged my fingers through his hair, pushed my body against his. He didn't stop kissing me. My heart thudded in my ears. As his lips moved against mine, I slipped my hand beneath his shirt, along the ladder of his ribs. He drew back slightly, sucking in a breath, and then I felt his mouth on my throat, his hands sliding down me.

He stopped abruptly, rolling away and leaving me dazed. "What—"

He clapped a hand over my mouth and nodded toward the door behind us. I tilted my head back. Horror washed through me as I saw what he'd seen.

My mother stood in the doorway.

If I were to make a list of the ten most embarrassing moments in my life, the number one spot would be taken by the time in fourth grade when Lydia Broderick read aloud to our entire class the love letter I'd written to her brother. In terms of trauma, nothing else could quite top that. But my mother catching me making out with her sidekick on the floor of her exercise room? That came in a very close second. Especially since she then marched the two of us upstairs and made us sit in the parlor to discuss the situation.

"Why are you awake?" I demanded, flopping onto the couch and crossing my arms. Mom usually slept until at least noon. The clock hadn't chimed eleven yet, but she was already showered and dressed, her H&H coat unzipped over a pink sweater, her blond hair pulled back in a bun. In one hand, she held the H&H folders she'd gone to the basement to retrieve. The other hand was on her hip.

"Good question, Audrey," she said. "Here's a better one: was that just a spontaneous attack of teenage hormones, or has this been going on for a while?"

I flicked a glance at Leon. He stood in the doorway, a very deer-in-the-headlights look in his eyes. Considering that hitting deer was something of a Whitticomb family tradition, this didn't bode well for him. And Mom appeared about ready to run him over.

"We were going to tell you," he said quietly.

That was true, I supposed. We hadn't made a conscious decision to keep our almost relationship secret, but since—according to Leon—we were still *thinking things through*, neither of us had wanted to talk to my mother about it yet.

"Oh? When would that have been?" Mom asked.

Leon started to speak, but I interrupted. "When we were ready," I said. "And I'm sorry, Mom, but it's not really any of your business who I kiss. I don't need your permission."

"Actually, it is my business. Recall that part where you're a minor and I'm your mother?"

"I'm not exactly in diapers anymore."

She snorted. "I would hope not, considering what I just walked in on."

I felt my cheeks burning, and for a moment I simply sat there, struggling for some form of coherent speech. Eventually, I blurted out, "You *like* Leon!"

"Of course I like him. That isn't the issue. Would you stop being so surly and let me speak?"

I opened my mouth to protest, then clamped it shut it again.

"You're misunderstanding me," she continued. She gave me a long, steady look. "I'm not mad at you, Audrey. Either of you. But I *am* concerned. I know that a Guardian's feelings for their charge can be very intense. Those bonds are messy, and they're complicated, and I just want both of you to be sure you know what you're getting yourselves into. Like it or not, you two are stuck with each other."

Exactly what Leon had said. That didn't make me any happier. I was about to repeat that it wasn't any of her business, but Mom wasn't finished with her speech.

"You may have these feelings now," she began, "but at your age—"

I couldn't let that one go. "At our *age*? When is the last time you had a relationship that lasted more than three months?"

Immediately, I wished I could call the words back. As far as I knew, her last relationship of any length had been with my father, and I hadn't meant to bring that up. I started to apologize, but Mom only sighed.

She turned to Leon. "Could you give us a few minutes? I'd like to talk to Audrey alone."

He hesitated, but the look on his face clearly said he'd rather be anywhere else at that moment—like in the middle of the ocean, surrounded by sharks, or in the death zone of Mount Everest.

"Oh, just go. It's not like you're helping anyway," I muttered.

He let out a short, strangled laugh. "And *you're* helping?"

I grabbed one of the couch pillows and lobbed it at him, but he vanished too quickly. The pillow sailed through empty air, landing in the hallway with a soft thud.

I turned back to find my mother watching me, her expression troubled. I would have liked nothing better than to melt into the floor, but since my body remained stubbornly solid, I folded my arms again and said, "Let me guess. We're going shopping for chastity belts."

"Go ahead, funny girl. Get all the jokes out of your system, because you and I need to be honest for a moment."

"That was pretty much all I had," I said glumly. "But don't you think you might be overreacting? Just a little? We were only kissing."

"From where I was standing, it looked a lot more like groping."

I didn't answer. I sat silent, reassessing whether or not that long-ago love letter really was more embarrassing than this.

"Don't try to pretend this isn't serious," Mom continued. "I've known for a long time how he feels about you. If I hadn't been so distracted lately, I'd probably have realized what was going on. I'm not going to lecture you, I just want you to be careful. No matter what happens, it's not going to be easy for him."

"Wait a second. Are you telling *me* not to break *his* heart? Aren't you being overprotective in the wrong direction here?"

"I'm sure he already knows that I'll break his kneecaps if he hurts you."

I groaned. "Mom. Seriously."

"*Seriously*, you and I are going to make a deal. Okay? I'll do my best to respect your privacy, and you'll promise to behave responsibly."

Since she'd sat me down for a safe-sex talk the moment I hit puberty, I was well aware of what she meant by that. Foreseeing a repeat of that talk in the near future, I nodded warily. "Okay…"

"But we're still going to have to establish some rules. Training sessions? Those are for training, not for exercising your libidos. And I don't think it's appropriate for Leon to live with us any longer."

"You can't kick him out!" I cried, feeling a surge of outrage.

"I'm sorry, Audrey. It made sense when safety was our highest concern, but now that the danger has passed, we need to consider other options. Options that don't involve my sixteen-year-old daughter living under the same roof as her boyfriend."

There. That was the moment I should have told her about the incident in the parking ramp. I should have explained that the danger hadn't passed. I should have told her about the Drought and Deluge, about the demon in the golden dress who had called herself Susannah. I should have spoken about the Guardian who had appeared out of nowhere and torn the Harrowers apart. I should have said *something*.

Instead, what came out of my mouth was, "That's stupid, Mom. He could just teleport straight into my bedroom."

"Not unless he wants to lose a few key parts of his anatomy," she said darkly. Glancing at the clock, she sighed again. "I have to run to a meeting. Think about what I've said, all right? We'll discuss this more later."

"Can't wait!" I called after her; then I trudged up the stairs to my room.

I didn't dream for the next few nights, but the memory of my nightmare lingered: Susannah standing watchful and silent, Daniel's chilled hand, the fear that sped through me. Even if it wasn't a Knowing, the demons themselves had been real. And since I was reluctant to tell Mom and Leon about the attack, I decided to get information from another source. I went to Mr. Alvarez. In addition to being my math teacher, he was the leader of the Cities' Guardians; if there was a threat to the Kin, he'd know about it. After Precalculus on Tuesday, I waited until the rest of the class had filed out, then asked him if there had been any recent Harrower incidents.

He seemed preoccupied. He was tapping his pen against his desk and didn't appear to notice the coffee ring his mug had left on somebody's homework. "Incidents? Not in the way you might think," he said, after I repeated my question.

"Is there a way that doesn't involve them trying to murder us on the streets?"

He looked up at that. "Several Harrowers have gone missing recently."

"Oh," I said. "I don't see how that's a problem."

"Neutrals. Harrowers who live in the Cities as humans."

"You keep track of them?"

"We're aware of them. When they start to vanish and we don't know why, it's cause for concern."

The beast within them sleeps, I thought. "Like maybe they're no longer neutral?"

"It could mean a number of things. Few of them good." He looked at me sharply. "Is there a reason you're asking?"

I didn't want to discuss Susannah's attack with him, either. Since he didn't seem to think there was an impending demon threat, I muttered an excuse and fled the room.

I wasn't the only one still bothered by the Harrower encounter. Tink, true to form, refused to acknowledge that anything had happened—her cuts had healed, and when I asked how she was feeling she shrugged the question aside—but Gideon was troubled. He hadn't been able to put the incident out of his mind. He was quieter than usual all week. Then, during lunch on Friday, he said, "I've been thinking."

"About?" I asked.

"Susannah."

Tink looked up from her magazine. "If you guys are going to keep talking about this, I'm going to the library."

"Then go to the library," Gideon said.

Unoffended, Tink shrugged, hopped out of her chair, picked

up her tray, and waved. "I still think you should just forget about it," she said. "Trust me. Whatever it is you're worried about, you're probably happier not knowing."

Once she was gone, Gideon turned his attention back to me. "I keep remembering what Susannah said to me."

"That you were friends? I think you should pass on that offer."

"She said I was *interesting.*"

"I don't think she was playing with a full deck." I paused, chewing on a fry. "Uh. Not that you aren't interesting."

He gave me a brief smile, then grew serious again. "I've just been wondering...do you think I might be Kin?"

The question took me by surprise, but I considered it. Gideon was adopted, so even though the Belmontes had no known link to the Kin, *he* might. He had no idea who his birth parents were. His family had always been very open about the subject, answering whatever questions they could, but Gideon hadn't been put up for adoption in the traditional way; as an infant, he'd been found abandoned somewhere downtown, without even a blanket wrapped around him.

He *could* be Kin—but I'd never felt it. I got a sense from most other Kin, a hint of connection, an underlying awareness of the thread woven between us. It was something that was always there, subtle but present. I didn't sense it in Gideon.

But before I could answer, he continued, "Do you think I could be the one the Harrowers have been looking for?"

"You mean the Remnant?" I frowned. For over a year, my

cousin Iris and her boyfriend, a Harrower named Tigue, had searched the Cities for the Remnant—a Kin girl born with the power to open passages Beneath—leaving a trail of bodies in their wake. Their hunt was the reason Iris had taken Gideon hostage two months ago—the reason he'd become aware of demons at all. The reason for his nightmares.

"Whatever it's called." He leaned forward, his brow creasing. "I never told you this part. When Iris showed up at my house, she—she said some things. She said you needed my help. That's why I went with her. She said there was a problem, and I was the only one who could fix it."

"The Remnant is supposed to be a girl, so unless you've been hiding a few things, it's probably not you. And if you *were* the Remnant, and Iris knew it, she wouldn't have needed me."

"You think she was just messing with me?"

"I think she was messed up, period."

"And you don't think I'm Kin."

"Do you *want* to be?"

"I don't know," he said. "Maybe."

"Well, we could try to find out," I suggested, digging in to my book bag and pulling out my Nav cards. "I'll do a reading."

As I shuffled, I focused on Gideon, noting the little details I sometimes overlooked: the tiny scar near his left temple, the ring of green in his brown irises. I thought of the morning I'd met him, the wide grin he'd given me, the dimple in his cheek, the tooth he'd been missing. Gideon was so familiar to me it was difficult to seek something that *wasn't* familiar, but I tried. Concentrate on what isn't there, I told myself. Maybe he *is* Kin. Maybe it's just not a close connection.

I began to lay out cards. The first was always the card that represented me, Inverted Crescent. I placed it in the center and moved to the next. Forty-three, The Prisoner. That was Gideon's card; he'd chosen it himself years ago, because he liked the design. Ever since, it had shown up in my readings for him.

A quick image shot through me as I placed the card on the table: Brooke Oliver laughing, turning away. She often appeared in Gideon's readings—predictable, since she was often in his thoughts—so I moved on. "No surprises yet," I said.

The third card in the reading was the Mapmaker, Tink's card. As my fingers grazed it, I caught an impression of the three of us. We stood on a sidewalk, our backs turned and our heads bowed beneath a black, starless sky. Snow swirled about us, catching in the glow of streetlamps. Beneath our feet, a thin light pooled, interrupting the paths of our shadows.

Footsteps echoed behind us. Susannah, I thought. Following us Friday night.

The image faded, and I set down the next cards. Four, Sign of Sickle. Forty-eight, Sign of Swords.

Iris's face flashed before me. It was so sudden, so real, that I jumped, nearly dropping the deck. At first she was smiling, a sad smile that made me think of the quiet way she'd moved and how her memories had always smelled of roses. Then her eyes went white. Her mouth widened, revealing sharp red teeth. I shivered, and the vision was gone.

"You getting something?" Gideon asked.

"Your nightmares are back."

He looked away from me. "They're getting worse."

I knew he didn't like to talk about it, so I didn't press. "Okay. Let's see what the cross cards have to say."

I set down the next card. Twenty-six. The Triple Knot. The only card with the same design on both front and back.

The triple knot was the sign of the Astral Circle. In a way, it represented the Kin. That might have suggested a connection— but the only impression I got was of the day Gideon and I had met, the bright aura that had clung to him.

I tapped my fingers against the cards. The Triple Knot, crossed by Year of Famine and Inverted Compass. No other images rose. My Knowing was silent, nothing but blank space.

"Well, they tell me nothing," I said. "Okay, last two."

Card seven. The Beast.

The final card was blank.

"Uh. That's weird." I flipped it over. It was definitely a Nav card—there was the triple knot on the back, black ink on a surface gone slightly yellow, the smudge of a thumbprint along one edge. "I must have brought the wrong set."

Ever since Esther had given me my father's cards two months

ago, I'd been using the decks interchangeably. I knew every card in Gram's set. As a child, I'd gone over each of them, learning their names, tracing the designs with my fingertips. I'd never examined my father's cards individually; I'd assumed they were the same.

"What does a blank card mean?" Gideon asked.

"I have no idea. I'll have to ask Esther." I bit my lip, gathering the deck back together. The reading might not have been telling me that Gideon was Kin, but it was trying to tell me *something*— and whatever it was, that something was related to his nightmares. Maybe I could find a way to help him with his dreams, after all. "Do you want to try again later?"

He started to respond, then stopped abruptly. Brooke Oliver, heading out of the lunchroom, paused by our table.

I glanced at her. Brooke was one of those people I sort of wanted to hate, just on principle. She never looked bad. Her blond hair was always perfect, all bright and glossy like a shampoo commercial, and her skin was always clear. If not for the fact that she'd suffered through two years of braces in junior high, I might have suspected she'd made some sort of sinister pact, and that there was a witch somewhere, stirring a cauldron and patiently awaiting the arrival of Brooke's firstborn child.

But because she was also a warm, friendly person, I couldn't actually hate her. As far as I could tell, the only true offense she'd given was her enduring ignorance of Gideon's devotion. And she couldn't even be blamed for that, considering he never managed to speak more than two garbled words in her presence.

Which was pretty much what he did now, when she approached, smiled at him, and set a blue spiral notebook near his lunch tray. "I think this is yours," she said.

Gideon said, "Hi." And then he just sat there with a dazed look on his face, like the time I'd accidentally hit him in the back of the head with a baseball.

"It got mixed in with my stuff somehow," Brooke said.

Since I was reasonably certain that he and Tink sat on the opposite of the room from her during U.S. History, I guessed that "somehow" meant Tink had surreptitiously placed the notebook in Brooke's backpack, probably out of a misguided attempt to give Gideon a reason to talk to her.

No wonder Tink had made such a hasty escape earlier.

When he continued to not respond, Brooke appeared a little confused. "Well . . . see you around?" she said, then headed out of the lunchroom.

"Thanks!" I called after her, since Gideon still hadn't located the unmute button.

After she was gone, he leaned forward and banged his head on the table.

How he could dance and flirt and carry on actual conversations with girls he'd just met, but couldn't utter more than a syllable in Brooke's presence was beyond me. He behaved like a perfectly normal person until she came within a five-foot radius. I considered offering to make him a blindfold, but he looked so forlorn that I just patted his shoulder instead.

This wasn't exactly a new issue. Gideon had adored Brooke most of his life. He'd known her even longer than he'd known me; they'd been in the same first grade class, though they had never been friends. His feelings for her were rather complicated—not to mention intense—but unlike Tink, I usually let the matter be.

I was more concerned with Gideon's reading. I traced my thumb along the blank card, which I'd left at the top of the deck. For half a second, an image flashed, too brief for me to identify.

I looked at Gideon. He still appeared dejected, resting his head against the table. His fists were clenched.

For no reason I could name, a chill ran through me.

I called Esther after I got home from school. I hadn't seen her for the past two weeks—she was busy with some vague Kin business she hadn't fully explained, and I'd been granted a reprieve from my Kin lessons—but when I explained that I needed help, she agreed to come by the house that evening. I was surprised, and rather thankful, that she hadn't insisted I go to St. Paul, since she was constantly trying to coerce me into attending family functions. After Iris's betrayal, Esther had insisted that we present a united front to the community. I'd agreed with her, for Elspeth's sake. Esther had taken this to mean she had free rein to transform me into her vision of the ideal granddaughter. She kept trying to dress me up and parade me in front of all of her friends.

So I wasn't exactly eager to throw myself back into her clutches—but I didn't know who else to ask about the blank Nav card.

When she arrived, I brought her into the parlor, where she stood gazing around at the old photographs and garage sale furniture with raised eyebrows. Then she seated herself in one of Gram's upholstered chairs, clasped her hands, and waited.

I sat on the sofa and fished through my book bag until I withdrew my father's Nav deck. I held the blank card toward her. "I wanted to ask about this."

Esther watched me expectantly.

"I don't know what it means," I said.

"It never appeared in your readings before?"

"I didn't have it." I set the cards on the table in front of me. "It's not in Gram's deck. This is my father's."

She looked thoughtful for a moment. "It would have been very unlike Angela to misplace a card."

"It's supposed to be in the deck?"

Esther inclined her head. "I assume that Angela removed it from her deck deliberately. Perhaps she didn't believe you were ready, and she lacked the forethought to explain the card's significance."

"It's not her fault she *died* before she could finish teaching me."

"Or perhaps she merely forgot," Esther responded, shrugging. "So, you want me to tell you what this card means?"

"Can you?" Though Esther had no real talent for Knowing, she had more knowledge and experience of the Kin than any other person I'd met.

"Perhaps not in the way you intend. Give me the cards."

Obediently, I reached forward and handed her the deck, watching her slow, meticulous movements as she shuffled. After a moment, she withdrew a card at random and handed it to me. I flipped it over. Card three, Anchor.

"There," she said. "If we were both asked what this card means, you would say one thing, and I would say another."

"I know that," I said. That was the very basis of the cards, as Gram had explained it. The Nav deck was different for everyone, dependent upon whoever dealt the cards. There was no written guideline.

"You attach meaning to the cards—to the symbols and names, and from those meanings you construct your interpretation of your readings." Esther paused to look up at me. "I'm explaining this to you because the blank card is different. Those with Knowing use the Nav cards to focus their abilities. The meanings you give to each card help you to do this. They allow you to rearrange your perceptions, to form a pattern from the images and ideas you're sensing. But the blank card does the opposite."

She shuffled the cards once more, pale blue showing through the skin on the back of her hands. On her left wrist, threads of color remained where Guardian lights had once pulsed through her veins. She turned the blank card over. "If the other cards are focus and control, the blank card is chaos. It represents infinite potential, infinite possibility. The realm of wonder and disbelief. It allows you to see around the edges, into what lies outside the pattern. Those things our closed minds cannot willingly accept."

"Then how do you use it?"

"By being open. By not assigning it meaning. From what I've been told, those who develop the proper skills see something different in the card each time it's dealt."

"It came up during a reading for my friend Gideon," I said. "He's been having... trouble. Ever since Iris took him to Harlow Tower."

Esther pursed her lips. She didn't like to discuss Iris. "He went through quite an ordeal."

"He thinks he's Kin. I was hoping the reading would give me an answer—or maybe some way to help him. But I couldn't get a sense from the card. I didn't see anything."

"Then you should ask yourself—what part of him are you blind to? What is it within him that you cannot accept? Here is what I suggest: do another reading for him. If the blank card doesn't reappear, well, then perhaps it was only a fluke. If it does appear, release your focus. Forget whatever question you were trying to answer. Stop seeking patterns. You may learn something." She rose from her seat, handing the cards back to me. "I still have some business to attend to, but I expect our lessons will resume in a few weeks."

I thanked her for helping me, then saw her to the door. After she was gone, I headed upstairs, making my way to Gram's room. Though most of Gram's belongings had been packed away or sold, there were a few items Mom and I hadn't touched. I moved to the closet. After sliding the few remaining clothes aside, I stood on my toes and reached up toward the shelf. My fingers grazed the dusty side of Gram's jewelry box. I pulled it toward me, easing it to the ground and opening it gently.

There was no jewelry inside, at least nothing that hadn't been strung together with craft store beads and bits of thread. Gram had used the box to collect small treasures, or so she'd claimed. Most of it was photographs and old letters on dry, crinkling paper. This was where she'd stored her Nav cards for years and years. Keeping them safe, she'd said, until I was ready for them.

And this was where I found the blank card, tucked beneath a photograph of my grandfather Jacky. I frowned, wondering why Gram had left it hidden here. She'd never even mentioned it to me.

Maybe Esther was right, and Gram hadn't felt I was ready. I thought of her whispering to me, the playful smile that lifted the corners of her mouth, the light in her eyes as she spoke, as though she were imparting the mysteries of the universe. She had loved secrets and stories. But the blank card was a secret she'd kept, a story she'd never told. And I couldn't believe she'd simply forgotten about it. My Knowing was a gift, she'd always told me—but she'd also cautioned me not to use it recklessly.

Maybe she had believed the card shouldn't be used at all. She had always said that there were some places it was best not to look.

I glanced at the blank card. Infinite potential. Infinite possibility.

I was still considering the question when I heard the front

door open and close—and then my mother bellowing for me to come downstairs.

"Do we need to have that talk about inside voices again?" I called back, hurrying to meet her.

"Can it, kiddo," came the irate response.

I found her in the kitchen, eating gummy bears and trying to beat the capricious coffeemaker into submission. Given what I could gauge of her mood—and the fact that she didn't always remember to check her strength—I was surprised she hadn't yet pounded it into pulp.

"One of these days," I said, crossing the room, "that thing is going to fight back. And then we'll all be killed in our sleep, smothered by coffee grounds."

Mom grunted, turning to face me. Without speaking, she leaned back against the counter and crossed her arms.

"You needed me for something?" I asked. I eyed her warily. Since we'd barely seen each other the past few days, she'd had no further opportunity to bring up the subject of Leon and me—or the possibility of kicking him out—and I wasn't eager to resume the conversation.

She hesitated a moment. A slight grimace flitted across her features. Then she said, "I hope you didn't have anything major planned for tomorrow, because you're booked."

I reached for her bag of gummy bears. "Booked how?"

"We're having dinner at L'Ora Rosso."

"Why? Wait. Who's *we*? Just the two of us?"

"And Leon," Mom said, sending a chorus of little alarm bells ringing through me. But before I could start panicking, or tell her that I didn't think a busy restaurant was really the best place for us to discuss the details of my relationship with Leon, she added in a low voice, "And . . . Detective Wyle."

That was so unexpected, it took a moment for her words to register. I gaped at her, openmouthed. Finally, after a few seconds of my finest fish impression, I asked, "We're having dinner with Mickey?"

She turned away, becoming suddenly engrossed in taking care of the dishes that had piled up in the sink. "I agreed to meet with him. I thought it was time we discuss his knowledge of Kin affairs."

Now I was even more confused. Mickey had discovered the existence of the Kin—and Mom's identity as Morning Star—two months ago, and, as far as I knew, he'd let the matter drop.

"Hold on. You 'agreed to meet with him'?"

"Reluctantly."

"Uh, Mom? I'm not an expert at this, but I'm pretty sure when a guy asks you to dinner at a classy restaurant, that's called a date. Not really the sort of thing you're meant to drag your daughter and your sidekick along to."

"It's not like that."

"Does Mickey know you've turned this into—" I broke off as a sudden, horrible realization struck me. "No. There is absolutely no way this is happening. I am going to be in therapy for the rest of my life if I have to go on a double date *with my mother*."

"Oh, please. If I haven't managed to screw you up by now, nothing will. Anyway, it isn't a date. It's"—she floundered for a moment—"a friendly meeting."

"A friendly meeting you feel the need to bring reinforcements to."

"I already changed the reservation to four."

Which meant, I supposed, that it had originally been for two.

"You can wrestle Harrowers one-handed, but you can't get dressed up and go out to dinner without calling for backup?" I gave her my sternest look. "Mom. This is not a superhero situation. What do you think he's going to do, Taser you?"

Her eyebrows snapped together. "Do you want your phone replaced or not?"

I couldn't decide if this was bribery or blackmail. Either way, it was hardly fair. I stole her bag of gummy bears and stalked out of the kitchen.

Later that night, I tried cornering Leon to get his help with Mom's descent into lunacy. I found him in his bedroom, surrounded by textbooks, simultaneously scrawling in a spiral notebook and typing on his laptop. While this was clear evidence that he actually had to study, like the rest of us mere mortals—considering he got straight As and I rarely saw him open a book, I'd begun to suspect him of omnipotence—it also meant he was distracted. It took me three tries to explain the situation to him.

And then, instead of agreeing with me that Mom was experiencing some bizarre form of dementia, he said, "If Lucy needs our help, we should be there for her."

"She doesn't need our help. She needs her head examined," I groaned. "But I have an idea. Tell her you won't go. Use your Hungry Puppy eyes on her."

He gave me a blank look.

"Don't act all innocent. You know exactly what I'm talking about. The big, sad eyes you use to get whatever you want. Maybe throw in a lip tremble for good measure."

"And you think Lucy is the crazy one here?"

I didn't even dignify that with a response. With a sigh of resignation, I left him to his textbooks.

I spent Saturday morning hoping for a blizzard. As soon as I woke, I hopped out of bed and peered through my window, searching for some indication that a storm was imminent. Frost and ice glistened on tree branches and along sidewalks, but none of the snow was freshly fallen. Above, a few high, wispy clouds were scattered in the blue. Otherwise the sky was clear. And since I had yet to discover a way to make my mood affect the weather, it seemed there was no escaping my fate.

Our reservation at L'Ora Rosso was at seven, and my mother, for once in her life, was determined not to be late. She started yelling for me to get ready around five thirty. I pulled on one of the dresses Esther had purchased for me when she'd begun outfitting me as a St. Croix, and then stood in front of the mirror, surveying myself. Though the champagne-colored cocktail dress didn't quite make me resemble a runaway bridesmaid, it was still a little fancy for dinner—but unless Mom wanted me to show up in jeans and a baggy sweater, my options were limited. I'd managed to tame my hair somewhat, and, to my delight, I found I actually looked rather nice.

I wondered what outfit Mom was planning. She owned exactly one dress, pale blue with a modest neckline, which was ten years old and got dusted off only when she was forced to attend funerals or weddings. But she must have gone shopping; when I saw her, she wore a slinky green dress that made her look like she belonged on a magazine cover. She'd left her hair down about her shoulders, and she was even wearing heels—but the effect was ruined by the fixed scowl on her face and the impatient way she kept tapping her fingers against her arms.

I narrowed my eyes at her. "A friendly meeting? Right."

She ignored me, heading for the steps.

Leon was downstairs waiting for us. I was accustomed to seeing him dressed up—the clean white shirt, the dark vest, and a tie—but somehow tonight felt different, even though I'd already informed him that I refused to consider it our first date. As I reached the bottom of the stairs, I felt strangely shy. My heart picked up speed, and I couldn't meet his gaze. I looked down at my shoes, fighting the blush that crept up my cheeks.

Then Leon spoke. "You look really..."

67

When he didn't finish the sentence, I glanced up to find him grinning. My shyness evaporated.

I grinned back. "Ditto."

We didn't say anything else. We just stood there smiling stupidly at each other—until Mom walked up to Leon and smacked him on the back of the head.

"I think I preferred the bickering," she said, then hurried us out the door.

We met Mickey at the restaurant shortly before seven. While he wasn't precisely enthusiastic about the inclusion of two unexpected teenagers, he at least had the grace not to appear annoyed. If anything, he seemed amused by our presence, his face quickly showing the laugh lines that marked the sides of his mouth.

He looked better than the last time I'd seen him. More relaxed. And he was much less rumpled than usual. His hair had been trimmed recently, there wasn't a trace of stubble on his jaw, and, for the first time since I'd met him, he appeared to have gotten a full night's sleep. He smiled when he saw us, shaking Leon's hand and greeting me with an easy "Hey, kid."

"Not my fault, I swear," I said, lifting both my hands in front of me.

His gaze flicked toward Mom. "I don't doubt it."

For her part, Mom looked distinctly peevish—especially when Mickey whispered something in her ear that sounded a lot like *coward*.

She didn't respond.

I watched them as we were led to our table. A nagging suspicion began to rise within me. There was a certain familiarity in Mickey's movements—and in Mom's. His hand hovered near the small of her back, not quite touching it. Once we were seated, she leaned forward to straighten his tie, then drew back abruptly, as though she'd thought better of it. My suspicion grew.

Still, I was beginning to think the evening might not be as bad as I'd feared. I'd wondered how Mom was planning to discuss the Kin in the middle of a busy restaurant, but before long, the answer became clear: she wasn't. She kept to neutral topics, and when she spoke, her tone was guarded.

Then, about halfway through dinner, Mickey reached into his coat pocket and withdrew a small envelope. He handed it to Mom.

"My father asked me to give this to you," he said. I glanced over at it. Inside the envelope was a picture of two young men in police uniforms. The first was my grandfather; the second could only have been Mickey's father, Hank Wyle.

"I hadn't seen this one," Mom said.

"Dad said you should keep it. He also asked why I haven't brought you by to see him yet. He'd like to know how Jacky's little girl is getting along." He paused, seeming to weigh his words. "I told him I'm working on it."

"I'm not sure that's a good idea," Mom said.

"Too normal?" Mickey asked.

Her eyes narrowed. "I'm not the meet-the-parents type."

"No kidding. It's taken two months of—" He broke off,

leaning back in his seat and running a hand through his hair. After glancing toward me, he cleared his throat and adjusted his tie. "It took you a while to agree to dinner."

As I looked back and forth between them, my suspicion became certainty.

This had never been about discussing the Kin, and Leon and I weren't here for backup. We were here as a buffer.

Mom didn't let many people get close to her. She didn't have friends; she claimed she didn't have time for them. And she never dated anyone who knew her secret. But whatever was going on between her and Mickey had been going on for a while—which meant that Mom had known very well this was a date. She'd just chickened out on going solo.

I felt a burst of indignation at the fact that she'd been lecturing me about relationships while she was well on the way to making a mess of her own. I decided to give Mickey some help.

"I'm going to the bathroom," I announced, jumping out of my seat. I grabbed Leon's hand, yanking him with me, and hurried away from the table before anyone had a chance to protest.

"That was subtle," Leon said as we walked through the restaurant.

I didn't reply.

"I assume we're not really going to the bathroom."

Once we were safely out of sight, I stopped and leaned against a wall. "No, my plan is for us to stand awkwardly in this hallway while Mom and Mickey talk." A waiter passed, giving us a curious look. I smiled blandly, then turned back to Leon. "And if you have any complaints, I would remind you that you're the suck-up who agreed to come along tonight."

"It's hardly my fault you've got sarcasm instead of a spine."

"She blackmailed me."

"She recently threatened *me* with severe bodily harm."

I had to give him that one. "You're right. You win. She's a tyrant."

He cocked his head toward the door. "Want to go outside for a bit?"

"Definitely. Though, right now, if you asked me to take a stroll on the surface of the sun, I'd probably agree."

"Don't you think that's a bit drastic? Tonight hasn't been *that* bad."

His hand touched my waist, guiding me toward the exit, and when I peered up at him, he was giving me another one of those looks that made me feel like my limbs were made out of Jell-O. "Well, it's getting better," I admitted.

We were nearly at the door when Leon tensed, halting suddenly. His arm curled around me, drawing me backward and holding me tightly against him.

"What—"

The word died on my lips. Ahead of us was a tall, lanky man who appeared to be in his midtwenties. His sandy hair was carefully tousled. His green eyes glittered in the warm light. With his air of nonchalance, the way he moved with a casual sort of grace, he would have stood out even if I hadn't immediately recognized him.

Shane. The Harrower who owned the Drought and Deluge.

He smiled lazily as he strode toward us.

Leon's voice was low and icy. "What do you want?"

"No time for pleasantries. We have a bit of a situation." Shane glanced at me, his smile turning rueful. "Terribly sorry to interrupt your evening, angel, but I'm afraid I require Morning Star."

When I was eight years old, on the night before we
moved to the Cities, I sat beside Gram on our porch swing in the
little house that had been my home and cried. She let me rest my
head in her lap. She stroked my hair, whispering that it would all
be all right. I didn't tell her, then, that I wasn't crying because I
was afraid to move, afraid to leave behind everything I'd known
and enter another world. That was exciting to me, an adventure,
filled with wonder.

I was crying because I sensed a greater change, a hush in the
air around me. Silence, where there should have been the hum of
insects and the soft beat of birds' wings. The sky felt charged, ready
to spark. I had goose bumps all down my arms. It was the first time
I'd sensed something like this. It wasn't the last.

*   *   *

Later, when I learned about my Knowing, I told Gram what I'd felt that night. She nodded slowly, taking my hand in hers, rubbing her thumb against my palm. "This might happen sometimes," she said. Perceptions that weren't complete, nothing solid, nothing I could name or put to words. Almost-Knowings, she called them. I might not have them often, but when I did, it was best to pay attention.

"But what are they?" I asked.

"Disruptions in the pattern. The shifting of the wheel. They're the moments when the hinge of the world begins to bend," she told me. "You sense the change in things."

Eventually, I realized she was talking about precognition. Many Kin had this, a latent sense buried so deeply within the subconscious that it only occasionally bubbled to the surface. My Knowing made me more attuned to it; on occasion, my perception had bordered on Seeing.

Now, watching my mother leave L'Ora Rosso with Shane, I didn't glimpse the future. But I felt it out there, waiting.

I hadn't heard Shane's explanation to Mom, how or why he'd tracked her down in the middle of dinner; I'd only seen her thoughtful expression and short nod. Then she'd turned to Mickey, quietly asking him to excuse her. I was seated at the table again, and I kept my eyes on her until she disappeared, focusing on details: the flicker of light that glanced off her bright hair, the jagged scar running down her right arm, the dark green edge of her dress.

Once she was gone, I turned back to the table, trying to calm myself. I didn't think Shane would hurt her. I doubted he even could. But I couldn't shake the feeling that something was about to happen.

Leon had wanted to accompany them, but Mom had instructed him to let her handle it. Now he sat beside me, tense and silent. Though he remained motionless, his eyes were alert, his entire body poised for action. He was all Guardian, restless, ready.

Mickey just seemed bemused. "Someone you know, I take it."

"He's a friend of the family," I said, hedging.

"Meaning—Kin." He stumbled slightly over the word. I wondered how much he and Mom had actually discussed the Kin, and how he'd dealt with the knowledge.

"Sort of the opposite," I said. I felt a rush of sympathy for him. He could win an award for the worst date in history. Not only had Mom dragged two uninvited guests along, she'd now left the restaurant with another man. Or demon, rather. I wasn't sure if that made matters better or worse.

Though perhaps Mickey should've known better than to ask a superhero out.

"I'm sure she'll be back soon," I added.

Mickey made a low noise and turned his head. After a moment of frantically searching for something consoling to say, I realized he was laughing.

That was when Leon left the table.

"Wait here," he said, rising so quickly and smoothly from his chair that he was halfway across the room before I saw that he was exiting the restaurant.

Mickey and I looked at each other.

"This happen a lot?" he asked.

"What, the way we're being picked off one by one in horror-film fashion?"

He smiled wryly. "That, too."

I hesitated. I still felt that difference in the air, that sense of expectancy, but it wasn't something I could convey to him. And even if I could, I probably shouldn't have. Mom had spent too much time emphasizing to me the fragility of humans and the consequences of getting them involved with Harrowers.

Instead, I tried to distract him. "So—you and my mom have been seeing each other?"

That *did* distract him. For several seconds, he seemed at a loss for words. Finally, he looked down at his hands and said, "You could say that."

He looked so uncomfortable I decided that this was a topic we both should avoid. I hastily changed the subject. "That was really nice of your dad," I said. "The picture. Did you ever meet Gram?"

"Mostly when I was too young to remember. Dad and Jacky had a falling out, and they didn't patch things up until I was already in college."

"I wonder why."

I didn't hear his answer.

Suddenly, that feeling I'd had, that almost-Knowing, came into sharp, painful focus. Every sense went on alert. The awareness was strong, strident, screaming inside me. Not an impression of danger—a sense of change.

And something else.

A familiar sensation crawled up my skin, the echo of something I'd felt before, lingering on the edge of my perception. The harsh, primal anger of the unknown Guardian.

I wasn't even aware I'd risen until Mickey followed suit.

"You should probably stay here," he said. "You don't look so hot, kid."

"I'm going to get Mom. I'll hurry. Don't follow." I darted toward the door before he could stop me, hoping he'd have the sense not to make a scene. I felt a tug of guilt at leaving him—he was now alone at the table, probably surrounded by curious onlookers, unable to chase me unless he wanted to turn our abrupt exits into an actual dine and dash—but I couldn't stop to worry about that. My Knowing was insistent, urging me onward. I remembered the Guardian in the parking ramp, recalled the blinding heat of his wrath, saw the hatred in his eyes and the blood on his face.

He was Kin; he wouldn't hurt other Kin, I told myself, but I couldn't slow the pounding of my heart. Once outside, I scarcely felt the chill of the air on my bare limbs. I knew exactly where I was headed. I moved quickly, leaving the restaurant behind and crossing to Loring Park.

The sky was clear above me. The lights of Minneapolis glistened, hiding the stars. The icy wind burned against me, but I ignored it, searching the snow-bright park. Harrowers clouded the senses, but I knew what I was seeking.

There. I saw a small cluster of trees, bare branches black in the thin light, the moon hanging among them. Below: the fall of three shadows; Leon's tall shape and wide shoulders; the beacon of my mother's blond hair, tangled by the wind.

Before I could reach them, a hand shot out, catching my arm and holding me in a firm grip. I spun, trying to jerk myself free, and found Shane smiling down at me.

"Hungry for trouble as ever, I see," he said, releasing my arm. "But it's probably best to let your mum handle this one."

I didn't see where he'd come from, but I was more concerned about where he *wasn't*—with Mom and Leon. I turned again, trying to identify the third figure. With effort, I made out a few details: female, slightly taller than my mother, pale hair cropped short, age indeterminate. I frowned. Though I couldn't see her well, I knew she wasn't human.

"Who is she?" I whispered.

"No need to fret. She's neutral."

"Did you bring her? What's she doing here?" I asked.

He shrugged. "Running scared. It appears there's a Guardian loose in the Cities who doesn't discriminate between the nastier element of the Harrower populace and those of us just trying to live out our sad, sordid little existences in some semblance of peace. She seems to think he's after her."

The Guardian from the ramp. It had to be. Maybe that was the reason I felt the lingering burn of his rage all around me, why he felt so near. "I think I've seen him," I said uneasily. "He sort of saved my life."

"How obliging of him. All the same, I'd prefer it if he didn't take mine."

"Is that why you're here, talking to Mom?"

"I'm more of an ambassador."

"So you *did* bring that demon."

"Don't get me wrong. I feel no soul-stirring allegiance to my fellows. But a Harrower begging help from Morning Star? That's a level of irony I couldn't possibly pass up."

"And that's your only reason?" I asked, frowning.

"You want the honest answer? You won't like it."

I crossed my arms. According to Mr. Alvarez, Shane was a Seer. He had the ability to glimpse the future—but he was rarely willing to share what he saw of it. "Is it going to be completely cryptic and unhelpful? Because I'll admit to being a little tired of that."

Shane turned away. He was silent a moment, tilting his head back to stare at the sky. When he spoke, his voice was soft. "This Guardian is a nuisance, but I expect he can be handled. His actions don't distress me. His presence—now, that's something else. I fear he's a herald of troubled times. The real threat is what he's come here chasing. Warn your mum. I'm not convinced she'll listen to me."

"This is something you've Seen?" I asked. I didn't think I'd ever heard him speak seriously.

"Call it . . . instinct."

I didn't answer. My own instincts were telling me that something was wrong, that something was close. I shivered, becoming abruptly aware of the cold around me, the biting wind, the snow at my ankles.

Ahead of us, the Harrower let out a high, piercing shriek.

I whirled. The ground was slick beneath me. I had no traction and found myself in the snow. As Shane helped me to my feet, I saw a burst of activity before us: Leon turning at the sound of my fall; the sudden glow beneath my mother's fingertips and throat. The blond Guardian had appeared out of nowhere and stood grappling with the Harrower.

Before Mom could intervene, the demon fell beneath a blow. The girl went down human but came up snarling, all talons and teeth, lashing out wildly. Moonlight rippled down scaled flesh, over eyes gone blank and round. But I sensed no malice in the demon, only fright—terror knifing through her, turning her words to whimpers and then into roars.

"Brilliant," Shane muttered.

Across the distance, I heard my mother's voice: "Get Audrey out of here."

The command was unnecessary. Leon was already advancing toward me with long, swift strides.

"She's perfectly safe with me," Shane said mildly, once Leon reached us.

"Yeah, right." Without giving me a chance to object, Leon dragged me to him, then reached behind my knees and scooped me up. My legs dangled over his arm, dripping snow. One moment, we were in the park. The next, we were in my bedroom.

Still carrying me, Leon flipped on the overhead light. "What the hell were you thinking?" he asked, sounding more exasperated than angry.

"I was worried," I said as I tried to squirm out of his grip.

He didn't release me but shifted his hold on me. A frown worked its way onto his brow. "God, you're freezing."

"Some of us aren't Guardians," I said. *He* was warm; he'd been standing outside longer than I had, but I felt the heat of his skin through the thin material of his coat.

"Precisely." He took two steps forward and dumped me rather unceremoniously onto my bed. "Stay here."

I propped myself up on my elbows. "You can't just—"

He silenced my protest by leaning across me and pressing me down into the mattress, covering my mouth with his. He kissed me just enough to leave me breathless, then stood up and gave me a crooked grin. "I've been waiting all night to do that."

And with that, he vanished.

The first thing I did was bellow Leon's name at the top of my lungs. I stood up on my bed, straightened my shoulders, and shrieked. Unfortunately, I quickly discovered that I wasn't nearly as good at shouting as my mother was. Not only did my shriek not have the intended result, it also hurt my throat. And it didn't even make me feel better. It only made me feel foolish, standing there on my mattress in a cocktail dress, soaked with snow, alone with my outrage.

I hopped to the floor, still fuming. After a minute or two of agitated pacing, I swapped my dress for jeans and a sweatshirt, tucked my hair into a ponytail, and headed downstairs to wait. While I waited, I rehearsed what I planned to say to Leon whenever he bothered to reappear. But as the minutes ticked past and I'd had no contact from him or Mom, my anger turned to restlessness, and then to worry. I paced the length of the living room, listening for any sounds that might signal their arrival. The house was quiet around me, big and dark and empty.

The hall clock chimed the hour. My thoughts drifted back to the events at Loring Park. The blond Guardian. The Harrower screaming. Shane's words echoed through me: *I fear he's a herald of troubled times.* I wondered what was happening. If more Harrowers had appeared. If there was fighting. Distantly, I hoped that Mom would remember Mickey.

Twenty minutes had passed when I heard a car slow on the street outside, and then pull into the driveway. I hurried to the hall and jerked the door open—and found Mr. Alvarez standing outside, looking somber and serious despite his spiked-up hair.

He'd apparently been in a hurry. He wasn't wearing his leather jacket, one of his shoelaces was untied, and he appeared to be holding the crumpled remains of a bag of Wendy's french fries. After giving me a brief greeting, he asked, "Lucy's still out?"

I was relieved to see a familiar face, even if the face belonged to my precalculus teacher, so I nodded and led him into the living room. "Is she expecting you? Because she sort of has her own situation."

"Same situation. We spoke earlier. She asked me to meet her here."

"I hope that wasn't your dinner," I said, when he tossed the empty Wendy's bag into the garbage. He gave me a look that told me any further comments on his dietary habits would be met with pop quizzes, so I shut up.

I was saved from making any awkward attempts at small talk by the return of Leon. He appeared beside me and touched my shoulder. I was so glad to see him it took me a moment to remember that I was annoyed. I smiled up at him without thinking. Then I glowered.

"You are in *big* trouble," I warned.

"You have an update, Farkas?" Mr. Alvarez asked.

"Lucy has him. They're on their way. Did you find out who he is?"

"I have some calls out. I was hoping to at least learn which Circle he's from, but I haven't heard anything yet. He went with Lucy willingly?"

"Theoretically," Leon said. "We'll find out—if he's still in the car when she gets here. I'm not positive, but I believe he can teleport."

The statement surprised me. I hadn't met any Kin besides Leon with the ability to teleport, though that would explain the Guardian's sudden appearance in the parking ramp last Friday.

"What happened to the Harrower?" I asked.

Leon turned away. "She's dead. Lucy stopped the fight, but the Harrower's injuries were too severe."

I swallowed tightly, recalling the rent, bloody bodies of the demons the Guardian had killed. Those demons had been hostile, vicious—but the one in the park hadn't been violent. She'd been terrified. I felt a strange, unexpected stirring of pity.

"That's bad," Mr. Alvarez was saying. "If he's in the habit of killing neutrals, we may have a problem. We'll need to get him under control."

"From what I saw, he didn't seem to have *any* control," Leon said.

"Then he'll learn it."

"Wait," I said. I turned toward the door, hearing the sound of a car approaching in the distance. For just a second, everything else seemed muted, far away. I listened to the engine, tires rolling across a street packed hard with snow. The car slowed. I felt that same familiar sense of anger up and down my skin. "I think they're here."

The Guardian's name was Drew. Drew Reingold, he told us. He stood in the parlor gripping the edge of the mantel with one hand, his arms and shoulders tensed. He came from the Circle in San Diego. He'd been in the Twin Cities a little over two weeks now, tracking a Harrower.

"She must be located as quickly as possible." His fingers tightened on the mantel, his knuckles going white. "And she must be killed."

I saw a flash of red hair, a gleam of gold. It was memory, not Knowing, but my heart thudded against my ribs. Susannah.

Leon, Mr. Alvarez, and my mother stood looking at Drew, their faces grim. Mom was still wearing her slinky green dress, but she was barefoot and her hair was tangled. Blood was smeared down her shoulder, a thin crimson streak turning brown. Near her, Leon leaned against the wall, his arms folded. His gaze strayed to mine now and then.

I lurked at the far end of the room, near the door. When they'd first arrived, Mom had made a halfhearted attempt to shoo me upstairs, but she hadn't pressed the issue, so I had stayed, doing my best to remain unobtrusive. Since Drew had given no sign that he recognized me, I kept my silence.

The last time I'd seen Drew, his movements had been too quick for me to form a clear picture of him. Now, studying him as he spoke, I filled in some details. I noted the fevered restlessness in his every motion, the blood that had dried on him. He was dressed simply, in dark jeans and a gray long-sleeved shirt; the clothing hung on his frame. Though Leon could charitably have been described as skinny, there was always an unmistakable air of health and vigor about him. This man was thin to the point of gauntness. I couldn't guess his age—maybe thirty, maybe older. Other features were easier. He was of medium height, perhaps an inch or two shorter than Mr. Alvarez, and his blond hair was once again pulled back in a short ponytail. His face was haggard, and the stubble on his chin was developing into a ragged, unkempt beard.

But none of that was what held my attention. There was something else about him, something that reminded me of the Beneath. Under the constant blaze of anger he carried, there lay a sort of desolation, a bleakness, as though some vital part of him had gone missing.

His eyes were the worst part. They were a soft blue-gray, the color of wet stone, striking in his hollowed-out face—but the look in them was one of bewilderment, of helplessness, like someone who had woken from a long sleep to find the world rearranged in his absence. Meeting his gaze was like touching an open wound. I flinched and looked away.

"You've been in the Cities two weeks," Mr. Alvarez was saying, "and you didn't think to contact the Kin? There's a reason we have support networks in place."

"I've been meaning to. There are matters you need to be aware of." Drew paused, turning, giving Mr. Alvarez a critical look. "You lead the Kin here?"

"The Guardians."

"But not Morning Star," Drew said.

"I prefer to go my own way," Mom affirmed. Her voice hardened. "That's not the same as going rogue."

Mr. Alvarez held up a hand. "We'll discuss that in a moment." He looked at Drew. "Tell us about this Harrower you're tracking."

Drew didn't answer immediately. He faced the wall, holding the mantel with both hands, bowing his head between them. The rest of us stood quiet, waiting. For a moment, I heard only Drew's short, shaky breaths.

Then: "She goes by the name Susannah."

It was what I'd been expecting, but a shiver ran through me.

"She showed up in San Diego a year ago," he continued. "Where she was before then—I don't know. Maybe near another Circle. Maybe biding her time Beneath. She's elusive. Cunning.

I can't gauge her true strength, because she makes others do her fighting. But she's powerful. Powerful enough to bring weaker Harrowers up from Beneath. She has sway over them."

I didn't think that was unusual—when it came to Harrowers, the weak often allied themselves with the strong; Tigue had certainly had plenty of willing minions to do his bidding during his search for the Remnant. But Drew explained that it was more than that. He didn't know if it was hypnotism or some other form of influence, but Susannah had a certain measure of control over her followers and was able to bend others to her will. And not just Harrowers, he said—humans as well.

"She was neutral," Drew told us. "Or she pretended to be. She was friendly with the Kin, with the Guardians. She introduced herself to us when she first arrived in San Diego. So that there would be no *misunderstandings*, she'd said. After that, she was quiet. She kept to herself. That was what we believed, anyway. In actuality, she had a few members of the Kin under her control. She used them to gather information about us."

"What happened?" Mom asked.

"It all changed a month ago. When she attacked."

"I seem to have heard something about this," Mr. Alvarez said. "There was a Seer who was killed."

"Valerie."

The word was quiet. Three soft syllables; almost a whisper. But heavy in the air. Full of longing. I caught a shiver of Knowing: The gray light before sunrise. The naked slope of a woman's neck, her dark skin. The lapping of water. Bare toes sinking into sand. I heard a low, throaty laugh and the sound of bells. I saw two hands slide together.

"She was your charge," Leon said. He locked his gaze on Drew for a long moment, then looked toward me.

But his guess wasn't correct, I realized. Not entirely.

Looking at Drew, I saw something I had failed to mark earlier: on his left hand, the warm gold gleam of a wedding band.

"Susannah killed her," Drew said. His face contorted, and he seemed to struggle to find his voice. Finally, he continued, "My charge is dead and I'm alive. Not how it's meant to work, I know. But that's how Susannah wanted it. She let me live because she wanted to remake me in her image. She had her pet Harrowers incapacitate me, and then she left Val dying in my arms, to teach me hate, she said. She wanted to see what I would become. And now—now I mean to grant her wish."

There was a long, uneasy silence. I stood immobile, my heart hammering. Drew turned, pacing. His breathing was ragged, his hands clenched. If Susannah had hoped to teach Drew hate, she'd succeeded. I thought of the savage way he'd attacked the demons in the parking ramp, recalled the blood on his brow. I felt the bright burn of his rage.

But my mind was racing for another reason. I was remembering the night I'd stood beside Leon's hospital bed, the night he'd taken a blast meant for me, the night he'd explained what it meant to be my Guardian.

It's not just wanting to protect you, he'd told me. *It's needing to protect you. It's physical.*

Seeing Drew's agitation, the way he couldn't keep still, the wild, stricken look in his eyes, the pallor of his skin—I finally understood what Leon had meant.

But another thought kept repeating itself in my brain.

Drew had loved his charge, and she'd died.

Drew had loved his charge.

I glanced at Leon, but he'd turned away from me.

Finally, Mr. Alvarez spoke. "Is that why you came here? To seek revenge?"

"I came to put an end to Susannah. With help, or without it."

"You'll have help," Mr. Alvarez promised. "But why is she here?"

"Because of Val. Because of what Val saw."

"A vision, you mean?" Mom said.

Drew's tone was steadier now. "That's right. But it's more than that. You have to understand about Val. She is—was—the most gifted Seer born to the Kin in generations. We always believed that's why I was called to protect her." His lips tightened. He looked down at his hands, and slowly unclenched his fists. "About a month before she was killed, Val had a series of visions, different from what she was used to. They were stronger. More intense."

I frowned. From what I understood of it, Seeing was a rare, uncertain ability, hazy and inexact. Though someone might have glimpses of future events, the visions weren't always definitive, and they were often open to wide interpretation. Esther had likened understanding visions to trying to complete a jigsaw puzzle with half the pieces missing: you'd have an idea of the final picture, but most of the details were absent. And since the ability was somewhat linked to Knowing, Esther warned me to be wary of anything I might occasionally See. *The future isn't fixed*, she'd told me. *Merely probable.*

"Val foresaw some Harrower plan?" Mr. Alvarez was asking. "Something they wanted to keep hidden?"

Drew didn't speak immediately, and in the momentary hush, I had that feeling again. The almost-Knowing that made me break into goose bumps, made my throat tighten and my heart lurch.

The shift of the wheel, I thought. The bend of the hinge.

"No," Drew said. "She saw the end of the Kin."

Silence fell, taut and heavy. I hugged my arms. Drew's

words, softly spoken, seemed like a spell. An incantation threaded
in the air, repeated and repeated.

The end of the Kin.

Images spun out before me. Not any sort of Knowing—just
fragments of my own imagination, fear channeled into form. I saw
the twisted layers of the Beneath: a world made of shadow and
bone; the glare of red stars; Harrowers all around, scaled, slinking.
I heard the sharp tap of claws on empty streets. I saw the light of
the Astral Circle, brilliant and burning, suddenly extinguished. I
saw figures in the distance. Faces turned from me.

Then Mom spoke, breaking the spell. "When?"

I let out a breath I hadn't realized I'd been holding.

Drew looked at her.

"You just told us the world is ending," she said. "I'd like to know how much time I have to prevent it."

"You're assuming you *can* prevent it," Drew said.

"I don't assume."

"Isn't that the reason you're here? To stop it?" Leon asked.

Drew looked at him. "I'm here for Susannah."

Mr. Alvarez cut in, his voice quiet but firm. "Tell us about these visions. Seeing isn't known for its accuracy. Are you certain that what Val saw was real?"

"Val died because of what she saw," Drew said. "Susannah learned about the visions and killed Val to keep her from Seeing anything else. That's real."

"I'm not questioning the validity of your loss. If we're going to fight this, we need to know what we're facing."

Drew's face contorted again. I felt his rage flare—so intense it was physical. I started to sweat beneath my goose bumps. He clenched his fists once more, loosened them, took an uneven breath. Finally, he turned away, toward the window, and spoke again. "The visions weren't completely clear. And they changed. Val saw them four times, and they were different each time. But there was one element that was always the same. She was certain of this part." He paused, taking another breath. "It begins here. At this Circle."

"That's why Susannah came here?" Mr. Alvarez asked. "She intends to start a Harrowing?"

"No. There was something else. In two of the visions, the end was triggered by a specific source. A Kin teenager. Val couldn't see this clearly, but she got a sense of it—a girl carrying an immense power. Something long forgotten, she said."

Mr. Alvarez's voice was grim. "The Remnant."

"That's just perfect," Mom muttered.

Leon's face was unreadable.

My thoughts spun. If someone wanted to destroy the Kin, using the Remnant would be the way to do it. Remnants were Kin who had inherited a specific power from the Old Race—the ability to create passageways Beneath. Anywhere. Potentially everywhere. Seventeen years ago, a demon named Verrick had begun a Harrowing because he'd had a vision of the upcoming birth of a Remnant within the Twin Cities. He might have succeeded in finding her, if my mother hadn't defeated him. And recently Iris and Tigue had killed girls all across the Cities, trying to locate this Remnant.

"Susannah is here looking for the girl," Drew continued. "My guess is—she'll find her, and she'll corrupt her. She's done it to others. She'll take her Beneath and keep her there until all of her humanity is stripped away and she's as dead inside as a Harrower. Susannah will control her utterly. Then she'll use her powers to open the Beneath."

And bring about the end of the Kin. I shivered. "Does this mean more bleedings?"

Drew's gaze shifted to me. I still couldn't meet his eyes. I looked away.

"We had trouble a couple of months back," Mr. Alvarez explained. "Another Harrower hunting the Remnant, targeting Kin girls."

Drew started pacing again, his hands moving restlessly. "Bleedings. No. I don't know. That doesn't seem her style. I don't know what methods she'll use, but she has—she has someone working with her. Someone with an incredibly potent Knowing. It could be she'll use him to find the girl."

I glanced up at that. When I'd first learned of the Remnant's existence, I'd tried—and failed—to locate her with my Knowing. But my abilities were limited. Even with Iris's Amplification, I'd found no clue of the Remnant's identity. I'd only had the certain, alarming sense that I wasn't the only one seeking, that somewhere, in the unguarded space where Knowing met Knowing, something had been looking back. The feeling had haunted my sleep for weeks, even after Tigue had been defeated and Iris had disappeared Beneath. Several nights, I'd woken in the silence of my bedroom, afraid I'd heard voices. Words. Whispers. Warnings.

But a demon wouldn't have to worry about what else might be looking. A demon could search unhindered.

Daniel, I thought, remembering the boy with the tattoo on his wrist.

"Did these visions have a deadline?" Mom was asking. "Did Val know when any of this was meant to occur?"

Drew shook his head.

"We need to act quickly. Whether or not the Seeing was

true, Susannah is a threat and cannot be allowed to locate the Remnant," Mr. Alvarez said.

Mom nodded. "I agree. We take her out. Immediately."

"We need to find her first," Drew replied. "She's been lying low. I've been tracking her, following her movements, but I lost her the last time she went Beneath. That was a week ago."

"Then we find her," Mom said.

Mr. Alvarez turned to Drew. "In the meantime, we can't have all the neutral demons in the Cities allied against us."

"The first thing Susannah did when she dropped her pretense of neutrality was convert others to her way of thinking. She gathers others to her. Collects them and controls them. I killed most of her faction before she left San Diego. She'll need to replenish her ranks."

"So you just decided to strike preemptively?" Mom asked.

"I didn't think you'd miss a few Harrowers."

Leon broke his silence in order to say, "There's one or two I could live without."

Mom shot him a look. "Not helping."

"The killings stop," Mr. Alvarez said. "The situation in the Cities is already unstable. Provoking hostilities puts the rest of the Kin at risk."

"So does allowing these Harrowers to run free. Neutral doesn't mean innocent. They'll pick a side quick enough—and they won't pick ours," Drew said.

"And actively hunting them will only make their survival

instincts kick in," Mr. Alvarez said. "We can't fight every neutral in the Cities *and* deal with the Susannah threat. Not without a needless loss of life. This isn't a debate."

Drew looked as though he were going to continue arguing, but after a moment he gave a grudging assent. Mr. Alvarez nodded and asked, "Where have you been staying?"

Drew lifted a shoulder.

"We'll find you lodging. Go to Harlow Tower downtown tomorrow, and talk to my uncle Bernard. I'll let him know to expect you."

"I'll be in contact," Drew said. I assumed that meant he was leaving, but instead he turned and walked to Leon. "This girl—she's your charge?" He jerked his head in my direction.

Leon nodded. His eyes were wary.

There was a sudden flash of color, Guardian lights glowing beneath the skin of Drew's hand as he grabbed Leon by the collar and slammed him against the wall.

"Guard her *better*," Drew hissed. Then he vanished.

Leon straightened, tugging at his shirt.

"What was that about?" Mom asked.

Leon didn't answer, but he turned toward me, watching me intently. I looked down at my feet.

"I'll bring the rest of the Guardians up to speed," Mr. Alvarez was saying, "and have them start searching for this Susannah. But Drew may prove to be a problem. I need you to handle him, Lucy. He seems a bit . . . volatile."

"He's completely unhinged," she said. Then her voice grew gentle. "He's grieving. I understand that, and I sympathize—to a point. That point ends when he becomes a danger to others."

Mr. Alvarez hesitated a moment, seeming to weigh his words. "Esther needs to be informed of the situation. The Kin elders will want the Remnant found. They'll want her powers sealed, Lucy. And Esther will agree with them."

Mom turned toward the window. "And so we sentence an innocent young girl to a life devoid of any deep emotion? Just like that?"

"I don't like it, either, but I'm not sure what choice we'll have."

"If the Elders want the Remnant, let *them* find her. Susannah should be our focus."

He nodded. "I'll contact the Kin in San Diego tomorrow and request whatever information they have on her." He turned to leave, giving a quick wave as he headed for the entryway, and then disappeared outside.

I looked from Leon to Mom and back to Leon. He stood in silence, not moving from his position near the wall. I swallowed.

"You've been pretty quiet, kiddo," Mom said. She crossed the room to me.

"That's because I'm still stuck on *end of the Kin*."

"That's not going to happen."

I didn't want to admit how shaken I was, so I just shrugged. "Are you sure? Because if we're all about to die, I'm not going to school anymore. I am not spending my last hours on Earth hearing about vectors."

Mom tugged me against her and started smoothing my hair with her hand. "We are not about to die. You are still going to school. And this is a Guardian issue, which you are absolutely staying out of, understood?"

"Okay."

"Okay." She squeezed me tightly. Once she was assured that I was all right, she released me and headed out of the living room, attempting to drag a hand through the tangled mess of her hair.

I followed her to the stairs. "What did you do with Mickey? I hope you didn't run out on him *and* stick him with the bill."

"I didn't do either."

I gave her a doubtful look, but she hurried out of sight.

"What did Drew mean?" Leon asked from behind me.

I turned to find him standing in the doorway of the living room, his expression grave. My lips parted, but no sound came out. I'd been dreading this conversation for days.

When I didn't speak, Leon took a step forward, then another. He reached toward me, caught my arm, and slid his fingers gently downward until they came to rest near my elbow. "Audrey," he said. "Drew knew something I don't. I need you to tell me what that is."

I lowered my gaze, looking down at his hand and the slender scar that trailed along the back of it. "Something happened last Friday."

"You were in trouble."

"I met Susannah."

"You *met* her." He seemed to struggle with speech a second, then asked, "How?"

"I was downtown with Tink and Gideon. Susannah followed us to a parking ramp."

"Drew saved you."

"He must have tracked her there. He killed the Harrowers who were with her."

"And it didn't occur to you that this was information you might want to share?" He gave a brief, humorless laugh. "Christ, Audrey. I thought we were past all this."

I felt my hackles rise and lifted my gaze to his. "Past all *what*?"

"Your willful ignorance of danger."

"It's not my fault some crazy demon girl decided to stalk me."

"That's not the point. You were in trouble, and you didn't tell me."

His tone made me bristle. I wanted to say, *I didn't think I'd have to*, but I kept my lips firmly closed. I knew he was right, and that I should have told him, but I wasn't going to admit that—not when I still didn't know why he hadn't appeared that night.

I tried to jerk my arm away, but Leon tightened his grip and held me where I stood. He scowled down at me.

My temper snapped. "Oh, my God, quit *looming*!" I railed. He was such a ridiculous giant, I almost needed a step stool to yell at him properly. I was sorely tempted to grab him by the tie and yank him down to my eye level. "Remember that talk we had about this whole domineering act of yours?"

He released me and took a step back, but the glower remained fixed on his face.

"Which reminds me," I said, "dumping me on my bed and disappearing? Not okay."

"I should have left Shane to look after you?"

"I'm not completely incompetent, you know. You could try letting me look after myself—or at least give me some *say* in the matter, instead of just deciding that you know best. Again."

"Ensuring your safety is my first priority. That isn't going to change."

"Then where were you last Friday?"

I had a second to register his look of surprise before I swung away from him, and turned to face the wall.

"First you were pissed because I protected you, and now you're pissed because I didn't?"

My eyes stung. I attempted to focus on the wall, the pale blue paint that Mom and I had applied last year, but my vision kept blurring.

Leon's hands curled around my shoulders. He tried to turn me around, but I twisted out of his grasp. "Are you going to look at me?" he asked.

"No."

A low sigh escaped him. "You didn't tell me you were in trouble *because* I didn't know. Is that it?"

Nodding stiffly, I said, "I thought it might mean you're no longer my Guardian. I'm not holding the Astral Circle's power anymore, and that was why you were called to protect me, isn't it?"

"I was called to protect *you*. I'm still your Guardian."

Finally, I turned back toward him. "Then..."

"Then something is wrong," he said. He paused, letting out a shaky breath. Our eyes met. He spoke quietly, echoing Drew's words: "I didn't know you were in danger. That's not how it's meant to work."

I gazed at him, wordless. He was always so confident, so sure of himself and his place in the world—but now, abruptly, he seemed a little lost. There was an uncertain look in his eyes I hadn't seen since the night we'd met, that summer twilight he'd shown up on his motorcycle and stood in the grass at the end of the drive. But he had smiled then, and he didn't smile now. He turned away.

"We'll figure it out," he said. "Lucy and I will need to be on the streets tonight. I should get ready."

I watched him leave.

10

The following afternoon, I went to see Shane.

I'd lain awake much of the night, my mind in a tumult. The evening had replayed itself behind my eyes. I'd seen the snow in Loring Park, a crescent of blood staining it crimson. I'd seen the grief that haunted Drew's movements, the shine of gold on his hand. I had drifted, half-conscious, as other images crowded my thoughts. The Beneath. Harrowers writhing as darkness spilled onto city streets. Susannah's pale eyes, the curve of her smile. My mother running, fighting, falling beneath a blow. Harlow Tower bleeding flame.

Then, near morning, as sleep finally took hold, I recalled Esther's words: *The future isn't fixed.*

Merely probable.

When I woke, I decided that Mom was right. The end of the

Kin wasn't going to happen—because we were going to make sure it didn't.

Not that I had any idea how to accomplish that. I wasn't a Guardian. I couldn't fight Susannah, not with any hope of surviving. And my Knowing didn't seem of much use. I'd failed to find the Remnant before, and the experience had convinced me it wasn't something I should try again.

That was when my thoughts turned to Shane. He was a Seer. He knew something he wasn't saying, something he had only hinted at. He'd told me to warn my mother. And the first time I'd seen Susannah, she'd been at the Drought and Deluge.

But when I brought the subject up to Mom, she told me she didn't think Shane would be of any assistance.

"Ryan might believe we can trust him, but I don't," she told me when I saw her that morning.

"But you helped him last night."

"I said I don't trust him, not that I fear him. He's not a threat. That doesn't make him our ally." She pulled her hair free from its bun, shaking it loose across her shoulders. Then she turned to me. "I meant what I told you last night, Audrey. I don't want you involved in this."

I nodded absently as she headed upstairs to sleep. Then, since I didn't consider asking a few questions to be involving myself in anything, I asked Gideon to drive me to the Drought and Deluge.

He was at my house already. I'd tried doing another reading for him, but I was too anxious to focus properly. The only images

I caught were of Brooke and Susannah, and those were only the briefest of flashes. Gideon told me it was all right, but I could tell he was disappointed that I still hadn't found any evidence of his being Kin. And though he didn't mention his nightmares, I knew they hadn't gone away. I promised him we'd keep trying.

He wasn't eager to go downtown again, but he didn't want me to go alone, either—even though Harrowers rarely attacked during the day. Demons weren't precisely allergic to sunlight, but they definitely didn't like it. I wasn't even certain I'd be able to find Shane.

"Why are you going, then?" Gideon asked.

"Because I have to do *something.*"

"What if he's not there?"

"Then I'll think of something else."

As it turned out, I didn't have to. When we reached the Drought and Deluge, Shane was standing outside, smoking.

"I guess you don't really have to worry about lung cancer," I said, approaching him. As Esther had told me, Harrowers might pretend humanity, but they didn't have it. They weren't susceptible to disease, and their human bodies didn't grow weak with age.

"The upside of immortality," Shane agreed.

"There's a downside?"

He grinned. "The girls you love grow old so quickly." His gaze drifted to Gideon, resting on him a moment before turning back to me. "Is this a social call? Somehow, I don't think your scowling savior would approve."

I didn't feel like talking about Leon just then. "I wanted to ask you a few things."

"Such as what I think the future might hold?"

"Sort of, yeah."

Shane didn't reply immediately. He'd finished his cigarette and stood leaning against the building, staring skyward. "As much as it pains me to disappoint you, you've wasted your efforts. I'm not privy to whatever devious plans this Susannah is hatching."

"But you know something. You told me to warn my mother."

"A fit of whimsy."

"It didn't sound like one."

He gave me a long, measuring look. At times, he seemed so human that I could almost forget he was a Harrower—but now his eyes reminded me. For all the warmth of his voice and smile, there was something distant and cold in his gaze. I glanced away.

I didn't think he was going to answer, but after a moment he said, "You want to speak with me, we speak alone."

Gideon had been standing there silently, a small frown on his face, but now he grabbed the sleeve of my coat. "That sounds like a bad idea."

Shane gave me no chance to protest. "Those are the terms. You needn't take them. You're free to leave." He turned and walked into the club.

"Bad idea," Gideon repeated.

"He won't hurt me. I'll try to hurry."

Inside, I found Shane standing in front of the mural of the Minneapolis skyline. His hands were tucked into his pockets, his head tilted to one side. I studied the painting: the buildings in it were stark white and gray shapes, red stars bleeding above them.

"Do you like it?" he asked.

"You did it yourself?" When he nodded, I asked, "Why paint the Beneath?"

"Because that's what I see."

His tone made the hairs on the back of my neck stand on end. I moved away, stopping at one of the nearby tables. "Did you know Susannah was here last Friday?"

He shrugged. "I'm afraid I don't keep tabs on everyone who frequents my club."

"But she's a Harrower."

"And naturally that makes us good friends."

"So, you've never met her, then?"

"I didn't say that."

"She knew who I was," I said.

He stepped back from the mural and perched at the edge of a table, crossing his arms and smiling at me. "I didn't tell her, if that's what you're asking. It was your little light show atop Harlow Tower that granted you infamy. That shine you carried burned rather bright."

I frowned. "What do you know of her?"

"That she's just about as nasty as they come. Not anyone you'd wish to spend time with. You should stay out of this one."

"Right. Because sitting around waiting to be annihilated is a *great* plan."

"I doubt it will come to that."

"Have you Seen something?"

"Ah—and now we come to it." He leaned forward, giving me a searching look. His smile turned mocking. "That's what prompted this little meeting of ours, isn't it? You didn't seek me out to discuss Susannah. You want to know what I've heard of this dead Seer—if I shared her frightful vision."

I hesitated. "You know what she Saw?"

"No. I'm well informed, but I'm afraid I fall somewhat short of omniscience. I don't know the details—only that this Susannah came here pursuing the dead girl's vision. Though from what you've said, I would assume that the Seer foretold doom and destruction and so forth."

The end of the Kin, I thought, closing my eyes briefly. "But you haven't Seen anything like that?"

"I See more than I'd like, truth be told."

"And more than you'll say."

"I've learned it's healthier to keep my own counsel. Since I've a notion to be around until the sun goes supernova, a certain measure of self-interest is required."

"So you're not going to tell me anything?" I felt a flicker of irritation. "You could've just said that in the first place."

In one fluid motion, he slipped from the table and stood before me, gripping the sides of my arms. His voice was low in my ear. "I'm terribly flattered that you came to me, but it appears you've forgotten a matter of some slight importance. I'm not like you, pet. I'm one of *them*. One of the monsters you see in your sleep. I might live up here, but I was born in the dark of Beneath. How can you be certain I don't hunger for the death of your Kin?"

I dropped my gaze, seeing the human hands that clutched me—and then they were not human hands. Through the layers of my coat, I felt the chill of his skin. I saw the ripple of silver, the flash of red. I twisted away.

"Don't care to look at me, angel? This is what I am. I'm not pretty. Try to recall that the next time you wish to know just what it is I've Seen."

He released me. I took a hasty step back, swallowing. I looked up at the mural again, at the harsh shapes and the broad, angry slashes of paint. I remembered what it had been like to go Beneath, how terrified I'd been. The emptiness hadn't simply surrounded me; it had crawled under my skin, pervading my senses. I had been alone, but not alone. I'd heard insidious whispers promising death. As I'd walked, I'd become aware of a presence, something that was always watching, always ravenous, waiting to feed. That brief time I'd spent Beneath had been enough to convince me I never wanted to see it again. I couldn't imagine having to live there.

"I'm sorry," I breathed.

To my surprise, Shane laughed—that warm, rich chuckle of

his. I glanced up to find him smiling at me, fully human once more. He clapped a hand over his chest. "Sweetheart, you wound me. I was trying to frighten you, not move you to pity."

"Why?"

"To remind you this threat is very real."

"I know that. That's why I'm *here*."

"Do you? Then I'll tell you this. Susannah is dangerous, make no mistake. If the Guardians have any sort of attachment to living, they need to leave her to your mother. Morning Star is the only one strong enough to stop her." He took my arm and guided me toward the exit. "I'll keep your visit between us," he said. "I suggest you do the same. Remember what I said, though, angel. Don't involve yourself. Some secrets are better left sleeping. I've Seen enough to know that you won't like where this path leads."

He hustled me outside to where Gideon waited.

The next few days passed quickly. With the arrival of Susannah—and the knowledge that she was seeking the Remnant—Mom and Leon were busier than ever. The entire Kin had been put on alert. That meant increased meetings and patrols, and several older Guardians who had semiretired were called back to duty.

I was still determined to find a way to help, but I hadn't been able to figure out how. My Knowing was of no use. I'd considered trying to use it to locate Susannah, but even with my Nav cards and the increase in my abilities, I didn't have nearly enough power to track her. Proximity continued to be a limiting factor, and even the attempt to search for her would have involved a level of risk. I remembered all too well the night I had used my Knowing on Patrick Tigue, how I had tried to read him, to look into the dark spaces where his secrets rested—and how he had looked back. That wasn't an experience I cared to repeat.

So far, Susannah had shown herself only once. Monday night, one of the Guardians—a woman named Rosa that I'd met a few times—was attacked in Uptown. According to Mom, she wasn't injured. The Harrower that assailed her had been relatively weak. She'd subdued it easily, and it had crawled back Beneath. Rosa had continued on her patrol. She'd gone half a block and then turned to find Susannah and Daniel watching her. She had been about to call for backup when the pair disappeared.

I thought that was rather creepy; Drew called it cunning, saying that Susannah never did anything without reason, and it must be part of some plan.

Drew was quickly becoming a familiar face. He'd been welcomed by the Cities' Guardians, but with a condition: he had to check in with Mom on a daily basis. To prove he was on his best behavior, I supposed, and not off slaughtering any neutral Harrowers he happened across.

"You don't mind that you got stuck being the one to keep him under control?" I asked my mother on Tuesday evening, after Drew had come and gone.

"He's not under control," Mom answered. "He's following our rules because it suits him to—for the time being."

But Drew was Mom's problem. I had other concerns. Whenever I wasn't occupied trying to come up with ways to prevent the Kin's impending doom, I was thinking about Leon. *Something is wrong*, he'd said. Though he hadn't elaborated, I understood what he meant: something was wrong between *us*. Somewhere, in the secret, unknown space between Guardian and charge, a wire had shorted. A disconnect had formed.

And that wasn't even the worst part. The worst part was the little voice that whispered in my head whenever I saw Drew, the way my heart clenched when I caught the glimmer of his wedding band or heard the grief that weighted his speech. The worry that wormed itself within me. The unhappy thought that perhaps Leon only cared for me because he had to, because that was what Guardians *did*. Maybe developing an emotional connection to your charge was some sort of biological protocol that was written into the calling. Maybe that was what Leon had meant when he said he wanted us to *figure out our feelings*.

Maybe he wasn't sure our feelings were real.

I didn't want to believe that, but Mom's words drifted back to me unbidden. Guardians' feelings for their charges were intense, she'd said. Messy. Complicated.

I couldn't have broached the subject with Leon even if I'd wanted to. There simply wasn't any good way to ask whether or not he thought his attraction to me might be a by-product of his Guardian programming.

Leon himself was focused on discovering why he hadn't

known I was in danger. There was a rift in our bond, he said, and we needed to find a way to fix it. That Wednesday, instead of having our usual training session, he handed me my shoes and coat and informed me we were going out. As soon as my shoelaces were tied and my coat was zipped, he drew me to him, wrapped an arm around me, and teleported.

There was an instant of blank space enveloping me, and then a cool wind touched my face. Leon's arm loosened. I took a step backward and glanced around, snow crunching beneath my feet as I turned. In the late afternoon light that streaked the sky, I saw evergreens jutting upward, the pale edge of a frozen lake, red picnic tables topped with snow. The smell of pine lingered in the crisp air.

I recognized the place almost immediately. Leon had brought me here once, a few months ago, after I'd first learned that I was Kin. It had been the end of autumn then, the ground littered here and there with leaves; now, winter lay across the area. The path that led to the water was white with frost, and ice clung to the grills that dotted the park. Little spikes of dead grass broke through the snow at my feet. Nearby, the small parking lot was dark and empty.

A low breeze tugged at my coat and hair. I brushed the snow from one of the picnic tables and perched on its edge. I glanced at Leon. We hadn't spoken much since Saturday night, and I felt a little awkward. "I hope this isn't our first date," I said lightly, "because I'm not really dressed for it."

"We had a first date," Leon said.

"Um, no. We had a disaster. And I already told you that it didn't count. Our first date is not going to include hospitals, Harrowers, apocalyptic predictions, or *my mother*."

"Unless you've learned to reverse time, I don't see how you're going to accomplish that."

"It wasn't a date!"

"It's possible you're fixating."

"I'm being serious." I turned my head to hide the smile that began sneaking across my face. Then, with both hands, I scooped snow from the table, packed it into a ball, and lobbed it at him.

He didn't bother to dodge or teleport. The snowball struck him square in the chest, a small explosion that left a dusting of ice crystals on his shirt. With quick strides, he closed the distance between us. He leaned over me, dropping his hands to the picnic table on either side of me so that I was caught between his arms. He didn't speak.

I looked up at him. "Aren't you planning to retaliate?"

"I have a better idea."

He smiled slowly. His gaze dropped to my lips. My heart skipped a beat. I lifted my face toward his.

Closed my eyes.

And then gasped as a handful of snow was deposited on my head.

I punched Leon in the shoulder and pushed him away. He moved back a few steps, looking entirely too pleased with himself. I was weighing my options, trying to decide the best way to get even, when he put his hands in front of him and said, "We're here for a reason."

"It'd better not be another pep talk."

His expression grew serious, and he turned away, toward the lake. Against the last flare of sunset, the pines behind him formed a dark silhouette. "We need to discuss the problem between us."

I shifted uneasily. "The rift in our bond?" I said. The short-circuit that had prevented him from knowing I was in danger.

"Yes."

"We can't discuss it at home?"

"I think best when I'm out here."

"I think best when I'm *warm*."

He swung back toward me. "Are you really that cold?"

"No," I admitted, though I pulled up my hood and tightened the strings for effect. I leaned back on my hands, gazing up at the sky. The first stars were coming out. Tiny pinpricks in the deepening blue. "Why here? You never said."

"My parents liked this spot. That was what my grandfather always said, at least. He brought me out here every summer."

"Oh." I drew in a slow breath. Leon's parents had died when he was only two years old. As far as I knew, he had no real memories of them. He didn't speak of them often, but I'd caught a glimmer of Knowing from him the last time we'd been here. I caught another now—a sense so fleeting I might have imagined it. The vision of a toddler laughing, crouching in water and sand.

Leon spoke again, interrupting my thoughts. "I've been

researching our situation. I'd like to avoid seeking outside help, if possible."

"Outside help? Like what, Guardian couples therapy?" Sudden horror struck me. I sat forward again, looking at him. "They don't actually have that, do they?"

"I meant the Kin elders."

"Oh. How have you been researching?"

"I read through a few histories kept by the Kin. Old Guardian journals and other documentation."

"Guardians keep journals? You keep a journal? Do you write about me?"

"*Some* Guardians keep journals. Most of them weren't much use to me, though—I was only looking for accounts of Guardians who were called to protect specific charges, so there were far fewer to choose from."

I hesitated. If Leon had found journals from Guardians in situations similar to ours, then there might be information on how common it was for a Guardian and charge to develop feelings for one another. "Could I see them?"

He looked skeptical. "You want to read them?"

"I like history." Well, I liked historical romance novels, anyway. That had to count for something.

"I didn't bring them home."

Which meant I'd have to ask Esther. I sighed. "So, did you learn anything useful?"

"Yes." His gaze was steady. "Our situation—it's happened

before. Three times. In each case, the bond was disrupted because either the Guardian or the charge . . . was fighting it."

It took me only a second to realize what he meant. I hopped down from the picnic table. "You think this is my fault."

"That's not what I said."

"It's what you were going to say. You're blaming your Guardian malfunction on me."

His eyes narrowed. "It's not *my* malfunction. It's ours. But yes, I believe you're the source of it." He paused. "It fits, Audrey. The rift didn't occur until after you found out that I'm your Guardian."

"That's stupid. Correlation does not equal causation. Or did you miss that day in school? And *you're* the one who was fighting it. You told me that. You said you didn't want to be a Guardian."

"That was years ago," he said. He turned away again, running a hand through his hair. "It doesn't matter. The point isn't who's causing the problem—the point is that we need to fix it."

"And how do we do that?"

"I don't know."

We were quiet for a long moment. Leon moved away from me and stood with his hands clenched at his sides. The breeze flapped against his shirt and ruffled his hair. I watched him, taking in familiar details: the broad line of his shoulders, his perfect stillness. The twilight was soundless around us. The scent of evergreens was heavy in the air, but now there was something else, as well.

That was when I felt it.

Abruptly, there was an expectant quality to the silence. A difference in atmosphere. A feeling of watchfulness. A cold that didn't come from the air, but from below, from—

Beneath.

"Maybe—" Leon broke off, sensing it in the same moment I did.

I called his name, my voice strangled and thick.

My warning came too late. The Harrower appeared out of nowhere and launched itself toward him.

11

The demon had not bothered with a human disguise.
As it crashed into Leon, I saw it clearly, its sleek body and jagged
claws. I felt its focus and fury. My own focus narrowed. The universe shrank to a single pinpoint in the space before me: the two
figures grappling in the darkening dusk, the light shining beneath
Leon's skin, an arc of crimson splashing in the snow.

In reality, all of this happened in only a few short seconds. But
in my mind, those seconds stretched endlessly, punctuated by the
sound of my heartbeat as it pounded in my ears. Everything was
in slow motion. Leon struck, parried, struck again. The Harrower
emitted a low, rasping hiss. Without thought, without reason, I
found myself moving forward—and then stopped short as a voice
spoke from behind me.

"You didn't say she was here as well."

I flinched and spun around.

Susannah and Daniel stood a few feet away from me, their hands clasped. I froze. In the semidark, their faces were shadowed, their expressions hidden. Daniel looked exactly as he had that night in the parking ramp, wearing the same thin, faded T-shirt, the same torn jeans. Susannah was clad entirely in white: pearls at her throat, white shoes, white dress. Her hair was a halo of red about her face. There was a pale gleam where the moonlight touched her neck.

"I didn't know," Daniel said.

She didn't glance at him, but I noticed her hand tighten around his. "I can't abide liars, Danny. You know that." Then she released him and stepped toward me, smiling. She tilted her head in Leon's direction. "This Guardian. He's yours?"

I didn't answer. I watched her carefully, my hands balled into fists.

She took another step. "You're the one he protects?"

I inched backward. "Yes."

"Pity."

Then Leon was between us. I felt his hand on my shoulder, gripping, dragging me toward him. But he didn't teleport. Not immediately. Around me, the world seemed to pick up speed, moving from slow motion to fast-forward. Heat surged through my body, sudden energy rushing into my veins. I felt Leon's hand jerk away from me and caught a glimpse of his startled face. Susannah moved toward us, taking quick steps through the snow, white against white. Then Leon's fingers closed around my shoulder again. His free hand shot out, shoving Susannah away, sending her flying across the park. I heard her gasp, heard Daniel speak, calling out a word, maybe a name—and then there was only darkness.

The void lasted longer than I expected it to.

Normally, when Leon teleported me, it took barely the space of a blink. This time, the emptiness expanded into heartbeats, breaths. I couldn't feel Leon's hands. I couldn't feel the chill of the evening or the wind burning against me. I couldn't feel anything. For a moment, I lost all sense of place, of self. I was anchorless. Adrift. I wasn't thought or body or being. I was nothing—and then, just as suddenly, I was something again. I was a girl standing in a cornfield, taking huge gulps of air, grateful for the solid ground beneath me.

Leon was at my side. He caught me by the shoulders, then ran his hands down my arms. He turned me around, then turned me again.

"You're not hurt?" he asked.

"Me? They didn't touch me. *You're* hurt." He was bleeding from a cut on his right arm, a thin horizontal slash just above the elbow. I reached toward him, but he shook his head.

"I'm fine."

"Where are we?" I asked. I glanced about. It was too dark to see much of our surroundings, but there didn't appear to be much to see, anyway. A few rows of dead cornstalks were spread out around us, and a squat yellow farmhouse sat at one end of the field. The glow of headlights cut through the darkness on a distant road. The sky was flooded with stars.

"I'm not certain," Leon answered.

"Then why did you bring us here?" I asked, setting a hand on my hip.

"I didn't," he said. "You did."

"Right. Since when can I teleport?"

"Since when can you *amplify*?"

I stared at him. "What are you talking about?"

"You amplified my powers. Did you know you were doing it?"

"I didn't even know I could." I frowned, trying to process this. "Are you sure?"

"I'm sure. I felt it when we were at the lake."

"But—how?"

He furrowed his brow. "The ability does run in the St. Croix bloodline."

That was true, though I'd never really thought about it. I'd spent most of my life being a Whitticomb—and only a Whitticomb. In spite of Esther's attempts to mold me into a St. Croix, I'd never felt like one. "You think I'm an Amplifier?"

"You just amplified. Do you have a better explanation?"

I didn't.

An Amplifier, I thought. Like Esther. And my father. And Iris.

"So *I* brought us here?" I asked.

"You amplified my powers," Leon repeated. He sounded a little embarrassed as he added, "And I overshot the distance."

"By how much?"

He'd taken out his phone and was using the GPS to pinpoint

our location. After a minute, he raised his eyes to mine. His smile was rueful. "About two hundred miles."

Leon was reluctant to teleport again. At least, he was reluctant to teleport *me*. He was worried we'd end up even farther away—or worse, that we'd land somewhere dangerous, like in the middle of a busy highway, or stuck inside a mountain. The mountain idea seemed pretty far-fetched to me, since we were in Iowa, not Appalachia, but Leon wouldn't listen. He was still looking at his phone, presumably trying to chart a way back to Minneapolis. I stood watching him, hugging my coat to me. The temperature had dropped, but the chill that spread through me had more to do with the thought of the blood drying on Leon's shirt than with the weather.

He had been targeted by that Harrower. And Susannah and Daniel had merely watched the fight, just as they had observed Rosa.

I let out a breath, watching it fog before me. The stillness and silence of the cornfield felt eerie. The rows of broken stalks reaching up through the snow struck me as somehow sad. Suddenly, I wanted very much to go home. I stepped toward Leon. "You said you could feel it when I was amplifying your abilities."

He looked up from his phone. "Yes."

"Am I doing it now?"

"No."

"Then teleport us."

His expression turned obstinate. "Not until I know it's safe."

"Then what are we going to do? Walk home? Hitchhike? Steal a car?"

"Give me a minute to think."

My voice came out in a low hiss. "Leon, we are in a cornfield. At night. You see that farmhouse? Any second now, some guy with a shotgun is going to come out here and threaten to release his hounds."

"Or offer to drive us into town."

"Or feed us into a wood chipper."

"Could you at least attempt to take this situation seriously?"

"I *am* taking it seriously. I am more than a little freaked out. I would like to go home. Now."

His expression softened, but it took another ten minutes before he agreed to teleport us. Even then he was hesitant.

"Just—don't do anything," he said as he drew me against him.

"Not a problem. I don't even know what I *did*."

Since Leon's normal teleportation range was limited to somewhere between thirty and forty miles, we traveled by degrees. Though he wasn't usually concerned about witnesses—the ability to teleport involved an instinctual knowledge of one's surroundings—he had decided upon further caution and had used his phone to plot a way home through less-populated areas. I found it a bit disorienting, moments of total darkness followed by bursts of color and sound, short pauses to catch our breath, and then darkness again. I held tightly to Leon, feeling the warmth of his skin beneath his shirt, the rhythm of his heartbeat. The cornfield became an empty park, and then a deserted lot, and then the slope of a hill dotted with pines. Cool air whistled past and was interrupted. When we finally reached the house, Leon himself was slightly unsteady. He explained that he wasn't accustomed to crossing such large distances in rapid succession, which did nothing to ease my anxiety. The cut on his arm was already healing, but I made him sit at the kitchen table while I grabbed a first-aid kit. To my surprise, he submitted, and even allowed me to roll up his sleeve and bandage the wound. Once I'd finished, he pulled out his phone, intending to call Mom and inform her of the incident at the lake, and give a report on Susannah.

She didn't answer.

He tried Mr. Alvarez next. The call went straight to voice mail.

Leon and I exchanged a look.

"Something's happened," I said.

"They're busy," he said. "Lucy will call back in a minute."

She did call back, but it wasn't in a minute. It was in twenty. She was in the waiting room of Hennepin County Medical Center.

As it turned out, Leon wasn't the only Guardian who had been attacked that evening.

Mom gave Leon a brief summary of events over the phone. Anthony Dawes, one of the younger Guardians, had been injured during his patrol. He was in serious condition, but stable, and expected to recover. Because he was unconscious, he was unable to verify precisely what had happened. There was no trace of Susannah.

The assault on Anthony had been similar to those on Rosa and Leon. A single Harrower had attacked him while Susannah and Daniel looked on. But this demon had been stronger than the others, more vicious; the fight had been savage. Though Anthony had killed the demon, his own wounds had been severe. He'd fallen unconscious on the street, his body slashed and bleeding. Eventually, a passerby had called an ambulance.

Mickey had been the one to alert Mom. He'd learned of the attack and had recognized the signs. A demon's ability to cloud the senses meant most witnesses wouldn't understand what they'd seen, but Mickey knew what to watch for. He'd called Mom as soon as he was certain. Because Guardians had accelerated healing, Anthony began to recover rapidly, but he still was hospitalized for a number of days. Mr. Alvarez, who was very protective of the Guardians and felt responsible for their well-being, had taken the incident personally. He instituted new rules: patrols were going to operate on a buddy system, and the moment any Harrowers were sighted, the rest of the Guardians were to be alerted. Susannah was not to be confronted alone. And Leon and Drew, the only two Guardians in the Cities who could teleport, were placed on call indefinitely. It made sense, since they would be able to assist faster than anyone else—but it also made me uneasy. Leon had already been targeted once. The thought of him being attacked again made my throat close and my heart constrict. Why Susannah was going after Guardians, if her real aim was the Remnant, no one was quite sure. Mr. Alvarez suggested she might want the Kin in disarray. Drew believed she just wanted the Guardians dead. I tried not to think about that.

I threw myself into trying to figure out how to use my Amplification and drafted Leon into helping me. Being an Amplifier meant I was no longer useless—provided I could learn how to control it. Thursday afternoon, we went to the training room and I attempted to trigger the ability.

"How are you planning to go about this?" Leon asked, once we'd reached the basement.

"I was hoping you'd have some ideas."

He thought for a moment. "We could start by providing you with powers to amplify. Give me your hand. I don't have much experience with Amplification, but I know that contact helps."

Tentatively, I held my hand toward him. He gripped it with his own, locking his fingers with mine, our palms sliding together. I gazed into the short distance between us, at the bridge formed by our arms. Leon was quiet, concentrating. After a moment, I sensed the change within him: the glow that began at his wrist, tracing its way through his veins up to his fingertips.

Nothing happened. "Now what?"

"It doesn't feel like you're amplifying."

"I could have told you that."

"Did you feel it before?" he asked. "At the lake?"

"I felt—heat. When you hit Susannah, right before we teleported."

He frowned, releasing my hand. "Let's try something else."

We went through a few of our training exercises, sparring for several minutes, in the hope that the activity of fighting might activate my power. Again, nothing happened. Leon tried startling me once, abruptly teleporting behind me, but the only thing that triggered was an elbow to the ribs.

I groaned in frustration. "If there's an *on* switch to this thing, I can't seem to find it."

"You don't know what caused you to activate it last night?"

"Uh, I was sort of panicking."

"You operated on instinct," he said.

Instinct, I thought.

The word stirred a memory from two weeks ago. The scene in the parking ramp flashed before me: the demon lunging for Tink, its claws catching hold; my strike connecting with its body; the force of the blow that had thrown it backward. Sharing powers was a part of Amplification. I must have inadvertently shared the demon's abilities that night, just as Iris had done with the Harrowers she'd fought. But I was reluctant to bring up my previous encounter with Susannah, since the discussion of who was causing the rift in the bond between Leon and me had been tabled. I lowered my gaze.

"How did you first learn to control your Knowing?" Leon asked.

"Gram helped me."

He was silent a moment. I glanced up to find him smiling apologetically.

"You're not going to like what I'm about to suggest," he said.

Leon was right: I *didn't* like his suggestion. Unfortunately, I also didn't have a better one. On Friday afternoon, I went to see Esther.

While Mom wasn't thrilled by the idea of my developing a new ability, she agreed that I should learn more about it, and drove me to St. Paul after school. She dropped me off at the sprawling St. Croix estate without comment, wearing the same gloomy expression she always wore when she was forced to deal with my grandmother. Mom might have accepted Esther's presence in my life as a necessity, but she avoided her as much as possible. Though there was a cautious truce between them, I doubted they'd ever be on easy terms.

"You're sure Charles will bring you home?" she asked as I hopped out of the car.

"Probably," I replied, though I wasn't even certain he would be present. My grandfather wasn't as involved with the running of the Kin as Esther was. The St. Croix family businesses kept him busy, and he was in no hurry to retire.

"Call if he can't," Mom said, waving as she drove away. She'd replaced my phone earlier in the week, with firm instructions to take better care of it or risk having it tied to my wrist like a mitten. I returned her wave, then headed toward the house.

I walked slowly, surveying my surroundings. The St. Croix estate had always reminded me of a haunted mansion from some old horror movie, even though the building lacked broken shutters that flapped in the wind, and there were no jutting towers surrounded by bats. With the lawn covered in snow, the rows of empty tree branches, and the bare, bristly hedge that surrounded the walkway, the house looked even more foreboding than it had in autumn. Most of the windows were dark. The sky above me was muted and colorless in the low, late-afternoon light.

As I approached, the solemn hush about the estate made me think of a funeral home. A space of mourning. Which, in a way, I supposed it was: Iris was gone, but her memory remained, imprinted upon everything she'd left behind. She was the shadow that lurked behind the eyes of my grandparents, the quiet ache ever present in the small, sad voice of Elspeth. Not for the first time, I wondered where Iris was, if the Beneath had swallowed her so totally that no spark of her life remained, no trace of her humanity—or if she'd surfaced elsewhere, in some other city, near some other Circle. We'd heard nothing. According to Esther, it was better that way.

It was her choice to betray us, Esther had told me, which I took to mean that she felt it was Iris's own fault that she'd gone crazy.

Now, when Esther met me at the door, she went very pale.

"Audrey!" she barked, clamping her hand on to my arm almost painfully. Without giving me a chance to speak, she pulled me into the house and steered me to her sitting room. Her face was set in lines of stern disapproval. "You should have called."

"I'm sorry," I said, feeling flustered. I sank into the chair she'd ushered me toward. I probably *should* have called, I knew, but I'd arrived unannounced before, and it had never been an issue. "I know you're busy, but there was something I was hoping you could help me with."

She turned away from me, toward the long windows in the far end of the room, where dark curtains fell nearly to the floor. "You should have called," she repeated. There was a tremor in her voice. She rested one hand on the back of a chair, her fingers trembling.

I was starting to worry something catastrophic had happened, but before I could apologize again, or ask what was wrong, Esther composed herself. She straightened her shoulders and faced me, not quite smiling, but no longer showing obvious displeasure. She appeared as unruffled as ever, clasping her hands together as she took the seat across from me. For a moment, we sat regarding each other. Neither of us spoke. Esther was dressed in one of the neat, soft-colored business suits she favored, and the string of pearls that seemed permanently affixed to her neck. Watching her, I realized how much she had changed since Iris's treachery. There was more gray in her hair than when I'd first met her last November, and there was a certain tightness to her lips whenever she spoke.

But the alert, piercing look in her gold-brown eyes was the same. She was giving me that look now.

"I guess you've been dealing with the Susannah situation," I said.

"Among other things. Is that why you've come? The Kin have faced worse. We've survived. We always will. You needn't concern yourself."

"When Harrowers start threatening extermination, I get a bit concerned."

"The Guardians will handle it."

"Guardians are the ones being hurt!"

She leaned back in her chair, giving me a shrewd look. "*Your* Guardian?"

I hesitated, then nodded slowly. "He was attacked."

"And one day he may be killed. You must understand this, Audrey. It is the duty of all Guardians to protect the Kin and to face death. It's a risk they take—but it is *only* a risk. Not a certainty. Now, it seems to me that what you're really worried about is this dead Seer's vision. That, too, is a waste of your energies. Visions are frequently misinterpreted. I am not inclined to put much stock in them."

"The future isn't fixed," I said.

"Merely probable." Her lips curved just slightly. "I'm glad to see you pay attention to at least some of my lessons."

"That's actually why I'm here," I said. "I need lessons. I've sort of been...amplifying."

Esther arched her eyebrows. "You've *sort of* been amplifying?"

"Well, okay, I definitely have been. Only, not all the time. It's happened twice, and it wasn't on purpose. I haven't been able to do it since."

"That's natural. Abilities begin with instinct. Only later do they come of your own will." She appeared thoughtful for a moment, tapping her fingers against her arm. "The gift does tend to manifest around this age. I should have had you tested earlier. As soon as our lessons resume, we'll try some exercises to determine your aptitude level, and then we will begin your instruction. I'll speak to your mother about scheduling additional time for training. I expect you will agree to this?"

I nodded. Though I wasn't enthusiastic about the idea of spending even more time with Esther, I did want to learn—and quickly.

"In the meantime, I would advise against too much outside

experimentation. Amplification is a useful gift, but it can be dangerous without proper control."

"When are we starting lessons again?"

"When my business is concluded."

I was about to ask for a more concrete answer when I heard a familiar voice from the hallway beyond. I hopped to my feet.

"You didn't tell me Elspeth was back," I said. I hurried past Esther before she could stop me.

Elspeth had been out of town the past few weeks. Esther had sent her to visit relatives overseas, hoping a change of scenery and distance from her grief would help her cope with Iris's betrayal. The last time I'd seen Elspeth, she'd hugged me tightly and struggled to smile, but she hadn't been able to hide the unhappiness in her eyes. Ever since Iris went Beneath, Elspeth had been listless and depressed. She skipped school and often refused to leave her bedroom—in stark contrast with the buoyant, cheerful girl she'd been when we'd first met. Her playfulness and her boundless energy had vanished. None of us knew how to comfort her. While I was skeptical of the idea that spending time with distant St. Croix cousins would be much of a cure, it had probably been smart to get her out of the gloomy estate and away from the oppressive winter weather.

With a quick glance down the hallway, I moved toward the sound of her voice.

I stopped short.

Elspeth stood a few feet away, near the staircase. She looked different. Before she'd left, she'd been painfully thin, but now she seemed to have gained a few pounds, and—though she was already tall—appeared to have grown an inch. Her black hair, once so long it hung nearly to her hips, had been cut as short as Tink's. She turned at the sound of my footsteps, and after recognition flickered, I saw panic bloom on her face.

But that wasn't what halted me, what made my skin turn to ice and my breath leave my body in a rush.

A man stood beside her. At first I saw only his back, the smooth lines of the suit he wore, the dark curling hair above his collar. Even before he turned, my skin prickled. I'd never met him, but I knew him. I'd seen him once before, in the vision of a long-ago night, in a memory not my own. I'd seen him standing at the edge of a lake, cupping my mother's elbow in his hand, drawing her into his arms.

The man who stood silent beside Elspeth, turning as she turned, so that I saw his face clearly and I felt the world stop, was Adrian St. Croix.

My father.

I stood staring. I heard nothing, not whatever words Elspeth was speaking, not the wild drumming of my heart. A hand came down on my shoulder. I registered, briefly, that the hand must belong to Esther, and I jerked away from her grasp. Otherwise I didn't move.

Adrian St. Croix. My father.

I continued to look at him, taking in details. His business suit was charcoal gray, tidy, well made. He stood with his shoulders squared. Although I knew that I closely resembled my mother, I studied him, searching his face for similarities, links I could trace between us. His hair was a rich brown, like mine, and it curled in just the same way. Though his eyes held the dusty St. Croix gold, I thought there might be something in their shape that I recognized in my own. Like me, he had a slight, almost imperceptible line of freckles across the bridge of his nose.

He didn't seem aware of my scrutiny. He hardly seemed aware at all. There was nothing left in him of the boy I'd seen in the vision, the sad, crooked smile, the mischief he couldn't quite keep out of his face. There was no humor in him, no warmth. When his eyes met mine, they seemed as flat and vacant as a Harrower's. He stood expressionless. Except for the bend in his nose where he must have once broken it, his face was smooth and boyish, untouched by age or care. From what my mother had told me, I knew he had to be close to forty, but he looked ten years younger—as though time had passed by him and not through him. There wasn't even the smallest touch of gray in his hair.

Heedless, uncaring, I reached out with my Knowing, but I could gain no sense of him. No impressions, no hint of a feeling or memory. No thoughts he kept close or images he carried. Not even the stubborn sense of inscrutability I sometimes got from Leon. It was as though there were nothing inside of my father but clean, empty air.

Finally, Elspeth's voice broke in. "This is a friend of mine from school," she was saying, twisting her hands nervously in front of her. "Audrey, this is my uncle. Adrian."

A short, stuttering "Hi" was all I could manage.

He held out his hand, but I just stared again. There was a fleeting look of confusion in his eyes, the only emotion I read from him. Then the moment passed, and he let his arm drop at his side. He nodded, saying it was a pleasure to meet me. His voice was kind, but there was no depth to it. I could only nod dully back.

Esther moved between us, her lips firm and flat as she took my father by the arm. She steered him toward the stairs, telling him she wanted to continue their discussion. Without looking back, she called to me, "Audrey, it's a school night. It's time you were getting home. I'll send Charles to you."

I watched them go, struggling with the desire to follow them up the long staircase and down the halls. As I hesitated, Elspeth spoke my name and led me away in the same manner Esther had guided my father. I felt too stunned to resist. I soon found myself back in Esther's sitting room, clumsily taking the same chair I'd recently vacated. Elspeth knelt in front of me, murmuring consoling words.

For a moment, I floundered. I seemed to be speaking, but none of the words formed sentences. Alarmed and strangely dizzy, I tried to steady my breathing. Eventually, I choked out, "Why is he here?"

"On business, I think," Elspeth answered. "I don't know the details. I just got home a few days ago."

"How long is he staying?"

"Grandmother hasn't told me. I'm sorry."

I shook my head rapidly. My shock was receding. The dizzy feeling began to ebb—and in its place, hot, swift anger was building. I clenched my hands, staring down at my knuckles.

Esther, I thought.

This was why she'd canceled our Kin lessons. To prevent me

from meeting my father. She'd wanted to keep him from me. No discussion, no deliberation, no chance for me to have my say.

Reading the look on my face, Elspeth quickly said, "She thought it was better if you didn't see him."

"She should have let *me* decide." It came out as a snarl, and I hadn't meant it to. I was furious, all knotted up inside. Feeling the warm sting of tears in my eyes, I wiped my face hastily with my fists.

"Would you have wanted to meet him?" Elspeth asked quietly.

I didn't answer. I wasn't certain. In some ways, my life had been shaped by his absence from it. Would I have wanted to meet him, knowing I could never know him? He was Adrian St. Croix, but he could never be my father—I understood that, even as I rebelled against it. His powers had been sealed along with his human heart. He was a shell that walked and breathed but felt nothing, not joy nor grief nor the love he'd once held for my mother. But he was still a part of me. He had helped form me. He was my blood, the same blood that Iris had demanded, the blood that I'd spilled on the roof of Harlow Tower. I'd sensed him there that night, sensed him more clearly than when he'd been standing before me. The flicker of his life, the memory of his laughter. Now that part of him slept. I hoped it dreamed. I hoped it was a happy dream.

"I wish things were different," Elspeth said. "For all of us."

I nodded, still sniffling. Elspeth gripped my hand and squeezed it. She smiled, but I noticed she was crying, too, slow tears that slid down her cheeks. I squeezed her hand back. Then Charles, our grandfather, appeared in the doorway. In a soft, somber voice, he told me that it was time to leave.

It took me until Friday evening to tell Mom that my father was in town.

I had planned to talk to her immediately, the second I saw her. I was furious with Esther for hiding him from me, and I definitely didn't intend to keep his presence a secret from my mother. But I wasn't certain how Mom would react. Though she hadn't seen my father in seventeen years, I knew she'd never quite gotten over losing him. A gap remained in the space where he'd been. She didn't need to tell me that. I heard it in the way she spoke of him, the funny little catch in her voice she tried so hard to disguise. I saw the distant, wistful look that came over her when she told me how he used to stand outside during thunderstorms, or the way he'd lie in the soaked grass and drag her down to him, or how he'd fall asleep during every movie she'd ever shown him—stories she was only now beginning to tell me. Mom could insist that she'd moved on, but I knew that the wild, hopeful girl she'd once been, the girl that sometimes lurked behind her eyes, still missed him, and probably always would.

When I finally managed to blurt out the words, Mom froze for a moment. We stood in the kitchen, heating up leftovers for dinner. Her back was to me. I saw her shoulders tense. Finally, she crossed to my side, pulling me into a quick embrace as she asked how I was feeling.

"Weird," I said, after she'd released me. That was something of an understatement. I felt completely off balance, as though the world had tilted and I hadn't tilted with it.

Mom gave my shoulder a squeeze.

"You're not upset?" I asked.

She hesitated a second before answering. "That he's in town? He's still a member of the St. Croix family. I'm sure he's been in town before."

"Don't you want to see him?"

Again, she didn't speak immediately. In the stretch of silence between us, I caught a flicker of Knowing: The memory of a cab ride in the darkness; that long-ago night when she'd defeated Verrick—the night my father had left. The note he'd slipped into her pocket. The way her heart had clenched. Now, her voice was soft. "I don't think so, honey."

I hugged my arms. "Esther didn't want me to meet him. That's why she canceled my Kin lessons. To keep me away from him." Words were thick in my throat. "Does he know about me? I mean, that I exist?"

"I'm not certain," Mom said. "He knew I was pregnant. But I'm not sure how much he remembers, or how much . . . connects."

Not a lot, from what I'd seen. Mom asked if I wanted to talk more, but I shook my head. I headed out of the kitchen and up the stairs to my room. I sat on my bed with my legs drawn up against me, thinking of my father's flat, unfeeling voice, his impassive face.

I was still sitting there an hour later when Leon appeared and stood in the doorway. I looked up at him, meeting his eyes. His gaze was steady, but he didn't speak. He just watched me.

"I saw my father," I said.

"I know."

I scooted over, and Leon came to sit beside me, his long legs stretched out before him. His fingers closed over mine. I leaned against him, glad that, if only for this moment, we were just Leon and Audrey, not Guardian and charge. I didn't want to think about what was wrong between us, that disconnect in our bond, or worry that his feelings for me might not be real. I just wanted to sit there beside him, holding his hand.

After a time, I spoke.

"When I was little, I used to imagine what my father was like," I said. I'd pictured him often, giving him different features, changing the color of his eyes and hair—though his face had always remained obscured. "Gram sometimes told me about him, but she wouldn't say much. So I made it up instead. I pretended he was a spy, and he'd been sent on some secret mission, and that was why we couldn't ever talk about him." I paused, biting my lip. I'd never told anyone this before, not even Gram. "That sounds pretty dumb, huh?"

"It sounds pretty normal."

"Were you the same way?"

"Did I imagine my parents were spies? No." He was quiet a long time. When he spoke again, his voice was low, almost a whisper. "I hated them."

I turned to face him. "For dying?"

"For dying together."

And leaving him alone. I thought of that image I'd glimpsed on occasion: Leon as a small boy, worried and waiting, watching the door for someone who would never again return.

"How did it happen?" I asked. His parents had been Guardians and had been killed during the Harrowing seventeen years before—but I didn't know anything beyond that.

"My grandfather never learned the details," Leon said. "All he knew was that they went to fight Verrick, and they didn't come home. Their bodies were found the following day. He stayed long enough to bury them, and then he took me up north."

I nodded. Up north was where his grandfather had raised him; I imagined a curve of highway stretching into the distance; the rise of pines; the long, cold shore of Lake Superior. If Leon hadn't been called, he might never have come back. "That was why you didn't want to be a Guardian," I said. "Because of them."

"That was part of it. I was angry at them for a long time. I couldn't understand why they both had to fight. I thought that they'd chosen to die with each other, rather than to live for me. And I couldn't forgive that."

"What changed?"

"I was called."

I nodded. Being a Guardian meant fighting. It meant putting the needs of others above your own.

Sometimes, it meant leaving behind those you loved most.

I looked down at the bedspread, our hands, the space where our fingers met. I wondered what his parents had been like. Tall, most likely. Since abilities tended to run in family lines, one of them had probably been able to teleport. But those details would merely be facts. His parents had died, leaving only the faintest of memories, a history of unknowable moments. I supposed that was the reason Leon liked to go to their lake. To be close to them, in the only way he could.

I thought of my own father.

He was alive, and he was close. And I had no idea when he would be this close again.

"I need to go to St. Paul," I said. I swung my legs over the side of the bed and stood. "I want to see to my father. Just to talk to him. While I can. He can't be my father. Not really. But I want him to know who I am."

I had no idea what effect—if any—that knowledge would have on him, but it struck me suddenly that Esther wasn't just keeping my father from me; she was keeping me from him. And he had the right to know.

Leon was looking at me, his eyes troubled. He rose from the

bed and came to stand beside me, touching my shoulder lightly. "Are you sure this is what you want?"

"I'm sure," I said.

"Then I'll take you to him."

Before we left, I called Elspeth to make certain my father was at the St. Croix estate. She told me that he was in our grandfather's study—and, unfortunately, Esther was with him. I was tempted to just show up anyway, but Elspeth agreed to run interference. She told me she'd find a way to get Esther out of the house. I didn't ask how.

Leon teleported us to the hallway, and I stood there a moment, my hand on the edge of the door, my heart hammering.

"Do you want me to go in with you?" he whispered.

I shook my head.

"I'll be right here," he said.

Giving him a shaky smile, I drew a steadying breath and entered the study. Inside, there was a lingering scent of cigar smoke, the dusty smell of old books. Shelves lined the walls, filled to overflowing. The room had a homey feeling about it that reminded me of my grandfather. A pair of his reading glasses had been left on a table. The huge leather reading chair was worn from use.

My father was seated behind the desk. He glanced up as I approached.

He looked much as he had the previous evening, dressed in a plain gray suit, his shoulders straight, his face expressionless. I didn't speak right away. I studied him, struck once again with a feeling of unreality, a sense that the world had been knocked askew. Part of me couldn't quite comprehend that he was actually here, that this man was my father. Again, I reached out with my Knowing; again, I found nothing, felt nothing. Blank space. Open air.

It was my father who finally spoke. "You're Elspeth's friend," he said. "Were you looking for her? I believe she's gone out."

"I was looking for you," I said. Then, since I didn't know how else to say it, the rest came out in a rush. "I'm not Elspeth's *friend*. I'm her cousin. My name is Audrey Whitticomb. I'm—I'm your daughter."

An awful silence fell. I couldn't seem to let out my breath. I just stood there, waiting for something, anything, to happen. But my father didn't have any sort of reaction, except to gaze at me blankly in the moment or so it took him to process what I'd said.

"I don't—" He paused. "Whitticomb. You're Lucy's daughter."

He recalled her, then. Her name, at least.

"Yes. She was pregnant. That was—that's me." When he didn't respond, I tried again. "Mom said you wanted her to name me after your mother. Do you remember?"

"Esther, if you were a girl. Jack, if you were a boy, for her father."

"Esther is my first name. I just go by Audrey."

He didn't answer.

"Mom said you were hoping I was a girl. Because you had a baby sister who passed away."

"Alice."

I nodded. According to Mom, my father had been ten when Alice was born, eleven when she'd died. He'd brought flowers to the cemetery every year. I wondered if he still visited her grave when he was in town, or if that was one of those things that had just faded away. But when I asked him, he said only that he wasn't often in the Cities, and then lapsed into silence again.

I fidgeted. "Could you say something?"

"This is unexpected," he said, though his face didn't register surprise. It didn't register anything. He was still looking at me exactly as he had when I entered the room, with the polite indifference of a stranger.

The knowledge of who I was didn't spark anything within him. There wasn't anything left to spark. It was what I had anticipated, what I had known, but I still felt a surge of disappointment. I swallowed the lump that formed in my throat.

He can't be my father, I'd told Leon, but that wasn't entirely true. Part of me had hoped.

"I'm sorry," I said.

"Why?"

"For disturbing you."

I wouldn't regret coming here, I told myself. At least now I was certain. I gazed at him, taking in the details of his face, trying to etch them in my memory: his gold-brown eyes, the line of freckles that dusted his skin, his crooked nose. He sat unmoving beneath my scrutiny, waiting for me to speak.

"I'm not expecting anything from you," I said. "I just...I wanted you to know."

"Thank you," he said. He hesitated a moment, as though searching for words. "I'm—glad you told me."

I nodded, giving him my best attempt at a smile. "Me, too," I said.

I turned away.

Mom wasn't upset that I'd gone to see my father. When I brought up the subject Saturday evening, she didn't even seem surprised. We were in the kitchen again, washing dishes. I leaned back against the counter, looking at her. She said she thought that perhaps it was something I had needed to do—so that I could accept the reality of who my father was.

I wasn't certain I did accept it. I understood it, but that wasn't quite the same thing. My thoughts drifted to Elspeth, how she had told me she that wished things were different. I wished that, too.

"*You* never went to see him, though," I told my mother.

She didn't answer me. Instead, she said, "Esther isn't going to be too thrilled with you."

"You say that like I should care."

"She's still your grandmother."

"You like her even less than I do. Why are you on her side?"

"I'm on your side. But it's possible you're being unfair. Esther wasn't trying to be cruel."

"She hid my father from me," I said.

A wrinkle appeared between Mom's eyebrows. "Her intentions were good. I'm sure she just didn't want you to be upset."

"So, what, now that she's a card-carrying member of the Keep Secrets from Audrey Club, you're suddenly defending her?"

"I think that may be a little bit of misdirected anger right there."

I didn't have a retort for that, so I was grateful when the doorbell rang and I had a convenient excuse to flee my mother and her furrowed brow. I hurried into the entryway to answer it. I jerked the door open, ignoring the cold blast of air that rushed in.

Tink stood outside. I had just enough time to register her presence—her thin coat tugged tight against her, her pale face lit by the glow of the yellow porch light—before she began babbling and pushing her way past me into the house.

"Good, you're here," she was saying. "I would've called, but I forgot my phone and didn't want to go back for it. I'm going upstairs." Without waiting for a response, she darted down the hall and up the staircase, presumably heading for my bedroom.

Mom peeked out from the kitchen. "Was that Tink?"

"Either that or a small blond tornado just blew in," I called back, following after Tink.

Upstairs, Tink had kicked off her shoes and flung her coat over my computer chair. She sat on my bed, hugging a pillow. Her nose was tinted red, and her eyes looked distinctly puffy.

"Weren't you going to that party with Kit?" I asked. "What happened?"

In her ongoing quest to demonstrate to Greg just how over him she was, Tink had concocted a plan to attend some party and hang all over our friend Kit. I didn't think this was a very convincing plan, but Tink had somehow persuaded him to go along with it. *He kisses better than Greg, anyway*, she'd confided to me yesterday. I didn't ask how or when she'd found that out.

But she wasn't at the party. She was here, wrinkling her new silver dress. I looked her over critically, taking in her hunched shoulders, her tousled hair, the faint trace of glitter along her face and neck. She seemed anxious and afraid, but I got no hint of Knowing from her, only the vaguest sense of what I couldn't see.

Feeling a surge of alarm, I asked, "Did something happen at the party?"

She blinked at me. "What? No. I didn't go. Kit canceled on me. At the last minute, of course."

I crossed to my computer chair, shoved Tink's coat out of the way, and sat, swiveling to face her. "You know, you really should've just asked Gideon."

Her troubled expression vanished. Her jaw dropped open, and she stared at me like I'd sprouted another head, or at least a few extra noses. "I can't have that boy's tongue in my mouth! It would break the laws of nature. Besides, he's saving himself for Brooke."

Since that last point was indisputable, I only shrugged. We were quiet a moment—Tink chewing her lip, me watching her. When she didn't seem inclined to volunteer any more information, I asked, "What's going on? Did Erica go to the party? Did she tell you something about Greg?"

She hugged the pillow tighter. "No. It's not—"

"Did you run into him somewhere, then? Or his girlfriend?"

"I'm not upset about Greg," she snapped.

"Right," I said, rolling my eyes. "The whole pretend-I-don't-care thing doesn't really work when—"

"Audrey, can you just shut up a second?"

I was startled into obedience.

Tink didn't speak immediately. She took a few shaky breaths, dropping her gaze to my bedspread. She let the pillow fall and traced the little floral pattern on my comforter with one hand. Finally, without looking up, she said, "It happened a few weeks ago."

An uneasy feeling bubbled up inside me. "What did?"

Still not looking at me, she lifted her left hand before her, flattening her palm so that I could see the pale blue of her veins threading upward beneath her skin. Slowly, light began to pulse at her wrist. Under her fingertips, the blue was joined by other shades: rose and amethyst and gold, warm green, deep indigo. Twining colors that softly glowed.

Her voice was little more than a whisper, but I didn't need to hear her speak to know her words. Her eyes met mine. "I was called."

"You were called," I repeated in a flat voice. My mind was racing, going back over the past few weeks in detail. I remembered Tink's recent evasiveness, the sense that she'd been hiding something, the nebulous feeling of anxiety surrounding her. I thought of her bare legs as we walked to the parking ramp, the way she hadn't felt the cold. I recalled the malicious tilt of Susannah's lips. I saw a Harrower slinking toward us.

Kill the Guardian, Susannah had said.

The words screamed inside me. She hadn't meant Drew. She'd meant Tink all along.

"I am such an idiot," I said, incredulity warring with comprehension. The powers I'd shared that night hadn't been the Harrower's; they'd been Tink's. Somehow, the possibility had never occurred to me. Tink was Kin, just like me—but I had never considered that she might be called.

I looked at her. She clenched a fist and held it against her chest. The light beneath her skin faded. I didn't know what to say, how to react, whether to comfort her or question her, to ask what it had felt like, being called. For one terrible moment, all I could feel was the burn of jealousy, knotting my stomach and closing my throat. I turned away, toward the window, gazing into the darkness outside that was nearly hidden by the climbing frost. "Why didn't you tell me?"

"I was hoping it would go away."

I swung the chair back around. "You thought you would get *un*called?"

"I don't know. This is really scary, Audrey."

Immediately, I felt bad. I left my chair and climbed onto the bed beside her. "You haven't talked to anyone about it?"

She shook her head. "I've just been ignoring it, or trying to. But the problem is—I can't really control it. Sometimes my hand will just *glow*. I've been wearing gloves everywhere, but tonight my mom found out about it, and she completely freaked out, and she threatened to call Mr. Alvarez to make him talk to me, so I ... left."

I frowned, thinking over what I knew of the subject. Most Kin children were placed in some form of combat training long before there was any chance that they might be called; at the very least, they were taught self-defense. Even Mom, who had kept the Kin a secret from me most of my life, had signed me up for martial arts training when I was eight. But the only classes Tink had had were a few gymnastics and dance courses, and she'd stopped taking those by fourth grade. Some element of a Guardian's fighting ability came from instinct, born in them the moment they were called—but not all of it. Tink would need help.

"Would you rather talk to Mom?" I asked.

"You are missing the point. I don't want to be a Guardian, and I'm not *going* to be one."

"I don't think you get a choice in this." As soon as the words had left my lips, I realized it was the wrong thing to say. "I'm sorry. I know you're scared—but you don't have to deal with it all by yourself. The Kin will help you."

"They won't."

I started to argue, but the look on her face stopped me. It wasn't the stubborn look she normally got whenever we discussed the Kin, all annoyed and obstinate; it was angry. "Why?" I asked.

She looked down. "You know how your mom's this great hero, defeating Harrowers and saving the world and all that? My dad—wasn't."

"What are you talking about?"

Tink rarely spoke of her father. I knew he'd died when she was little, but it was another one of those subjects she preferred to avoid. Now, there was a catch in her voice. "My dad betrayed the Kin. He did something terrible, and he got six Guardians killed." A tear rolled down her cheek. She wiped it angrily away. For the space of a second, she was open and vulnerable. I caught a sliver of Knowing: Tink as a young girl, wearing a blue cotton dress and holding her mother's hand. From nearby, the sound of a man's voice, vaguely familiar. *We're a part of her. She's a part of us.* Then it was gone, drowned out by other voices, harsh words, cold, sneering faces. The child that was Tink fled down a long hall. The image faded.

Tink gulped in a breath. "Trust me when I tell you, I may want nothing to do with the Kin, but they want even less to do with me."

"Then *I'll* help you." I reached forward and gripped her hand. "And so will Mom. And Leon."

Before Tink could respond, Mom hollered up from below us. "Girls, get down here!"

Tink sighed, swinging her feet over the side of the bed and heading for the door. "That probably means my mom is here."

But it wasn't her mother waiting for us at the bottom of the stairs. It was Mr. Alvarez. He didn't look happy. His hair and clothing were damp with snow, and he had on the stern teacher face he used whenever he caught someone texting in class.

Tink swore when she saw him, folding her arms and planting herself at the bottom of the stairs. "Go harass someone else."

"Your mother contacted me. She asked me to talk to you."

"You can save it, because I've heard it," Tink said, doing her best to sound bored.

"Then you'll hear it again. Being called changes things. You need to acknowledge that. You can no longer pretend you're not Kin."

"You are wasting your breath."

He ignored her. "You'll need to begin training as soon as

157

possible. I've spoken with two other Guardians, and they've agreed to take on the responsibility. For the first few weeks, they'll switch off nights, until we can determine who better suits your needs."

That got a reaction. Tink jumped to her feet and took a step toward him. "My *needs* involve being left alone," she shot back. "I have no interest in any of your Guardian bullshit. How do you not get that?"

"Your life changed the second you were called. Ignoring that fact won't alter, or solve, anything." His voice was quiet, almost kind, but it didn't soften the bluntness of his words or the grim look on his face.

Mom watched him uneasily. "Maybe this isn't the best tactic," she said. "She's just a kid."

"We all were." He sighed. "Give us a minute, Luce. You, too, Whitticomb."

I had a few qualms about abandoning Tink, who stood looking mutinous in her silver dress and bare feet. From her expression, I expected to see little clouds of steam spiral out of her ears at any second. But Mom gestured for me to follow her upstairs, and, after mouthing an apology to Tink, I went.

Once we entered her room, Mom busied herself getting ready for the night. She exchanged her jeans for black pants and pulled her hair back into a bun. "Did you know she'd been called?"

"Not until a few minutes ago. I should've figured it out earlier, but I guess I've been a little preoccupied."

"How do you feel about it?"

I hesitated. Mom didn't have much of a Knowing, but she could read me pretty well. "I don't know," I said. "I didn't really expect it." That pang of jealousy flared under my skin. I knew I could still be called. Both of my parents had become Guardians at fifteen, but that didn't necessarily mean anything; it wasn't dictated by parentage. Some Guardians were eighteen or nineteen before they were called. But part of me had the urge to cry out that it wasn't fair that Tink had been called when she didn't want it, and I did. I sighed and turned away from Mom, saying, "Do you know what happened with Tink's father?"

"I don't know the entire story," she said, then paused as we heard the sound of bare feet padding down the hall.

After a moment, Tink appeared. Her coat hung over her shoulders, and her shoes were dangling from her hands. "I'm going home," she announced.

"You okay?" I asked.

She wrinkled her nose. "Ugh. I feel like I just signed away my soul."

"You made a deal with him?"

Tink nodded glumly. "He said that if I agreed to try training for two weeks, he'd lay off. And if I didn't, he'd sic the Kin elders on me." She shuddered. Having met the Kin elders—a group of sharp-eyed old women who were three broomsticks and a black cat short of a coven—I understood her trepidation.

"If you need any help, I'm here," Mom offered. "I know it can be a frightening time."

Tink, probably fearing another lecture, took that as her cue to leave. She thanked Mom, hugged me briefly, then vanished back down the hall.

Later that night, Mom told me the story of Tink's father, Howard Brewster.

"It was more than eight years ago. We were still living up north," she said. Mom sat in the parlor with a cup of cocoa. I curled up on the sofa, my legs tucked beneath me, watching as her face clouded. "Most of the Kin prefer not to talk about it."

Six dead Guardians, Tink had said. In my mind, I saw lights shining within the gentle bend of a wrist. Lights that ebbed.

Mom's voice was low as she spoke.

She'd never met Howard Brewster, she told me, but she knew about him—what little there was to know. He'd been a quiet, unassuming man, with no close friends or relatives in the area. Instead of taking an active role within the Kin community, he'd kept to himself. He wasn't a Guardian, and if he had any powers—a blur of Knowing, or the innate gift for Healing some of his ancestors had had—he'd never disclosed them. There were others like him, Mom said, Kin who gradually distanced themselves, preferring to live simply, hoping to forget the signs of their heritage, the danger that lurked. Howard had married outside of the Kin; that was common enough, though some among the older generations of Kin still frowned upon it. Then, after his divorce from Tink's mother, Howard had committed what many saw as an unforgivable crime.

He'd fallen in love with a Harrower.

"Like Iris," I breathed. I saw again the pain and devotion in my cousin's face, the silver sheen of the necklace she'd worn, the triple knot twisting, the ring on Tigue's finger. Love—if it had been love—had ruined them both, I thought, recalling all the blood and the secrets that bound them together. Dead girls who had died for Iris's terrible dream.

My mother shook her head. She turned her mug in her hands, gazing down. "No. From what I can tell, this Harrower—I don't know her human name—was truly neutral. I'm not sure what Tink has heard, but Howard didn't betray the Kin, at least not intentionally. Not in the way that Iris did. His sin, if you want to call it that, wasn't treachery. It was idealism. He believed there should be peace. He believed it was possible."

"Peace," I repeated, feeling a little mystified.

"Between human and Harrower."

"*Idealism* is an understatement."

"Maybe it just wasn't the right time," Mom said, but she sounded doubtful.

Peace might have been Howard's intent, she told me, but it wasn't what he'd achieved. The incident had occurred eight years ago—and a little over eight years since the Harrowing and Verrick's defeat. The Kin had been scattered, weakened, still struggling to recover from the long shadow of grief that lay across the Cities. The Guardians were weakened as well: many had died at Verrick's hands, and others, like Mom, had left the Astral Circle. Those that remained were the very old and the very young, teenagers only recently called.

Mom's voice was flat, cool, but as she spoke I caught the faint edge of guilt that rose up within her, words that slid within words.

"There were maybe a dozen active Guardians remaining at the time," she said. "Not enough to form a real defense if trouble arose. From what Ryan tells me, Howard never hid his relationship with the Harrower, and the Guardians were very suspicious, even before he began talking about brokering a peace."

For months, everyone was on edge. And then the betrayal had happened.

Not Howard Brewster, and not the Harrower that he somehow loved. Another demon, claiming to be neutral, had turned on them.

Mom didn't know the precise details, only that Howard and his girlfriend had planned to meet with several other Harrowers, and had invited the Guardians along, to prove their intentions were genuine. By the end of it, dozens of Harrowers had been killed, along with seven members of the Kin: six Guardians and Howard Brewster. There had been only two survivors.

I was silent, taking this in, when Mom told me that one of those survivors had been Ryan Alvarez.

"That's how he ended up leading the Guardians," she said.

"What, by default?"

She smiled briefly. "No. He took charge."

Mr. Alvarez, she said, had spent months traveling about the state, stitching together the tattered remnants of the Kin, contacting those who had strayed from the Cities and urging them to return. With the Guardian leadership dead, he'd stepped in to supervise the training of the young Kin who'd been recently called. And he'd attempted to put an end to the enmity toward Howard Brewster. He'd contacted Tink's mother and tried to bring Tink herself back to the Kin.

"I'm afraid not everyone was kind to her," Mom said. "And Ryan was a little naive back then. I don't think it occurred to him that people would be less than welcoming."

I nodded slowly, but as I listened, a sudden memory sparked. I caught the image of a hazy summer twilight when we'd still lived up north, recalled the sound of a gasping engine as a car made its slow way up the dirt road. I was curled up on the porch swing beside Gram, my head on her shoulder. She sang softly. We watched the fireflies come out, little lights in the grass. Beyond us: the long approach of dark.

The car had stopped in our driveway, and a teenage boy with a mop of black hair had stepped out. I hadn't seen him clearly; I'd been sleepy, drifting into dreams with the gentle sway of the swing, Gram's voice in my ear—but as I thought of him, it seemed to me he'd worn a grim, determined expression that I later came to know well.

Now, I looked at Mom in surprise. "Mr. Alvarez came to you, too?"

"He told me that Morning Star was still needed," she said, with a short nod. She was gazing past me, maybe remembering that same long-ago evening. Slowly, she rose from her seat at the couch and turned to the window. "That's when we came home."

In spite of Esther's warning about the dangers of experimenting with Amplification, I was anxious to learn, and I wasn't going to rely on her to teach me. As far as I was concerned, I was done with Kin lessons. But now that I had a way of helping Mom and Leon, I meant to do everything in my power to prepare myself for whatever came next.

Unfortunately, there weren't any other Amplifiers in the Cities who could instruct me. Mom had some knowledge of the ability, since she and my father had fought side by side for years, but he had never explained to her precisely *how* the sharing and increasing of powers worked. It was something that had been intuitive with him, she told me. Instinctual.

She did give me a few details, however. Similar to Knowing, Amplification was in some part dependent upon relationship: my father had always had an easier time amplifying her strength than assisting anyone else. She knew it was possible to share powers without also amplifying them—though that took effort—but the reverse wasn't true. She knew my father had used demons' abilities on occasion, though he hadn't liked doing so. And she knew, of course, that it was his Amplification that had formed a link between him and Verrick.

Elspeth was able to provide more information. On Sunday night, she raided Esther's library for some documentation on the subject and stopped by to help me pore over the volumes she'd located. I already knew some of the material. Direct contact helped, but wasn't strictly necessary; concentration allowed the bond between Amplifier and subject to be maintained without physical connection. I learned that Amplifiers themselves differed in aptitude, some providing only a minor increase in abilities, others doubling or tripling their subjects' strength.

But none of the files, none of the documents and anecdotes, told me how to activate it. It was something that came naturally to a person. The only thing coming naturally to me was frustration. I set the books aside.

Then, when I asked Elspeth to help me with training—in the hope that we could trigger the ability—she shook her head, looking panicked.

"You need formal training," she said. "And you need to go slowly. You should read through the books first, and then wait for Grandmother. She'll help you understand everything. Amplifying can be dangerous—we can't just mess around with it."

"That's why I want to learn. So that I can control it. It's only dangerous if I don't know what I'm doing."

Her voice was quiet. "Iris knew what she was doing."

I hesitated. Iris had used her Amplification on Harrowers, sharing their abilities in order to kill them. And she'd changed because of it.

"I wouldn't be sharing a demon's powers," I said. "I'd be sharing yours."

"For now, yes. But I know you, Audrey. You're not going to want to just sit around waiting when there's trouble. You're going to want to fight."

Well, she had me there. I did want to fight. I wanted to help. And now that I was no longer powerless, I intended to do everything I could to learn about that power. But I wasn't about to go out onto the streets and search for Harrowers to brawl with, either.

"I want to *help* fight," I said. "I'm going to figure it out eventually, even without your help. *Or* Esther's."

"Fine. Figure it out yourself," she snapped. And then she started crying.

The last thing I wanted to do was cause Elspeth more pain, so I dropped the subject. For my apology, I raided the kitchen for the last of Leon's sugar cookies, and we spent the remainder of the evening discussing her trip overseas. But once she was gone, I went over each of the books again, searching for anything I might have missed.

Focusing on my Amplification meant I was able to set other

troubles aside for a time—but not indefinitely. Monday night, Leon reminded me of the problem with our bond and said that he was intent on fixing it. Of course, he was also insistent on the fact that I was the one causing the problem, which started another argument—or would have, if Drew hadn't appeared for his nightly check-in.

Susannah hadn't been seen since Wednesday night, but there was other unsettling news. Several neutral Harrowers within the Cities had gone missing. No one knew where. They'd simply vanished, dropping their human lives and aliases without word or warning. If they'd gone Beneath, they hadn't resurfaced.

"I didn't touch them," Drew said, when Mom asked whether he knew anything about their whereabouts. "And I should have. I warned you this would happen. Susannah is too persuasive, her influence too great, for most Harrowers to withstand."

"We can't know they've gone over," Mom protested.

"Where else would they be?"

Leon snorted. "Probably hiding from you." He and Drew had settled into a state of mutual dislike, which I didn't fully understand, and tried to ignore. But, recalling the agonized shriek of the Harrower that night in Loring Park, I thought Leon might have been correct.

Drew turned toward him. "I would've thought you'd agree with me. You have more to lose than most."

Leon didn't react, except for the subtle tightening of his jaw. He glanced at me, then away.

That night, I dreamed of Susannah.

She stood across from me in a snowy field, the demon named Daniel beside her. The one Drew had mentioned, I thought; the one with the Knowing. Their hands were clasped, tattoos winding together like a snake coiled about their wrists. They watched me. I watched them. All around us, Harrowers writhed. Guardians bled beneath the moon. A wind rose, howling and cold, swirling through Susannah's hair so that it rose like fire in the night. She turned her back, releasing Daniel's hand. He didn't move. His sad eyes lifted to mine. And there, in the stillness of sleep, I felt awake, aware. For just a second, Knowing met Knowing, and it seemed that Daniel was telling me something he couldn't quite speak. He said my name.

I woke up wondering if Harrowers dreamed.

Tuesday morning dawned bleak and gray. I shuffled around my room, feeling half dead as I pulled on the jeans I'd tossed across my computer chair the night before, then dragged a sweater over my head. Downstairs, Mom was already at the kitchen table.

She looked up when I sat beside her, squeezing my shoulder. "The past few days have been a bit of a roller coaster for you, haven't they?"

More like a blender, I thought. I picked at my food until Gideon arrived.

With everything else going on in my life, the routine of school was something of a relief, even though I was behind on homework. On the drive in, I pushed thoughts of Harrowers aside, and by the time we reached the parking lot, I was beginning to feel more awake. The morning was mild, the roads damp with fog and melting snow. The temperature had risen above forty, which much of the school population—Gideon included—took for T-shirt weather. I simply hoped it meant that we'd finally begun the long, slow creep toward spring. Months of snow and sludge, brown grass, and bare trees made me yearn for anything green.

I wasn't the only one preoccupied these days. Mr. Alvarez was so distracted he forgot to quiz us in Precalc for the second day in a row. My friend Erica thought it a sign of the apocalypse and started checking the calendar in her planner for solar eclipses. I was actually a little disappointed, since Precalc was the one class I was caught up in.

At lunch, I planned to do another reading for Gideon, but we were delayed by Tink's bad mood. She slammed her tray down on the table with such force that her chicken sandwich bounced upward and a piece of broccoli went rolling under her chair. Then she just sat there scowling.

Gideon and I exchanged a glance.

"Don't mention the G-word," I whispered to him.

"Which G-word?" he asked. "*Greg* or *Guardian*?" The only thing Tink had told Gideon about being called as a Guardian was that she didn't want to talk about it—but since she was still needling him about Brooke, he apparently didn't feel the need to adhere to her wishes.

I rolled my eyes. "Good job mentioning *both of them*."

"I thought so." He grinned.

"Ha-*ha*," Tink said. "Aren't you guys hysterical. As it happens, my anger is currently directed at an entirely different letter of the alphabet."

"*F* for freshman?" Gideon said.

"*A* for Alvarez."

I made a guess. "He introduced you to your trainers?" Tink hadn't warmed to the idea of being a Guardian—especially since she'd had to rearrange her work schedule at Caribou Coffee to accommodate training.

"One of them. And you know what he did? He saddled me with *his girlfriend*."

I'd met Camille, Mr. Alvarez's girlfriend, once or twice before and hadn't found anything objectionable about her. "I think she's nice," I said.

"I don't care if she's nice. This is his way of getting around his promise," Tink replied. "He told me he would leave me alone about the Kin, remember? Now I'll just have Camille nagging me instead."

Knowing Mr. Alvarez, I figured she was probably right about that. "Are you still going to keep your end of the deal?"

"Two weeks, that's all I agreed to. After that, I'm done," she said. Then she grinned. "Besides, I don't have time for all of this. I have it on good authority that Lars Lyman is going to ask me out."

Gideon looked confused. "I thought you were still stuck on Greg."

She lifted a hand. "Over it!"

"But . . . Lars Lyman?" I asked. Lars was friendly and easygoing, cute in a football player sort of way, and he gave discounts to every Whitman High student who stopped by his family's pizza place, where he worked after school—but he wasn't someone I would have matched Tink with. He was a senior, which might have added to his appeal, except that he'd also been a senior *last* year.

"What?" Tink asked, shrugging. "I've been helping him in math."

Since she could nap her way through that class and wake up with an A, I thought that was a nice gesture on her part. Still, if my choices were between being a teenage superhero and eating greasy pizza with a guy who was repeating twelfth grade, I'd have been in my mother's closet that very second, stealing her hoodies.

Gideon still seemed puzzled. Tink turned toward him. "This is good news for you," she said. "Lars and Brooke are friends. It's perfect. We'll all go to a movie together, and I'll make sure you get to sit by her."

"Because that won't be obvious at all," I said. *Subtle* was not a word in Tink's vocabulary. I could imagine exactly how she'd accomplish this. She probably wouldn't even ask about seating arrangements—she'd just push Brooke directly into Gideon's lap.

"Obvious is the entire point," she said. "You know, faint hearts and fair ladies and all that. He won't get anywhere by turning invisible whenever she walks by."

Gideon had gone quiet, but the glares he started aiming at Tink made me think it wise to position myself between them.

"If he kills you, can I have your stuff?" I asked her.

"Nope. When I die, I want to be placed on a pyre with all my worldly possessions. And anyway, Gideon has no reason to murder me. My intentions are wholesome and pure. I'm only trying to help those who cannot help themselves," she said. Then, after bidding us a quick farewell, she dashed off without even finishing her lunch.

I turned to Gideon. He was looking a little panicked. "I don't think she'll actually make you go to a movie with them," I said. "But it would give you a chance to talk to Brooke."

"I *can't* talk to her," he said.

Not without that blindfold, anyway, I thought—but I sensed he meant something else. "Why?"

"I don't want to ruin things. Can you please just drop this?"

I wasn't sure what there was to ruin in endless pining, but I supposed that when you'd had a crush as long as Gideon had, pining was what you clung to. As long as she didn't reject him, he still had hope.

"Okay," I said, and we decided to move on to his reading. I pulled out my cards and began shuffling. "I'm not entirely sure this will work," I warned. "I haven't really gotten the chance to practice, and my focus is still a little off. We might not get anything."

For a second, as I shuffled, I felt a shiver of apprehension, thinking of the blank card and how Gram had hidden it away. But, I reminded myself, this was *Gideon*. The worst thing I was likely to discover about him was that he'd once flushed his sisters' toys down the toilet. Or maybe that he'd been lying all this time when he swore he hadn't laughed the day I'd shown up at school with my shirt on backward—and I couldn't exactly blame him for laughing.

To Gideon's disappointment and my frustration, the reading went much the same as the other two had. The cards that appeared were nearly identical, and I got the same senses and impressions I'd had before—images of Iris, of that night at Harlow Tower, gold lettering and dark windows, the snow-swirled roof, teeth and scales and the silver ripple of Harrower flesh. Memories Gideon couldn't escape, visions that darkened his dreams, but no hint of a connection to the Kin.

The blank card appeared again at the end of the reading. I tried to do as Esther had suggested. To release my focus, forget my questions. Break the pattern, I told myself; be open to potential and possibility and chaos. I tried to shut out the world until there was silence around me, within me, until my mind was as blank as the card.

But I didn't see anything. Only the card itself, faintly yellowed with age.

"Still nothing?" Gideon asked.

"Sorry," I said. I reached for the cards, intending to return them to my book bag. Then I stopped.

As I touched the blank card—lightly, my fingers grazing its surface—Knowing shot through me. It was nothing distinct, just the blurred image of what might have been a face. It blinked before me, and then it was gone. I touched the card again, trying once more to do as Esther had instructed, but the Knowing didn't return.

Gideon was looking at me. "Did you see something?"

"I saw... someone. I think. I don't know." I hesitated. I hadn't recognized the hazy image that had flashed before me, but it had felt different from the rest of the reading. The other impressions I'd gotten had been of recent events. This had seemed older. Older—and somehow sad.

I wasn't certain what it meant, though it occurred to me now that maybe there wasn't a connection to the Kin after all. Maybe Gideon's nightmares were merely some forgotten childhood trauma that had been brought back by his ordeal with Iris. Though I supposed I'd be aware if anything truly traumatic had happened in his life, considering I'd known him for half of it.

I decided I might as well ask. "Did you ever have these nightmares before?"

"No. I mean, I had nightmares—but not like this." He paused, frowning. "I had trouble sleeping for a while after Miss Gustafson died."

I remembered that story. When Gideon was in first grade, his teacher had been killed in a car crash three weeks before the end of the school year. He'd been devastated by the loss. It was a memory burned into him—the first time he had experienced death. Until then, he'd never known anyone who had died, who was there one moment and not the next. A sudden gap.

But while her passing had had a profound effect on him, I wasn't certain it was quite on the same level as being held captive by demons and threatened with death.

I sighed. "Well, we made progress, anyway. I got *something* from the card. We'll keep trying."

I had martial arts after school that evening, which always cleared my head and calmed me. I found comfort in the simplicity of physical motion, action and reaction, the stretching of muscles, falling and blocking. By the time class was over, I'd worked myself into a pleasant sort of exhaustion. The temperature had dropped outside, but I didn't mind the cool air against me as I waited for the bus. The low clouds from that morning had scattered, leaving the night bright and clear. I took in long breaths. On the bus, I listened to music on my phone, tilted my head back, and watched the streets slide by in a blur of signs and stoplights. The moon was nearly full, an imperfect circle, distant and gleaming.

I arrived home to find Mickey's car parked out front. He was inside, arguing with Mom.

They were in the parlor and didn't hear me enter the house. I picked my way carefully through the hallway and up the stairs, not bothering to remove my coat and shoes until I reached my room.

Deciding it was best if I minded my own business for once, I barricaded myself in the bathroom, stripped off my sweaty clothing, and hopped into the shower. The chill from outside that lingered on my skin gradually receded, and after I toweled dry and put on my pajamas, I intended to curl up in bed with my homework and then go through more of the documents on Amplification that Elspeth had left behind.

But when I got out of the shower, Mom and Mickey were *still* arguing. This time, curiosity won. With quick, noiseless steps, I moved to the top of the staircase and seated myself there, my elbows on my knees. I felt a twinge of guilt at eavesdropping, but Mom's voice was so loud I probably could've heard her while shut up in my bedroom wearing headphones.

Mickey was quieter, but his words still carried. "I understand the risks," he was saying.

Her response was immediate. "This isn't about risks. It's about weakness. *Your* weakness."

"You sure know how to make a guy feel manly."

"I don't give a damn about your ego. I'm concerned with reality. Getting involved in Kin affairs will only get you killed."

His voice was gruff. "I'm already involved. It's too late for me to pretend I don't know anything. I won't confront this woman—"

"She's not a woman."

"Whatever she is, then. I won't confront her. I'll just keep a lookout. That's all."

"I'm tired of arguing about this."

"And I'm damned well tired of being shut out." There was

a short silence; then Mom started to speak. Mickey cut her off. "Look," he began. "I'm not asking to fight at your side, and I don't want to stand in your way. I just want to be of use."

"You can't be."

Another silence, longer this time. When Mickey spoke again, his voice was low, his words too muffled for me to catch. I didn't hear what he said, but I heard him leave. Heavy footsteps across the parlor, into the hallway. He turned near the door, looking back at Mom. She hadn't followed. He hesitated a moment longer, his hand on the doorknob. Then he left. He closed the door gently behind him, but the sound of it echoed through the hall.

Once he was gone, Mom stepped out of the parlor and turned toward the stairs. She halted when she saw me.

"Nice going," I said.

"Zip it," she said crossly, walking past me up the stairs.

I followed her. "You don't think that was maybe a little harsh?"

She paused near her bedroom, her hand gripping the edge of the door. "He'll survive his injured pride. There's no guarantee he'd survive another Harrower encounter. It's better for him to stay away."

"He's looking for Susannah?"

Her face was grim. "For whatever alias she's using while here in the Cities. We're not even certain she has one. He spoke to a couple who witnessed one of the attacks. They didn't see the Harrowers, but they saw enough of Susannah to give a description."

"He did help you out with Anthony." When she didn't answer, I added, "Anyway, you should probably be nicer to him. He seems to like you a lot."

She turned toward me, frowning. "Why are you bugging me about this?"

"I want you to be happy."

Her expression softened. "Oh, honey," she said. She grabbed me, giving me a tight hug. "I am happy."

But I heard the little catch in her voice, and I knew her statement for the lie it was.

Elspeth was still unwilling to help with my Amplification, and none of the books she'd lent me provided me with ideas on how to activate it, so I threw myself into what training I could. I spent Wednesday afternoon sparring with Leon—and doing my best to avoid the subject of our Guardian bond—and on Thursday I attended an extra class at the dojo.

Once class was over, I made my way toward the bus stop slowly, lost in thought. Night thickened around me. The air was more crisp than cold, the sky clear. I tuned out the noise of traffic: the hum of car engines, the distant sound of police sirens. A pickup truck missing its muffler sputtered past me. Nearby, a kid on a bicycle skidded to a halt at the end of the avenue, narrowly missing a badly parked minivan. I turned a corner and found myself alone on the street.

Two blocks from the bus stop, I snapped to attention. I

straightened, tensed. In the meager light ahead, the shadows divided. What I'd taken for a tree became a boy, and the boy stepped toward me.

I caught my breath. I couldn't see him well, but I knew him immediately—his lanky body, his blue T-shirt, the hole in his jeans. Daniel.

Susannah's other half was solo at the moment. He stood about twenty feet in front of me, pausing the second our eyes met.

Instinct screamed that I should flee, but there was something different about Daniel, and that difference made me hesitate. The Beneath clung to him, like a mist around his body, spiderweb thin—but not in the way that I'd felt from other Harrowers. Daniel didn't have their malice. There was no hint of their deep hunger and hate within him, their writhing anger, their cold cunning. No glimmer of silver broke through his dark skin, no flash of red teeth showed between his parted lips.

"Don't run away," he said. Not a command, but a plea. "Audrey."

He knew my name. Just like in my dream.

I stood immobile as he approached. His movements were hesitant, uncertain—he didn't carry himself with the sleek, languid grace of Susannah, but he didn't have the awkward shuffle of weaker demons, either. As he shortened the distance between us, he kept his eyes pinned on me. Around us, the wind rose up, harsh and biting.

That was when I saw it. Daniel was shivering.

His T-shirt was thin, almost threadbare. The tear in his jeans flapped in the cold air. The wind bucked against him. And he was shivering.

"I've been trying to talk to you—I *need* to talk to you," he said.

I stared at him as Knowing wrenched within me. He wasn't a Harrower.

He was human.

I flinched and moved backward, reeling. Confusion rapidly turned to concern. My gaze dropped to his tattoo, the design identical to Susannah's. Daniel might not have been a demon, but he was living among them. He'd been Beneath, and not just for an hour or a day. I sensed that. I could feel the Beneath within him. It was a part of him now, breathing in him, around him. Its whispers echoed in my ears. Whispers that spoke of death.

But below all of that I sensed something that was raw, grieving. I heard the drumming of his human heart. And I realized with a start that it wasn't my own abilities that told me these things. Daniel was using his Knowing on me.

"What do you want?" I asked. When he didn't approach again, I searched the space around him. He was alone, but he might not remain that way. I assessed him as I spoke, watching the way he held himself, his gestures. He hadn't moved like a fighter. If it came to it, I felt reasonably certain I could defend myself, unless he had powers I wasn't aware of.

"Please," he said. "I'm not here to hurt you."

"What about your girlfriend?"

He recoiled as though I'd struck him. A shudder ran through his body. His face became contorted. But all he said was, "We don't have a lot of time."

I sensed Susannah before she spoke. Dread climbed up my spine.

"And it appears you've wasted it. What a shame."

We turned.

She stood before us on the street, near the edge of the sidewalk. Her strapless dress was emerald green. She'd exchanged her pearls for a diamond necklace that glittered at her throat. Her long hair curled against her shoulders. The streetlamps lent her face a chilly glow. She smiled like a shark, giving us the full benefit of pointed red teeth before becoming human once more.

"It seems my pet has slipped his leash," she said. "Come here, pet."

For one fleeting second, Daniel turned toward me. Connection rippled between us. Our Knowing collided. Impressions sped through my consciousness: broken glass, Susannah laughing, a woman's sharp scream, blood. Then the Beneath, only the Beneath, everything the Beneath.

The moment passed. Daniel's expression went blank. He looked at Susannah. Two long strides and he was beside her. Her arm looped around his waist, and she leaned her head against him, crooning words I couldn't hear. He nodded jerkily.

"All better," she said.

Now was the time to run. I knew it, I felt it, and I willed

my body to obey. But Susannah's eyes held mine. My stomach clenched. If I ran, there was no way she wouldn't catch me.

"I've been curious about his interest in you. He says you'll be of use, but I have to wonder if he has some other motive. He won't tell me why you're so much in his thoughts these days. He ran off tonight, and he came straight to you. Why is that?"

I swallowed. "He didn't say."

She glanced briefly at Daniel and asked, "What do you think? Should I kill her?"

"We can use her."

"You keep saying that, but I have yet to see proof."

"She'll know. Wait."

Susannah's words were soft, silky. "What do you want with her, Danny?"

"She'll know," he repeated.

"That's not why you came to her. That's not why you left me."

Something flickered in his eyes, quickly banished. Sadness crept back into his voice. "I want to go home."

"I'm your home," she murmured. She turned toward him.

I ran.

As I ran, I reached for my phone. I didn't care about direction or distance. I doubted I'd get far, but that didn't matter—I just needed to buy myself a few seconds, long enough to make a call. But I hadn't taken more than three strides before my arm was wrenched behind my back, my knees were kicked inward, and the sidewalk rose to meet me.

I landed hard. The impact reverberated through me, even as Susannah jerked me back to my feet, turning me around to face her. Her grip was so tight on my wrist I feared she'd crush the bones. Her other hand went to my neck, squeezing—and then she lifted me, held me above her as I choked and struggled.

"Don't be rude. We weren't done talking." Her grip on my throat tightened, then twisted. "You set something in motion that night on Harlow Tower. Did you feel it? That was the night the little Seer bitch had her first vision. The night she saw the doom of your Kin. It all comes back to you. You set it in motion—but I intend to finish it. I'll find the girl, open the world your kind trapped us in. But my Danny says you have a part to play yet, so I'll let you live."

Her fingers loosened. She tossed me backward onto the sidewalk. I cried out, a hoarse rasping that sounded alien to my ears.

"We should go," Daniel said.

Susannah wasn't finished. "I said I'd let her live. I didn't say I'd leave her whole."

She went after me again, grabbing me by the arm and yanking me up. This time, it wasn't fingers that wrapped my flesh.

It was claws.

Pain stabbed through me, so intense I thought I might throw up. My skin felt hot, so hot it seemed that steam must be rising from me into the chill of the air. Tears coursed down my face. I struggled to free myself, but Susannah held on. Her talons sliced through my coat and shirt, into skin. My vision blurred. I saw only shapes and fragments, bits of color: the scuffed, stained cement of the sidewalk, the silver of ice along the curb, the fall of Daniel's shadow before me. Someone spoke, but the words didn't touch me.

Leon, I thought dazedly.

Just as quickly, my mind rebelled.

In that moment, I was glad the connection between us was broken. Glad that the link was severed, or at least silenced, that Leon wouldn't know to come to my aid. He was strong, but Susannah was stronger. They would fight and he would die. I felt it with a certainty deeper than the pain that spread through me. But as long as our connection was cut, he was safe. I clung to that. I hadn't consciously fought the bond before; I did now. I warred against it, against myself, against the longing inside me to hear his voice, to see his face. With everything in me, I willed him away.

I gasped in breaths. I heard Susannah laughing. My mind was in disorder, every thought scattered except the feverish need to keep Leon from me—but within the chaos, an idea sparked. A memory flickered and grew. Iris, the memory whispered. *Iris.*

Iris had fought demons.

By using their own powers.

I felt the clutch, the scrape of Susannah's claws, my blood spilling against her, scarlet against green. I reached out with my senses, with my fear and desperation and with my Knowing. I reached out with intuition and instinct and need.

The jolt of connection shook us both. Susannah's grip faltered. I twisted about, catching her with my free hand, refusing to let her go. I felt the awful strength within her, a force so much greater than that of any of the other Harrowers I'd faced. That strength surged through me. Potent, dizzying, almost overwhelming. With it came the feel of the Beneath. A chill so deep it went beyond cold and even beyond burning. It blinded me, choked me. I gagged, feeling as though the air in my lungs had turned solid and my blood had stopped flowing. Everywhere, I sensed Susannah's hate. Her power became my power, but so did her malevolence, her fury, the darkness that writhed inside her. My consciousness narrowed. I knew wrath and I knew hate, Susannah's feelings and my own blending together. I knew nothing else—until she broke away. She tossed me to the sidewalk and retreated, her expression startled. I stared up at her, seeing the gleam of silver beneath her skin.

I didn't pause to think. I jumped to my feet and hurled myself toward her. My fingers caught her neck, locked there, digging in. She lifted an arm, thrusting me away, but I held on. Distantly, I was aware of my own skin breaking, of her claws sinking in to my shoulder, but I pushed back awareness, pushed back pain.

She broke free a second time, throwing me to the ground once more. I hit the sidewalk. I had a split second of blindness, and then felt a rush of dizziness as the connection between Susannah and me shattered. My thoughts reeled. I climbed to my knees. I saw Susannah ahead of me, Harrower form flickering behind her human guise. Her teeth were bared. There was a wild look on her face that might have been anger, might have been fear. I was preparing to launch myself at her once more when Daniel stepped between us.

"She can't help us if you hurt her," he told Susannah, keeping his back to me.

"If this plan of yours works, we won't need her."

"If it doesn't, we will."

"Why is it you can't find the girl on your own?"

"She's hidden from me."

I sucked in air. My entire body ached. I focused on Susannah, watching in case she moved to attack. Her eyes flicked to mine, and I realized with revulsion that I could see into them, through the flat blue color into the space where she kept her hatred, the part of her that was always Beneath.

"For you, Daniel," she said, though she kept her gaze on me. "But remember: if you run from me again, I'll peel the flesh from her body, piece by piece."

Her arm snaked around his waist. In the darkness, their bodies seemed to melt together. Then they were gone, and I was left staring at a long stretch of sidewalk and an empty street.

Curled up on the cement, I fumbled in my pocket for my phone. My fingers shook as I made the call. I cradled the phone to my ear. It rang once, and then Leon answered.

"Come get me," I breathed. "Please. Come get me."

My eyes closed. Darkness swam all around me. I pressed my cheek to the sidewalk and, as consciousness ebbed, I thought only of how warm the concrete seemed.

18

The next few hours were a blur, a patchwork of moments stitched together, full of worried faces, voices speaking rapidly, sharp light above me, the sterile hospital smell of disinfectant. I drifted in and out of consciousness, retreating into the safety of slumber whenever I could. I woke in Leon's arms, shifted, hid my face in his shoulder, slept again. Later, I stirred to the sound of my name. Feeling warm and drowsy, I nodded numbly to questions that seemed to come from far away. I registered that I was in the emergency room, that a nurse was speaking to me. Mechanically, I obeyed his instructions. My awareness divided into small, separate details: the nurse's voice, low and soothing; the pale blue fabric of his scrubs; the cool feel of metal; the far-off sound of footsteps. I watched everything with detachment. X-rays were taken, tests were run. I had no broken bones, but my left arm needed stitches. My coat and shirt were ruined, slashed in several places, stained brown with blood. My mother arrived, looking pale and frantic. She hugged me tightly, then immediately began interrogating the hospital staff. Finally, it was determined that my injuries were superficial and I wouldn't need to be admitted. I was given pain medication and sent home.

At home, there were more questions.

The feeling of unreality followed me. We went into the kitchen, where Mom led me to a chair. She crouched before me, tucked my hand in hers, and asked what had happened. My throat was raw, and speech was difficult. I answered in whispers and hisses. Then weariness descended once more, a heavy gray fog that filled my senses. My eyelids slid closed. I fought them open; they closed again. And then the dreams began.

In the dreams, I saw Susannah. I saw her smile, saw her tilt her head. Her hair was a cascade of fire that burned down her back. She shut her eyes, stepped out of her human skin. Her flesh melted away, pooling like mercury. She became formless, abstract, endless. But her presence remained. She was the watchful darkness Beneath. She was red stars shining above a barren street.

Daniel stood beside me.

"What were you trying to tell me?" I asked.

He lifted a finger to his lips. "She's listening," he said.

And then "I'm sorry." His cold hand clutched mine.

When I woke again, I was in my bed. Morning light filtered through the blinds, warm on my face. I lay there a moment, feeling groggy and disoriented, then sat and blinked away sleep. Pain raced up my arm when I moved, but I swung myself out of bed and made my way to the bathroom, pausing at the mirror. I grimaced. My neck was bruised, my left arm swollen and bandaged. Dark circles had formed under my eyes. My hair was so ratty and snarled it would have been an insult to birds to call it a nest.

"How are you feeling?" Mom asked when I trudged downstairs. She was at the kitchen table eating cereal, but rose when I entered. She felt my forehead.

"Like week-old roadkill."

"You sound like it, too." She gave me shoulder a gentle squeeze. "I already called you in sick. Go back to bed."

I was too exhausted to argue. I did as instructed, returning to my room after I'd taken more pain medication and had gulped down a glass of water. The medicine made my limbs feel heavy, as though I were walking underwater. My thoughts slipped out of focus. I curled up in bed with the covers pulled tight, and before long, sleep stole over me.

That afternoon, Esther arrived at the house and invaded my room, ignoring my protests. I'd woken only fifteen minutes earlier, and though I felt more lucid, I didn't particularly want to deal with her. I slumped back down on my bed.

"You and I need to have a discussion," she said.

"You're not supposed to bother an injured person."

"I'm persuaded you'll live."

I assumed she was there for a lecture, so I sighed and waited, keeping my focus on the bedspread. When she didn't speak, I chanced looking at her. She sat with her hands clasped in her lap, appearing every bit as tidy and serene as usual—if a bit out of place seated on my computer chair. Noticing my gaze, she frowned lightly.

"You've had quite the adventure, it seems."

I bit my lip. "It wasn't my fault."

"Did I say that I blamed you?"

"Usually when I'm attacked by a demon, it's followed up by someone yelling at me."

"I believe I'll leave that to your mother. Tell me about this Harrower you fought. You used your Amplification on it?"

I nodded.

"That is a perilous undertaking," Esther said. "You cannot share a demon's powers without also sharing its corruption."

"I didn't have a lot of choice."

"I wasn't criticizing. Merely stating fact. You need training, Audrey."

"What do you think I've been trying to do for the past week?" I asked, feeling a flash of annoyance. "*Without* your help."

"I will expect you to resume your lessons with me."

"Once my father is conveniently out of the picture again, right?"

Esther's tone was wintry. "If you believe there is anything convenient about Adrian's absence, you are very much mistaken."

"He's my *father*," I said, folding my arms.

"He's my son. And there is not a day that passes that I don't mourn the man he was. But I can't change the past. There's nothing to be gained by wishing otherwise." She let out a slow breath. "I am not here to discuss Adrian."

Of course she wasn't. I narrowed my eyes. "My throat hurts. I'm tired of talking."

"Good. Then you can listen. I spoke with your Guardian. You aren't being fair to him, Audrey."

Immediately, I bristled. "What are you talking about?"

"He informed me of the issue you've been having. He should have informed me sooner." She leaned forward slightly, watching me with that direct, piercing gaze she had. "You are fighting the bond."

"That's between us." I swallowed tightly. I knew, now, that Leon was right, that I was the one causing the rift. I'd felt it as I'd struggled against Susannah, willing him not to come to me, to stay in safety. But it wasn't something I wanted to discuss with Esther, especially since I could no longer claim it was unintentional. I might have severed the bond unconsciously, but last night I'd done everything in my power to make certain it remained that way.

Esther wasn't deterred. "It isn't easy, caring for someone and seeing them in danger. Worse still to be the cause of that danger. But you do him a grave injustice."

"By keeping him safe?"

"When a Guardian is given a specific charge, they don't simply desire to defend that person; it is a physical need. This boy was called to protect you, and now you're denying a part of who he is. It's selfish."

"Selfish! I don't want *him* to get hurt."

"Because of your feelings for him."

My heart lurched, thudding against my ribs. "Is that what he thinks?"

"It's the truth, isn't it?"

"No. Even if I didn't care about him, I wouldn't want him to get hurt for me—I wouldn't want anyone to."

"Perhaps. But you wouldn't fight so fiercely against it."

I didn't answer. I wanted to deny it, but I couldn't. Ever since the night Leon had been wounded in my place, something inside me had shifted, rebelled. I just hadn't been able to admit it. I looked away, toward the window. Outside, the late afternoon light had gone gray. I dragged in a breath, clenching my fists.

"This is your problem to resolve, Audrey. I suggest you do so quickly."

My words were soft. "What if I don't want to fix it?"

"Then that will be your burden to live with." I didn't look at her, but I heard her rise, heard her footsteps as she crossed my room, heard her pause. "And his."

By Saturday, my throat had mostly healed, and the pain in my arm had receded into mere soreness, but I was still hovering at the edge of exhaustion. Mom questioned me again in the morning—about the attack, about what Susannah had wanted—and I answered as best I could. I closed my eyes, seeing Susannah step toward me, hearing the lilt of her voice, feeling the chill under her skin. With a shiver, I hugged the blankets to me and returned my attention to Mom. I told her I didn't believe Susannah had been after me. I told her about Daniel.

"He was trying to tell me something," I said.

Mom furrowed her brow. She leaned forward and kissed the top of my head before departing. She'd only had a few hours of sleep, but she told me she had work to do, meetings to attend. Since Leon had a shift at the bakery, and she didn't feel comfortable leaving me alone, she instituted an hourly texting policy.

"What if I'm asleep?"

"Then you can expect to be woken up," she said.

I stayed in bed until early afternoon, when Gideon called and talked me into hanging out with him. I didn't bring my Nav cards along—I was feeling too rattled to focus properly—so we spent the day in his room, eating his grandmother's brownies and getting ourselves killed in video games. Eventually, after we'd both agreed that our zombie-shooting skills landed somewhere between rather pathetic and criminally incompetent, we decided to call it quits.

I was hoping to avoid the subject of Susannah, but as soon as we'd set down our controllers, Gideon glanced at me and said, "Ready to talk yet?"

I busied myself looking through his collection of games.

He sighed, rolling back and forth in his desk chair. "Audrey, you're covered in bruises. Are you going to tell me what happened?"

"I wasn't planning on it," I admitted. Gideon had enough troubling him; I hadn't wanted to make his fears any worse by discussing demon attacks. But I supposed there was no escaping it. I seated myself on the floor and leaned back against his bed, looking at him. "I got into a fight with someone."

He stopped turning the chair. "I'm guessing this someone wasn't human."

"No."

"Was it the girl from the parking ramp?"

I nodded and saw alarm flicker in his eyes. "But you don't have to worry," I added hastily. "She has no reason to go after you. You're safe." Unless he was Kin, as he suspected—but I didn't say that.

"Well, now I'm worried about *you*." He looked away. His voice was quiet. "And I don't feel safe. I keep getting this feeling... like something bad is going to happen."

"Your nightmares?"

"It's more than that. I can't describe it."

"You went through something pretty awful," I said gently.

"So did you. You *keep* going through awful things, and you're fine."

"I'm not fine. I'm a complete mess."

He frowned. "You haven't said anything."

"I know. I'm sorry. It's just been a really weird couple of weeks." I hadn't purposely been keeping things from him, I explained; I'd just been preoccupied. Now, though I didn't mention Val and her visions of the end of the Kin, I told him about my Amplification.

And about meeting my father. I tried to keep my voice even, but Gideon knew me too well. Concern clouded his face.

"You met your father," he repeated. "Audrey, that's huge. Are you okay?"

"I don't know." I laughed shakily. "Like I said: complete mess."

I normally would have stayed for dinner with the Belmontes, but since I didn't want to answer any questions from Gideon's family about my bruised appearance, I headed home as afternoon darkened into dusk. Outside, the air was warm, the sidewalks muddy. Snow melted into little rivers that ran along the gutters. The hedge in front of my house was beginning to bud. I paused beside it, lightly touching the small shoots of green that rose from its branches. I hoped a late freeze wouldn't kill them.

The lights were off inside the house, everything quiet except for the slight creaking of floorboards and the faint rattle of the wind against the door. I paused in the doorway to text Mom, then made my way into the kitchen. Dishes were piling up again, but I ignored them. I rummaged through the fridge and pulled out the milk.

I was at the counter, eating a sandwich, when Leon appeared.

He stood in the doorway, hesitated a moment, then moved toward me. My pulse sped up. In the past two days, I'd seen him only once or twice, and that was in passing. We hadn't yet spoken of Esther's visit.

I smiled cautiously. Assuming he'd come from the bakery, I asked, "Did you bring cookies?"

That was when I noticed the blood on his shirt.

Nervousness evaporated as worry shot through me. It wasn't a lot of blood, just a thin trail that led down his left side, near his ribs. But it was fresh, bright scarlet, not yet fading into brown.

Leon noticed my gaze. "It's not mine," he said, catching my arm as I turned to fetch a first-aid kit.

I looked up at him. He hadn't released me. "Whose is it?"

"It's Harrower blood. I think. There was another attack. Drew and I were called in."

I swallowed, recalling the fight in the parking ramp, the Harrower that Drew had ripped open. No longer hungry, I freed myself from Leon's grip and put the remains of my sandwich into the fridge. "Is everyone okay?"

"Everyone human."

"Susannah was there?"

"She went Beneath," he said. I started to question him further, but he stopped me. "Audrey, we have to talk."

I'd known this was coming, but I was dreading it. My skin felt hot. I retreated to the far end of the counter and leaned back against it. "About?"

"Us."

"This can't be leading anywhere good," I said, keeping my tone light and trying another smile, but Leon didn't smile back. His expression was sober, serious.

"This thing between us," he said. "It's putting you at risk."

It took me a second to realize what he meant. Not the rift in our bond; our feelings for each other. I gaped at him, incredulous.

"Hold on. This *thing*? We don't even have a relationship, we have a *thing*?"

"You're the one who keeps insisting we haven't been on a date yet."

"And so the definition you settled on was *thing*?"

"Are we really going to argue semantics here?"

"I'd rather not argue at all," I said.

"Then stop fighting me."

"It's not *you* I'm fighting."

His gaze didn't waver. "Fighting the bond means fighting me. I'm your Guardian. I'm always going to be. I need to be able to protect you. And that's more important than what either of us feels."

My stomach plummeted. My eyes stung. But instead of dwelling on what he'd just said, I turned my thoughts in another direction. "Is this what normally happens between Guardians and their charges?"

His tone was sharp. "What do you mean?"

"Drew and Val. You and me. Does it always happen? Because of the calling? Is it just—part of it?"

It was his turn to gape. "You think my feelings for you are a product of my guarding you?"

"Are they?"

"Christ, Audrey, haven't you heard a word I've said? My feelings for you are the *problem*."

"You could've just said *no*," I said, feeling like my legs had been kicked out from under me. Since they hadn't been, I whirled away.

He caught my arm, turning me back toward him. I blinked back tears, unable to meet his eyes.

"You don't understand," he said.

I jerked my arm free. "Obviously."

"What I mean is . . . it's intense. Being your Guardian and—" He broke off, running a hand through his hair. "You've seen Drew. You've seen what Val's death did to him. He's a mess."

"You don't even like Drew."

"But I understand him. His charge is dead. He's going to spend the rest of his life haunted. He failed to defend the one person he was called to guard, and now he's taking the only course he has left."

"He wants to kill Susannah."

"No. You don't get it. He doesn't want to kill her. He wants her to kill him. He was supposed to die for his charge, and that's exactly what he means to do." He paused. His eyes were steady on mine. "I would die for you, Audrey. I'm not afraid of that. I'm afraid of what happens if I don't."

I stared at him. Some part of me had short-circuited—my brain or my heart, I wasn't sure which. Little alarm bells were screaming inside me.

I turned and fled.

Despite my lingering fatigue, I couldn't sleep that night.

I tried. I burrowed under the covers, cocooning myself in blankets and sheets, hugging a pillow against me as I closed my eyes and attempted to shut out the world. But I couldn't shut out my thoughts. Leon's words stayed with me.

He would die for me.

I knew that. I'd held the evidence of it in my hands: his body heavy in my arms, both of us sinking to the ground, his blood spreading darkly in the snow. That was what his being my Guardian meant. Shielding me. Defending my body with his own. It was what I had struggled so desperately against the night I'd fought Susannah. But hearing the words made it somehow worse. Actual instead of just possible. Leon was willing to die for me.

It was the sort of thing that sounded romantic in theory; the type of wild, passionate declaration you hear in movies. But this wasn't a vow. It wasn't a promise. It was fact. Cold, hard, inescapable. And it didn't feel romantic. It felt terrifying.

I rolled to my side and stared at the clock on my nightstand. Ten minutes after two in the morning. Eleven. Twelve.

Restless, groggy, I swung my legs over the side of the bed and left my room, padding into the hallway. Mom had stopped home briefly before leaving again for the night, but I knew Leon had remained behind. I crossed to his door without thinking and stood outside it with one hand raised. I didn't know what I would say, but I felt compelled to say something, to do something. I told myself to go back to my bedroom, but I couldn't make myself leave. Instead, I pressed my palm flat against the door and simply stood there.

The door was jerked open abruptly. I stumbled slightly forward. Leon caught my shoulders, steadying me.

"What are you doing?" he asked.

I looked up at him and went from drowsy to alert in the space of two seconds. His bedroom blinds were open. I saw moonlight streaming in through his window. I saw silvery shadows that clung to his face, turning his blue eyes almost black. I saw his sleep-tousled hair, the faint trace of stubble along his jaw. But mostly I saw that he was wearing his boxers. And nothing else.

It wasn't as though I'd never seen him without a shirt before. He'd been living in my house for a few months now, and even before that, he'd spent most of his time here. But this was different. Maybe because of the darkness, or the late hour, or how small the distance between us was. Barely a step. I felt myself blushing furiously.

All I said was, "Um."

His eyebrows drew together. "Go to sleep."

"I can't," I said, doing my best to pretend I wasn't acutely aware of all the clothing he wasn't wearing. "I tried. I wanted to apologize."

"At two in the morning?"

"I wasn't really thinking," I admitted.

"Apologize for what?"

"Running away, I guess." I paused, trying to sift through the jumble of my thoughts, through words I couldn't seem to arrange. "It's just—I hate the idea of you getting hurt because of me. And I don't like that you have to protect me."

His face took on that familiar serious expression, and his grip on my shoulders tightened. "I *want* to protect you. That's what I was trying to say. Not just because I'm your Guardian."

"But that's the thing. I want to protect you, too."

Leon didn't speak. He touched my face. Then he lowered his mouth to mine.

I closed my eyes, swayed into him. I slid my arms around him, pressing my hands against his back. A slight shock ran through me as my fingers met bare skin, a shock followed by a shiver, though the heat of him seemed to melt into me. One of his hands tangled itself in my hair; his other arm encircled me, molding me to him. I kissed him greedily, not letting go. Somewhere in the foggy recesses of my brain was the thought that this was the reason Mom wanted him to move out—but I ignored it. I concentrated on the kiss, on learning his skin by touch, on the giddy realization that there was only the thin, worn layer of my flannel pajamas between us. I felt his hand on my spine, the drumming of his pulse.

"This was not a good idea," Leon murmured against my lips, but he didn't release me. He took a step backward, then another, bringing me with him. When he'd backed into his bed, he sat down on it, pulling me onto him and kissing me until I was dizzy and gasping. His hand slipped beneath my shirt. I moved onto the bed, dragging him toward me, and we lay there, mouths meeting, hands seeking, until distantly I remembered that time was passing—time that wasn't marked in breaths and heartbeats but in minutes and hours. But those minutes kept sliding together, and I didn't want to stop them.

It was Leon who pulled away first.

He looked just as dazed as I felt. His face was flushed, his eyes glazed. He seemed to struggle for coherent speech. For a second he just sat there looking down at me. Eventually, he said, "It's really late."

I glanced at his clock and felt a jolt of surprise. We'd left three a.m. well behind us.

"I should go," I said.

But I didn't leave. I rolled to my side, resting my head on his pillow.

Leon lay back down, facing me. He reached forward, gently tracing his finger across my lips. He smiled. "You should go."

"I should."

Instead, I closed my eyes. His hand gripped mine. I fell asleep with my fingers laced through his.

The sun was high when I woke. I was in my own bed, blankets tugged up around me. I had the vague memory of stirring at the sound of Leon's voice, of his lifting me, of early light pushing through the window, and the chatter of birds outside. I'd murmured something, and then sleep had claimed me again.

Since I didn't find Leon splattered on the carpet when I went downstairs, I had to assume he'd returned me to my room before Mom had come home. She'd left a note for me on the fridge, saying that she'd be gone most of the day and that she expected more texts. I wondered how long it had been since she'd slept.

With Mom gone and Leon working another shift at the bakery, I was left to my own devices. But before I could make any sort of plans, Elspeth called and told me she was coming over.

She didn't waste any time in informing me of the purpose of

her visit. As soon as we'd reached my room, she said, "Did you really share that demon's abilities?"

I looked at her. It was still strange to see her without the thick, glossy curtain of hair, but the pixie cut suited her. Her gaze was lowered. She was easy to read, even without a Knowing. I didn't need psychic powers to feel the worry coming off her in waves. She stood, arms crossed, waiting for me to speak.

"I had to," I said, moving to her side. I gripped her arm gently. "She attacked me. It's not something I plan to repeat, I swear to you."

"And you're . . . all right?"

I bit my lip, remembering how the cold of the Beneath had ripped through me as I'd grappled with Susannah. If Iris had felt that every time she fought a demon, it was no wonder it had altered her.

"I'm all right."

Elspeth must have sensed my hesitation. "Was it awful?"

She needed to hear this, I realized. Not because of me. Because of Iris. "It wasn't just sharing her powers," I said. "It was more than that. I could feel how angry she was. I felt her hatred. I felt the Beneath."

"Why did Iris keep doing it?"

I'd wondered that. I couldn't imagine wanting to share a demon's powers on a regular basis—or ever, for that matter. But Iris had blamed herself for her parents' deaths. Maybe she'd felt she deserved that agony.

"I think she was just hurting a lot," I said.

Elspeth nodded. "I wish I could have helped her. I wish she would have let me." She paused, wiping her face with her hand. "I've been dreaming about her. Not like she was the past couple of years, but when we were little. Before our parents died. Sometimes I think she's dead, and then sometimes I know she isn't. Have you . . . have you sensed anything?"

"Like in a reading?

"Or anything."

"Nothing that could help. I'm sorry."

She nodded again, then shook herself lightly, straightening her shoulders. She looked at me. "You still want to learn?"

"To Amplify? You want to help me?"

"Not helping didn't really do any good, did it? You ended up in danger, anyway." She paused. "Grandmother won't be very happy about it."

"Does anything make her happy?"

"Obedience?"

I laughed, leading Elspeth downstairs to the training room.

"You've figured out how to activate it?" she asked, once we'd reached the basement. She stood in front of me on the exercise mat.

"Maybe. Not exactly. I was able to trigger it when I fought Susannah, but I'm not certain I can repeat it."

Elspeth lifted her left hand. Colors pulsed at her wrist, up the lines of her palm, spreading to her fingertips. "Let's try it, then."

I touched her arm.

"Nothing yet," she said.

"Give me a minute."

I began with Knowing. I thought of Gram, the exercises she'd shown me when I was little, teaching me to focus, to feel, to seek with my senses. Knowing was a means of connection, just like Amplification; it required being receptive. I attuned myself to Elspeth. I concentrated on her steady breathing, the way she stood. Impressions flickered through me: a garden; the scent of honeysuckle; the hum of bees. I saw Iris as a little girl, dirt on her dress, daisies in her hands. I saw Esther's stern face. I heard the far-off sound of laughter.

But it wasn't only Knowing that I needed. I had to move past that. Letting instinct guide me, I tried to shift from Knowing into Amplifying, from sensing into sharing. This was in my blood, I told myself, a part of me; it should be effortless, like breathing, or sliding into a dream. I closed my eyes, opened them again. Nothing happened. Elspeth remained silent, watching, Guardian lights shining from her hand.

I got it on the third attempt.

I felt the link form between us, sudden heat beneath my skin. Energy flowed through my arms. Power hummed in my veins. The air came alive around me, vibrant and sparking. The connection crackled. I felt different. I felt—strong. I wondered if this was what it was like to be a Guardian.

"Well, I'm sharing," I said. "Am I Amplifying?"

Taking me with her, Elspeth stepped slowly across the room,

pulled back her right fist, and struck my mother's punching bag. It sailed into the air on its chain, and we had to duck away as it swung back down.

"That would be a yes."

"You can't feel it?"

"I can. I just wanted to test it out."

I withdrew my hand from her arm and let my focus drift. After a moment, the connection between us dissolved. "Okay. Now to see if I can do it again."

For the next hour or so, I practiced activating the ability. It came easier each time, and I was able to establish the link more quickly, but it still took effort and heavy concentration. Though I was glad to have gained some measure of control, I was frustrated by how long it took me to establish the link, time I wouldn't have in an actual fight. But I reminded myself that learning to use my Knowing had been gradual; understanding Amplification would be, as well.

Finally, Elspeth needed to leave for a meeting with some of the younger Guardians, and our training session came to an end. Since Iris's disappearance, Elspeth hadn't been very active in the Kin community, but the current crisis meant she was needed. Her curfew had been altered so that she could assist with patrols.

Before she left, she asked about Gideon.

"Is he doing okay?" She paused near the top of the stairs, turning away.

She'd had a crush on Gideon a few months back, but she hadn't mentioned him recently. Having your sister kidnap and threaten to kill the object of your affection wasn't really conducive to romance—but her feelings did lend some credibility to the theory that Gideon was connected to the Kin. As Esther was fond of telling me, Kin were drawn to Kin.

I told her he was fine. I didn't want to mention the lingering effects that his abduction seemed to be having on him. Elspeth already had enough to worry about.

I spent the rest of the afternoon catching up on homework. It was difficult to focus, but I managed to force myself through the readings for chemistry and U.S. History, and to go through a few precalc problems. Near dusk, I ventured downstairs to make myself dinner.

Drew was sitting in the kitchen.

"Drew?" I stepped through the doorway, flipped on the light, and blinked. He was at the table, his head in his hands. After a second, he turned to look at me. "Are you all right?" I asked.

His eyes were swollen, rimmed with red. All he said was "I was waiting for your mother."

In the dark. Alone. "Oh," I said. I took a cautious step forward, surveying him. The haunted, wounded look hadn't left him. Below the raw edge of his fury—so strong even now that it seemed to tint the air around him—was the familiar impression of confusion and helplessness. Though he was clean-shaven today, the hard yellow light of the kitchen emphasized the hollows in his face. He looked tired and awfully thin.

I didn't know what to say, so I just stood there in awkward

silence, fidgeting. Drew turned from me, once again sinking his head into his hands. His shoulders were slumped, his breathing ragged.

I thought he had forgotten me, and I was trying to decide whether or not to leave, when he said, "I frighten you."

There didn't seem much point in denying it, so I answered, "A little."

He let out a shaky laugh. His voice was hoarse. "I frighten myself. Val would be horrified."

As he spoke, Knowing shot through me. Valerie. Little fragments of her that wandered through his thoughts, his speech. Memories he had gathered. Images that lived within him: the bright laugh, the black hair. A single day drenched in sunlight. Whispered endearments. Her body going slack in his arms. The final sigh that escaped her lips.

Instead of leaving, I stepped into the room and sat down at the table beside him. "Do you..." I swallowed. "Do you want to talk about her?"

For a second, I thought he would answer, that he would tell me. I thought maybe he needed to. Then he looked up. His eyes met mine, and this time I didn't look away. The bewilderment was still there in his gaze, but there was something else, too. The knowledge that, no matter how he tried, he could never truly speak of her. That the sum of a person could not be divided into sentences and syllables. No combination of adjectives and nouns could recreate her, not when she'd been made up of motions and colors, of sounds, of moments strung together. He could see the white cotton dress she'd worn the day he'd met her, how closely it had hugged her body; he could recall the sway of her hips as she walked, the smell of soap and perfume that followed her—but none of these things could convey who she'd been. He could, perhaps, describe the quality of her voice, but he could never again hear it.

Even when we die, Gram used to say, *we're still a part of the people who carry us.* Drew carried Val. It was the only way he could keep her.

Leon's words from the night before came back to me. Drew didn't want to kill Susannah.

He wanted her to kill him.

Looking at him, a feeling of overwhelming sadness seized me. I realized the truth of Leon's statement. Drew's death wouldn't help Valerie; the loss of his life wouldn't bring her back into being—but this had nothing to do with logic. It wasn't about reason. She was dead, but he was still bound to her. He wanted to lie beside her in the earth, to let the world go on above them, green and growing.

Unable to think of anything else to say, I asked, "Can I do anything for you?"

His gaze moved from mine. "Don't pity me."

"Okay." I ran my finger along the tablecloth, lightly tracing the design. I bit my lip. "You never said Daniel was human."

"I never said he wasn't."

"Who is he? Do you know?"

"He was Val's brother."

The answer threw me into confusion. "He's your brother-in-law?"

"Was."

"What happened?"

"Susannah took him. The night she killed Val."

Now I was incredulous. "And you're not even trying to get him back?"

"I did try. I found them the week before I came here. I got Daniel alone, tried to snap him out of it. But he was still under her control. He stuck a knife in me and returned to Susannah. Whatever she did to him, he's hers now. He's been Beneath too long."

Like Iris, I thought, remembering the way she'd looked on Harlow Tower, the way her eyes had gone as white as a Harrower's.

But Iris had made her own choice. Daniel hadn't.

I shook my head. "No. He's been trying to communicate with me. He escaped from Susannah in order to tell me something."

"It's just one of her tricks."

"I don't think so. I could sense him."

I want to go home, he'd said.

Drew looked at me. Some emotion I couldn't name flickered in his eyes. He started to speak, then stopped. Whatever he had planned to say, he never said it. His phone rang.

A chill spread through me as I watched him answer. The call was brief, only a matter of seconds. Drew hung up, looked at me.

"I have to go," he said. "It's another attack."

*　*　*

After Drew left, I retreated to my room and sat on the bed, my legs drawn up against me. Outside my window, blue deepened into black. My heart thudded. My mind raced. Drew's being called in meant Leon must have been, too. Susannah's face flashed before me, her pale eyes and her wide, slow smile.

In an effort to calm myself, I pulled out Gram's Nav deck. I took my time shuffling, letting my hands linger on the cards. I had no real subject in mind. Gram had done this on occasion—readings for the sake of readings, Knowing just to know. Leaving yourself open to the universe, Gram had called it. Instead of focusing, I let my thoughts drift.

They drifted to Daniel.

He'd been trying to communicate with me using his Knowing. I'd felt it. But his Knowing was stronger than mine; I'd felt that, as well. He had found me, but I didn't think that I could find him. I recalled the image of him I'd had in my dream. *She's listening*, he'd said. I shuddered.

Twenty minutes had passed when I heard the front door slam. Jolted from my thoughts, I let the cards spill from my hands. I hurried downstairs.

I saw Mom first, clad in black pants and Morning Star hoodie, one hand on her hip. Mr. Alvarez had followed her into the house. They stood in the entryway, arguing. Neither of them glanced at me when I came to a halt at the bottom of the staircase.

"We can't fight her if we can't *find* her," Mom was saying. "And we can't find her if she's always Beneath. In the meantime, we're just making ourselves easy targets."

"All right, Luce, what do you suggest? We invade the Beneath?"

"Believe me, I'd like to."

"We're not going to win this with brute strength."

Mom snorted. "Well, we're certainly not winning it with brains."

There was a short silence. Mr. Alvarez hesitated, turning away. "I've spoken to Esther. I was right. She and the elders want the Remnant located and her powers sealed."

I thought of my father, speaking in a monotone; his empty gaze. My throat tightened.

"And I suppose you just agreed with them," Mom said.

"We don't have many alternatives."

"You really believe this vision of the end of the Kin?"

"The elders do." He sighed, rubbing his face with his hands. "Either way, it's not our decision. It's theirs."

"Nice attitude."

"This is personal for you, I understand that, but—"

"Oh, go to hell."

He sighed again. "We can talk about this later. I need to get back." He turned and headed out the door. She didn't stop him.

After he was gone, I crossed the hall to stand beside her. "You're not actually going to kill him one of these days, are you?"

"It is tempting." She let out a slow breath, then turned toward me, looking me over critically. She reached forward to tuck a stray piece of hair behind my ear. "How are you feeling? Your bruises seem better."

"I'm okay. Where's Leon? Was he there tonight?"

"He was there. He's out patrolling with Drew."

I felt a surge of alarm. "Wait. With Drew? Who decided *that* was a good plan?"

"It's easier if they're together if they need to be called in."

"Also much easier if they decide to tear each other limb from limb."

Mom rolled her eyes. "Leon knows to be civil."

"Um, if you say so."

She just shook her head.

Mom needed to leave again, but she stayed long enough to grab a quick dinner. It took some prodding on my part, but eventually, she told me what had occurred. The attack had followed the same pattern as the others, she said. Two Guardians—working together per Mr. Alvarez's buddy system—had been waylaid by a single Harrower. While the Harrower went after one Guardian, the other had called Leon and Drew. Susannah and Daniel had stood nearby, waiting, watching in silence. They'd gone Beneath the moment Drew appeared. The other demon had been killed. Mom, Mr. Alvarez, and a few of the other Guardians had been alerted, but hadn't arrived until after the danger had passed.

A little knot worked its way into her forehead as she spoke. I sensed her frustration, a thread of tension running beneath each word, each gesture. She was a fighter—and, as she'd told

Mr. Alvarez, she couldn't fight an enemy that wouldn't face her. Anxiety gnawed at me. So far, Susannah always seemed to be one step ahead.

Noticing my worried look, Mom smoothed her brow and spent the next ten minutes trying to reassure me. They would find Susannah, she said. They would defeat her. It was just a matter of when.

But Monday morning, I woke to the news that Susannah had launched another attack during the night.

Mr. Alvarez was in the hospital.

The Guardian he'd been patrolling with was dead.

At school, the official explanation was that Mr. Alvarez had been in a car accident. I didn't know what specifics had been given, but during Precalc, a few of my more obnoxious classmates embellished the story, adding that he had suffered terrible burns all over his body, as well as the loss of limbs. The substitute teacher spent most of the hour giving the students stern glances. I kept my silence, feeling sick to my stomach.

Mom had told me Mr. Alvarez would recover. She hadn't seen him, but when she'd stopped by the hospital, she'd spoken to his father and uncle. Mr. Alvarez's injuries weren't life-threatening, but they weren't minor, either. He had a couple of broken bones and a few cracked ribs. He'd needed surgery. Even with a Guardian's accelerated healing, he would need time to convalesce. As far as fighting went, he was out of commission.

The precise details of the attack were unknown. Mr. Alvarez

had been sedated from his surgery and hadn't been able to provide any information. They did know that Leon and Drew hadn't been alerted, and neither had any of the other Guardians.

Ryan isn't reckless, and he isn't stupid, Mom had said that morning. *He wouldn't try to take on Susannah by himself. She must have prevented him from calling for backup.*

Mom didn't know if that meant there had been more than one Harrower attacking, or if Susannah herself had finally acted. Until Mr. Alvarez himself was able to explain what had happened, the rest of the Kin would have to remain in the dark. The only other witness was dead.

I hadn't known Peter Winslow, the Guardian who was killed, but Mom had. He'd been part of what she termed the Old Guard, the generation of Guardians that had come before her. Many of them had been killed seventeen years earlier, during the fighting with Verrick; Peter had survived, and in later years had gone into semiretirement. He'd returned to duty because of the current threat. Mom had never been close with him, she said—but my father had. Back then, Peter had been something of a mentor to the younger Guardians.

"Ryan is going to blame himself," Mom said. "It was his decision to call in the Old Guard."

A wake was scheduled for later in the week.

I didn't mention the attack to Tink, but Tuesday at lunch, I could tell she knew. While her typical response to anything upsetting was to withdraw, she'd clammed up even more than usual.

She was visibly shaken, speaking in monosyllables and barely listening to me. Eventually, I was able to coax a few sentences from her. She'd heard about the assault from Camille, who had canceled their training session in order to go to the hospital and be with Mr. Alvarez. As far as Tink was concerned, this meant her instruction as a Guardian was at an end.

"There is no way I'm continuing after this. They can't *make* me be a Guardian," she insisted; it was the most words she'd managed to string together all day.

I didn't argue with her—but I also didn't agree. I'd had the opposite reaction to the attack. I wanted to learn to fully control my Amplification, and I wanted to learn fast. On Tuesday evening, instead of going to martial arts, I convinced Leon to help me practice.

The moment I saw him, I felt my heartbeat quicken. I remembered falling asleep in his bed, the feel of his skin. We hadn't seen each other alone since then, and I had to resist the urge to just drag him away somewhere and start kissing him. With effort, I pushed the thought away and focused on training. I told Leon that mastering Amplification would allow me to better defend myself, and he agreed. The issue of our Guardian bond hung unresolved between us—and I doubted that Leon's spending more time around Drew was going to help matters—but, by unspoken agreement, we didn't mention it.

We made our way to the basement. Now that I knew *how* to

Amplify, I wanted to concentrate on actually using the ability. Leon held up his hand, lights glowing within his wrist. Tentatively, I laid my fingers against his arm.

Amplifying turned out to be much easier with Leon than it had been with Elspeth. The connection came almost immediately, and it was stronger. I felt heat flare in my veins. I felt the rush of power and energy, the sudden electricity in the air. But it was more than that. It was alignment, attunement, both physical and not. The drum of Leon's pulse blurred into mine, echoing through my body. The light beneath his skin gleamed brighter.

I broke contact, easing my hand away. For a moment, the link between us remained. I held my breath, trying to hold the connection, trying not to count seconds. Then my concentration slipped, and the connection snapped. I sighed in frustration.

"It's going to take more than one or two training sessions," Leon said.

"When did you start teleporting?" I asked.

"When I was seven."

"And? What happened?"

"I fell asleep in bed one night and woke up in the neighbor's backyard."

"How long did it take to figure out how to do it?"

He didn't answer.

"You got it right away, didn't you? I hope you know how obnoxious that is."

He grinned.

I sighed again. "I'm making it my mission in life to find something you are *really* bad at."

We continued practicing for the next twenty minutes. I was able to hold the connection for longer periods of time, but it still wasn't something that came naturally. Finally, I became tired of attempting it. I suggested we move on to using my Amplification while sparring.

Leon grew wary. "I'm not taking you out patrolling with me."

"I wasn't going to ask you to," I said.

Yet.

He looked skeptical but eventually gave in.

Sparring proved more difficult than I'd anticipated. Because I wasn't able to consistently maintain the link whenever we broke contact, my strikes lost their momentum and my movements were hindered. And Leon wasn't accustomed to his powers being Amplified; he was cautious, careful to control his strength, to the point where he was barely fighting back. Annoyed, I caught him by the arms, letting the link crackle between us. I intended to fling him away from me. One quick motion, with little force behind it. But I failed to check *my* strength. I didn't just fling him away.

I flung him into the wall.

I ran to him with a cry of dismay, but he was on his feet before I reached him. He only laughed.

"We should probably work on that," he said.

Further training was put on hold, however, by the arrival of

Mom, Drew, and several of the other Guardians. With Mr. Alvarez still in the hospital recovering, the rest of the Guardians were looking to Mom for guidance; she wasn't particularly pleased with the role. There was some disagreement over what course of action to take. Searching for Susannah had made the Guardians into targets, but sitting at home and hoping the threat went away wasn't much of an option. And while staying inside might have been safer for the Guardians—since, in general, Harrowers preferred to attack in open spaces—not patrolling left the Cities vulnerable to *any* demon who passed through the Circle, not just Susannah. Finally, it was settled that the patrols would continue, but that the Guardians were to check in with one another at regular intervals. I volunteered myself as the call center. Mom quickly shot the idea down.

They didn't discuss the Remnant, but that night I dreamed of her.

I had dreamed of her before. Nothing concrete—nothing to identify her, no face I recognized, no whispered name. I saw only indistinct images that slipped through my subconscious: the blur of a back, muffled footsteps, a raised hand. Now, the impression I had was of a figure far away, standing in an empty hall. The Remnant moved. I saw a shoulder, the sweep of hair. I watched her step away.

And as I watched her, Susannah watched me.

I didn't see Susannah, but I felt her gaze, little pinpricks along the back of my neck. I tensed. The Remnant turned toward me.

You shouldn't be here, she said without speaking. *You'll tell her.*

"I won't," I promised. "I would never."

Then Daniel stood before me. He gripped my hand, just as he had the night I'd first dreamed of him. I tried to struggle, but couldn't. I couldn't flee or even wrench my hand away. Cold flooded the space around us, filled me, turned the air in my lungs to ice.

Daniel's grasp held firm. He was mouthing two words. Again and again.

I'm sorry, he was saying. *I'm sorry.*

At last, as I pulled my hand free, Susannah stepped forward and smiled.

There were no further attacks during the night, but there were other developments. Esther and the Kin elders had made it official: they wanted the Remnant located. How they planned to do this, I had no idea.

Mom was dubious. "Saying something and actually doing it are two very different things. They've had seventeen years to find the Remnant. I doubt they're going to find her now."

I hesitated. "If they do ... are they even going to give her a choice about having her powers sealed?"

"I don't know. I would guess not. They're weighing the future of the Kin against the future of one person. Again."

"You can't agree with them."

"I don't agree with them," she said. "We'll need to hope—for everyone's sake—that she remains hidden."

But the news that the elders wanted the Remnant found, coming directly after my dream, left me unsettled. At school, I found it difficult to focus. The substitute in Precalc was going easy on us, but I still couldn't make myself pay attention to anything she was saying. It didn't help when Greg cornered me after class. He'd heard about Tink and Lars. And he wasn't happy.

"What do you care? You broke up with her," I said, blinking at him.

Greg pushed up his glasses, which were sliding down his nose. "I thought it would make her jealous. She wasn't supposed to start going out with someone else."

I groaned. "Greg, I am really not in the mood for this."

"Would you talk to her?"

"*No.*"

Tink herself seemed to be having a meltdown, and I didn't know how to help her. If it had been possible, I would have gladly taken her Guardian powers; as it stood, the best I could do was offer consoling words—which did nothing to console her.

"My life is *over,*" she said. We were in the library, sitting on the floor between two stacks of books, speaking in whispers. "I'm not going to get to do anything I wanted to. Maybe I still go to college, but after that? I get to spend the rest of my life fighting things that shouldn't even exist, in order to protect a bunch of people who hate my guts."

As far as I knew, Tink's only plans after college involved winning the lottery and having a tragic love affair, and I didn't think being a Guardian decreased the odds of either. I didn't mention that. "No one hates you," I said. "Is that really what this is about?"

She drew her legs up against her, wrapping her arms around her knees. Her voice was small. "I can't fight."

"That's what the training is for," I said. "It takes time. But you'll get it, I promise."

"No, that's not what I mean. I can't *fight*. I'm not like you, Audrey. I'm not brave. I always just want to run away. I keep thinking this has to be some huge mistake—that I wasn't the one who was supposed to be called."

"I don't think the calling makes mistakes."

She turned toward me. "Oh, yeah? You're thinking it, too. *You* should've been called, not me." She wiped her face. "Do you remember how we met? I was hiding in the girls' bathroom. Sadie Mills was threatening to beat me up because she thought I'd stolen her nail polish."

"You did steal her nail polish."

Tink rolled her eyes. "The important part is that I hid there for three hours. If I couldn't even face Sadie Mills, how am I supposed to face Harrowers?"

"That was fourth grade, and everyone was scared of Sadie," I pointed out. "And you didn't run away in the parking ramp. You *did* fight."

"Because I thought we were going to die." She leaned forward, resting her forehead against her knees. "I don't want to die, Audrey."

I started to say, *You won't*, but stopped myself. She was right. She might die, and no promises or platitudes would change that.

When she'd first told me she'd been called, I'd been jealous. I hadn't fully considered what it would mean. The risk of injury. The risk of death. Those were aspects of being a Guardian I was all too aware of, but the idea of Tink's being placed in real danger hadn't entered my thoughts, not even with the memory of Susannah's words echoing in my head. Now I found I couldn't reassure either of us. Instead, I told Tink the only thing I could. "I don't want you to die, either."

She looked up and gave me the ghost of a smile. "At least we're in agreement," she said—and then decided she didn't want to talk about it anymore. Instead, she moved on to the subject of Lars, and spent the rest of the day talking about their upcoming date.

The wake for Peter Winslow was held that evening. Most of the Guardians made appearances, though they arrived in shifts in order to maintain the patrols. I accompanied Mom and Leon to the funeral home and, as we stepped inside, I thought of the last wake I'd attended. It had been Gram's. I remembered standing beside Mom, numb from crying, unable to adjust to the very idea of Gram's absence. Now, I gazed across the room at Peter's widow. She looked tired and wan. She wasn't the only one. Peter had been the third Guardian to die within the past few months. Three wakes, I thought. Three graves collecting flowers. Three headstones. Three families that would never again be whole.

And more to come, if Susannah wasn't stopped.

We didn't stay long. We gave our condolences, then paused to speak with a few members of the Kin. I wasn't closely acquainted with anyone there, so I stayed near Mom and Leon, feeling uncomfortable and troubled. We were on our way out, heading toward the door, when a voice stopped us.

"Lucy."

Mom froze beside me. Then she turned.

"Adrian," she said.

21

He stood watching us without expression. His eyes were as empty of emotion as they had been the last time I'd seen him. His voice was as flat. He held out his hand, and Mom took it.

I felt my heart leap into my throat and lodge there. I looked at them: Mom, in her pale blue dress, her lips tightening as she tried to smile; my father with his tidy business suit, that face that didn't show his age. Two strangers who knew each other's names.

"It's been a long time," my father said.

"Seventeen years," she answered.

"You look well."

He remembered her, but that was all she was to him, a face with data attached. He didn't remember what she'd meant to him. Maybe he knew that he had spent years beside her, but he didn't know how that had felt. He didn't know that he had loved her. And he must have remembered that Peter had once been his friend. But these were only details. Information without sensation. Statements of fact. Pieces of history out of some blurred recollection of the unreachable past. That was all. There was no emotion in these memories. No connection between brain and heart. Only a faint confusion and a sudden dead end.

"I think you've met my daughter," Mom said.

His gaze moved to me. "Our daughter."

"That's right."

He acknowledged me with a nod, keeping his eyes on mine, and I nodded back. I shifted awkwardly. I looked at the floor. Black shoes. Bare hardwood with a glossy finish. From nearby came the sound of hushed voices and the scent of roses. Mom introduced Leon.

"It's nice to meet you, sir," Leon said. His hand closed over mine. I slid my fingers through his.

"How long will you be in the Cities?" Mom asked.

"I leave tonight. My flight is later this evening."

A short silence fell. I could feel Mom's hesitancy, the tension rising from her in waves. Twice, she started to speak, then broke off. The silence lengthened. "We should get going," she said at last.

My father nodded again. "It was good to see you."

He turned. He started to move away.

My mother stopped him.

She took a single step forward. Her hand rose to her throat, trembling slightly. When she spoke, her voice was soft, almost a whisper—but he seemed to have heard it. "Adrian," she said.

He faced her again. He looked at her, and for a single, fleeting instant, he really looked. In that second, it seemed that time had not only stopped, but reversed. That the earth had spun backward on its axis, that all the years that stretched between them had evaporated, that the only distance that divided them was these few short steps. Knowing shot through me, clear and shining, an abrupt sense telling me that part of him still lingered, half-conscious, almost aware. Some part of him stirred now and then, some doubt, some uncomfortable certainty inside him that this man he'd become was not the man he should have been. But the moment passed, and then there was only confusion within him once again, a vague puzzlement that there was something he ought to know, but didn't. He waited.

"Are you . . . okay?" Mom asked.

I looked at him, then back at her.

She needed to hear this, I realized. She needed to know that he was all right, that it was okay for her to move on. For seventeen years she'd been treading water, and now this was it. Sink or swim.

I took in the details: that brown hair that curled like mine, still dark, without a trace of gray. His St. Croix eyes. The little wrinkle that appeared in his brow, the first expression I'd seen on him. My gaze met his once more, and with everything inside me, I willed him to answer yes. Voiceless, angry, helpless, hoping—I screamed it at him. *Tell her you're all right*, I pleaded. *Forget that when you look at her something goes quiet inside. Forget there's a void inside you that you've never understood. Forget how you wake up sweating sometimes and wonder where you are and why your life is nothing more than what it has become. Please. Please.*

"I'm okay," he said.

He walked away, and this time, she let him.

Mickey was waiting outside the house when Mom, Leon, and I got home. His car was parked a short distance down the road, shadowed by the maple trees that lined the avenue. He stood near our hedge, at the end of the walkway, with his hands shoved into his pockets. He was dressed plainly, in jeans and an old Twins sweatshirt, his hair slightly tousled by the wind. In the thin evening light, his face was inscrutable.

Streetlamps blinked on as we approached, turning the twilight yellow. My gaze flicked to Mom. She was frowning as she looked at him, her entire body tense. Mickey could not possibly have had worse timing, I thought. Before Mom had the chance to speak, I hurried down the sidewalk toward him.

"How long have you been here?" I asked.

He shrugged. "About ten minutes."

"You should've gone inside. Our door is, like, two hundred years old. It can't be that hard to break in."

"I prefer to be invited."

"Like a vampire?"

The corners of his eyes crinkled. "Or a law-abiding citizen."

My mother and Leon had reached us. Mom didn't bother to say hello, just glanced at Mickey and then jerked her head in the direction of the door. Mickey followed us into the house and paused in the doorway. I moved past them, switching on the hall lights. Mom turned to face Mickey, leaning against the wall with her arms folded.

"I need to talk to you," Mickey said.

"You couldn't have called?"

"I wanted to see you."

Leon had made a hasty exit upstairs. I started to follow, intending to give Mom and Mickey some privacy—or at least to absent myself from what was bound to be yet another awkward conversation—but Mickey's next words stopped me.

"I'm not here to argue. I found that woman you're looking for."

I halted near the bottom of the stairs, my hand tightening on the railing. I swung back toward them. Mom had straightened up, her eyes alert.

"I told you stay out of it," she said.

Mickey grunted. "You're welcome."

"You're certain it's her?"

"Red hair, medium build, occasionally scaly? Yeah, it's her."

Mom sucked in a breath. "Please tell me you haven't been doing surveillance on her."

"What else was I gonna do? Generally, if I'm planning to accuse someone of being a creature from the netherworld, I like to have proof."

"Finding that proof could have gotten you killed."

"It didn't."

Mom was silent. She lifted a hand to her forehead, rubbing her temples. Finally, she let out a low sigh and asked, "Where is she?"

"She's got a place in Uptown. Doesn't spend a lot of time in it, from what I can tell, but she was there when I left."

I supposed that meant Susannah didn't spend all of her time Beneath. I wondered if she had an actual alias here, if she spent her days pretending to be human, speaking to people she passed on the street, smiling, doing her best to blend in, the way Shane did. Or maybe it was for Daniel's benefit; since he actually *was* human, presumably he still needed to eat.

"How long ago?" Mom asked.

"Maybe half an hour."

She turned toward the stairs and bellowed for Leon. He promptly appeared, took one look at her face, and hurried down the steps.

"Mickey is going to give you Susannah's address," she told him. "I need to change clothing. Then we go."

My skin prickled. "You're not going to call in the other Guardians?" I asked as she passed by me on her way to the second floor.

She shook her head. "It's better if we go alone." Then she was up the stairs and out of sight.

As I stood there, watching the space where she'd been, I remembered Shane's warning. Only Morning Star was strong enough to stop Susannah, he'd said. My eyes moved to Leon. He stood beside Mickey, waiting in silence, his face unreadable. His gaze met mine briefly. Then he glanced away.

Cold spread through me. My heart kicked against my ribs. I thought of the wake we'd just left. The finality of it. The tall vases overflowing with white flowers, the sheen of the hardwood floor, the hush in the air. The widow. The casket. I thought of Mr. Alvarez lying in a hospital bed. I thought of Drew, holding Val lifeless in his arms.

I moved to Leon and gripped his hand. It was cold, like mine.

"Take me with you," I breathed.

He gaped at me. "Have you lost your mind?"

"I can help. I fought Susannah before."

"You were nearly killed before."

"I know how to use my Amplification now. I can fight with you. I can *help*."

"You can help by staying where we know you'll be safe," Mom said. She'd returned dressed in dark pants and a Morning Star hoodie, her hair pulled back. Without giving me a chance to argue, she turned to Leon. "Ready?"

He nodded.

Mom crossed to my side, hugging me briefly. She kissed my forehead. "This will all be over soon." To Mickey, she said, "Thank you."

Leon grasped her shoulder, drawing her against him. They vanished.

Mickey and I waited in the living room.

I curled up on the sofa, wrapping myself in an old crocheted blanket of Gram's. I tried not to stare at the clock, but I heard it ticking, seconds easing into minutes, those minutes passing. Mickey sat in a nearby chair, wearing the same slightly stunned look he'd had ever since Leon had teleported with Mom. I supposed he was silently adding another item to the ever-expanding list of strange occurrences he'd witnessed recently.

He noticed me watching him. "You okay?"

I shrugged.

"Your mom's pretty tough." When I didn't answer, he added, "I never got used to this part as a kid. The waiting."

"Are you staying?" I asked.

"If you don't mind."

"I don't mind."

"Have you had dinner? Is there something I can fix you?"

"We need to go grocery shopping. So unless you can make a meal out of stale cereal and lettuce, probably not."

He smiled and shook his head.

"You cook?" I asked.

"What, your fortune-telling didn't tell you that already?"

I returned his smile. The minutes continued to drag on. Mickey tried to keep me occupied by sharing stories about my grandfather—memories from his own childhood, things his father had told him, like the pranks that Jacky used to pull, and the calls they'd been on together. Though I knew most of the stories already, from Gram, I appreciated the effort. But beneath Mickey's words and his smile, I felt his own unease. It was alien to him, the idea of waiting instead of acting, of staying behind instead of charging forward. It wasn't that Mom's warnings were meaningless to him, I sensed—but that his desire to be of aid overrode the urge for self-preservation. I wondered if it had been the same for my grandfather.

My grandfather, who had been killed by Harrowers because he, too, longed to help. "Let's talk about something else," I said.

"All right. You pick."

I started to speak. Stopped. Knowing surged through me, heightened awareness running up and down my skin. I heard a voice. Heard someone cry out. Heard claws clicking across concrete. I smelled blood, and something rank. Then all the air seemed to go out of the room, and I thought only—

"We need to go."

I shot to my feet, the blanket falling to the floor. A figure had appeared in front of us. But it wasn't Mom or Leon.

In the faint yellow glow of the living room lights, a sneer twisting her human lips, stood Susannah.

22

A scream strangled inside me. I froze, a hundred thoughts racing through my mind. Scenarios played out before me: Mom was dead. Leon was dead. They were lost forever, trapped in the unceasing waste Beneath. Val's vision of the future had been called forth. The end of the Kin. The end of everything.

But even as panic squeezed my throat, I took in details and began processing them. Susannah was severely injured. She was having difficulty maintaining her human form. Pale skin faded into scales, faded back again. Her hair had clumped into thin, strawlike bristles. The demon showed itself in her face, in bared red teeth, in one eye blue and blinking, the other egg white, lidless. Her hands convulsed, changing between talons and fingers, clenching and unclenching. Through the flesh of her neck, her spine was the color of blood.

She was alone. Daniel was nowhere to be seen, and she hadn't brought any Harrowers up from Beneath with her. That meant she was weakened, I guessed, maybe even dying. Mom and Leon weren't dead, then. They had done this. Susannah had fled. Susannah had—

"Don't look so distressed," she said. Her voice was lilting, but there was an edge of anger in it. "I'm only here for a visit. Morning Star was kind enough to call at my home. I thought that I'd return the favor."

Mickey had risen to his feet. He stepped in front of me, drawing a gun I hadn't even realized he was wearing. "Get out of here, kid."

"Stay put, unless you want to see how quickly I can rip a man's spine through his throat."

"What do you want?" I asked.

"To send your mother a message. At first, I thought that crippling you might be fun—though after our last encounter, I'm afraid that would take too much time. I left Morning Star a bit of a mess to clean up, but she's bound to appear sooner or later. So I've come up with a better idea. I have a sense about these things."

Mickey fired. Three shots, rapid and deafening, small explosions that rang in my ears. Mom must have told him just where to shoot, and his aim was perfect—but the effort was futile. Weakened though Susannah was, she didn't even flinch. All three bullets struck her. They didn't penetrate her skin. They burned as they touched her body, then fell away, leaving scorch marks in the hollow above her collarbone.

"That wasn't very nice. Put down the little toy, Detective."

He swore.

As Mickey lowered his arms, I ran past him, rushing toward Susannah. I wasn't certain what I intended—I hadn't been able to share abilities without Amplifying them yet—but I needed to act. I had fought Susannah before; I could do it again.

But the last time we'd clashed, my Amplification had taken her by surprise. This time she was ready for me. She moved faster than I could see, faster than I could even think. She caught me by the neck, pulled me into the air, and flung me from her before I had the chance to attempt sharing her powers.

"None of that," she hissed.

I struck the wall sideways. My shoulder took most of the impact; then I was on the floor, my head rocking back. My vision swam. Black spots swirled before my eyes, and nausea rose up within me. I twisted onto my stomach, lifting myself up on my arms.

Susannah's attention had shifted. She stepped toward Mickey.

Horror flooded me, seared me. Alarm screamed inside me. I wanted to tell Mickey to run or to fire again—anything. But my words came out in choking gasps. And Susannah had reached him.

He had no opportunity to struggle. Suddenly, she had her claws pressed to his neck; tiny spots of blood welled up where she touched him.

"Don't worry, Detective. I'm not going to kill you. I have something far more exciting planned."

I climbed up onto my knees. Mickey didn't move, but his eyes met mine. Across the distance between us, my Knowing was clear and sharp. I saw what I always sensed from him, images he carried, the memory of summers and open spaces: rivers that lapped his ankles, tall grasses, the northern lights that lingered forever in his mind, the scent of pine. But now there was something else, too. Not fear—but a sort of sadness. His lips moved, forming a word. I couldn't hear it.

Susannah wrapped her free arm about him. "Have you ever been Beneath? I think you'll like it." She stood on her toes and whispered something to him.

The light died in his eyes.

And before I could move, they were gone.

There was broken glass on the floor. I noticed it as I pulled myself up, using the coffee table as leverage. A photo frame had fallen from the wall; Gram and I smiled out of it, our arms linked. Small shards dug into the carpet. I eased sideways, away from it, thinking that it was somehow important not to touch the glass. Then I was on my feet. I stood, not moving, feeling the shock of silence that followed Susannah and Mickey's departure, like the hush that followed a hurricane. My legs wobbled just slightly. I heard the sound of my breath. The sound of my heartbeat. The sound of the clock.

And then the sound of a voice.

"Audrey?"

I turned. Drew stood in the doorway of the living room. He made his way to me slowly, looking about the room.

"What happened in here?" he asked.

"It was Susannah."

His gaze sharpened. I felt the swell of rage in him at the sound of her name, but all he asked was "Where are Lucy and Leon?"

"They went to fight her. They haven't come back."

"Are you hurt?"

I shook my head. Dull pain throbbed in my shoulder and thigh, but it would pass. Drew took hold of my hands. I looked down and found my fingernails biting into my palms.

"He left you here," Drew said.

He. Not they. Leon, he meant.

"They thought it was safe."

Safe. It should have been. We'd never been attacked here before. Most Harrowers preferred to fight in open spaces, I knew that. Most Harrowers weren't strong enough to come up from Beneath this far from the center of the Circle. Most Harrowers wouldn't have dared to enter Morning Star's home.

But Susannah was not most Harrowers.

And maybe that meant no place was safe anymore.

"Let's get you out of here," Drew was saying.

I jerked away. "No. We need to wait for Mom and Leon." I wouldn't move—I couldn't move—until then.

They appeared a minute later, teleporting directly into the

living room. Neither of them looked to be injured, though Mom's hair had come free of its bun, and there was a hole in one of her sleeves, revealing bare skin. I didn't see any blood. Distantly, I was aware of a sense of relief—but I was too shaken to do anything but stare at them.

"Audrey?" Mom said. And then: "What in the hell—?"

Leon moved to my side, gripping my shoulders. I looked at him, then past him, to Mom. My words came out in a garbled rush. "Susannah was here. She did something to Mickey. She took him Beneath. The way she took Daniel. I couldn't stop her."

"Susannah was *here*?" Leon echoed.

The color drained from Mom's face. She stood frozen. The only word she said was a single, whispered *"Dammit."*

"He's alive," I told her. "She said she wasn't going to kill him. She said she had something planned for him."

Alive—but Beneath. I thought of him there with Susannah, bound to her, unable to break free. I felt the chill of the void. I saw red stars gather. I saw him walking through streets that twisted with decay, moving aimlessly until the roads became wastelands, empty and endless. I imagined the abyss pressing in, telling him there was no hope, no escape, telling him to long for death, just as it had told me.

I thought of Daniel. *He's been Beneath too long*, Drew had said.

"We have to help him," I said.

Mom had started pacing. She dragged a hand through her tangled hair. She took in long, shaky breaths. I looked at the tear in her sleeve, the eight points of the star on her back. There was blood on her, after all, I saw: a thin trail down her neck, where a talon must have grazed her flesh.

After a moment, she stopped and turned toward us. "Leon, take Audrey to Esther. I want both of you to stay there tonight. Drew, I need you to speak with the other Guardians."

"What are you going to do?" I asked.

Her gaze was steady on mine. "I'm going to talk to Shane."

Leon and I were given guest bedrooms at the St. Croix estate in St. Paul. Whether or not the house would actually be safer than my own, I didn't know—but at least we weren't alone. Esther was grim-faced as we spoke to her. She listened without comment as we explained the situation. Afterward, she said little, but she placed a hand on my shoulder and let it rest there a moment.

"It's good you weren't hurt," she said.

My father, I learned, had already left for the airport.

Once Esther had excused herself, saying that she had matters to discuss with the elders, Leon told me about the fight with Susannah. He came to my room, and we sat beside each other on the bed, our backs pressed to the wall, our legs stretched out. His hand rested against mine as he spoke, our fingers almost touching.

Susannah hadn't been alone, he said. She'd had three other demons with her, Harrowers either too weak or too careless to maintain human form. Daniel had been at her side, as usual, but she'd sent him Beneath with one of the other Harrowers as soon as the fighting began. She hadn't attempted to flee, herself. At least, not then.

Mom had gone straight for Susannah. Leon had handled the remaining two Harrowers himself.

I'd seen Leon fight before. I'd seen the strength running through him, the confidence and grace of his movements, the swiftness of his strikes. I'd seen the Guardian lights that pulsed in his skin. I could imagine that now, but I didn't want to. Biting my lip, I shifted closer to him.

Susannah was powerful, Leon said, more powerful than any other Harrower he'd seen—but she was no match for Mom. Mom had repelled each of her attacks and had eventually gotten close enough to wound her. But before Mom could finish her off, she'd vanished. They'd assumed she'd merely gone Beneath and stayed there, as she had during every other fight.

"She said she left you with a mess to clean up," I said.

Leon grimaced. The mess, he said, was Harrowers. Susannah had sent more demons up from Beneath. But instead of simply fighting, the demons had gone into the streets, seeking other targets. Mom and Leon had been forced to pursue them. And Susannah had bought herself time.

I closed my eyes, shutting out images of Susannah's half-human face, of her claws sinking into Mickey's neck.

"We would have returned earlier," Leon said softly. "We would have let the Harrowers go. But we didn't know you were in trouble."

It didn't take me more than a moment to catch his meaning. He was talking about the Guardian bond. I twisted to face him, a flare of anger rising—along with something that might have been guilt. I swallowed tightly. "You mean *you* didn't know."

Leon didn't speak. He gazed resolutely forward.

"So it's my fault Mickey was taken?"

"I didn't say that."

"You didn't have to."

His brow furrowed. "The point is—we can't continue to ignore the problem."

"What do you expect me to do?" I snapped. "I can't just shut off my feelings."

"You could try to stop fighting the bond."

"I'm not okay with you getting hurt for me. I am never going to be okay with that."

The word *never* seemed to echo between us. Leon's hands clenched. A muscle in his jaw twitched. Without speaking, he swung his legs over the side of the bed and left the room. I heard the sound of his bedroom door closing from across the hall. I rolled onto my side and squeezed my eyes shut.

I didn't go to school the follow morning. My absences were beginning to add up, but at the moment, I didn't care. Since Elspeth had convinced Esther to let her stay home as well, we spent the afternoon practicing my Amplification. We worked for a few hours, and I was able to make some progress—though not as much as I would have liked. Leon was moody and uncommunicative, but he was also unwilling to leave my side. He lingered nearby, a glower fixed on his face. I wasn't exactly thrilled with him, either; I did my best to ignore him, and focused on training.

Late in the afternoon, Mom arrived to check on us. She hadn't slept. Shane had agreed to search the Beneath for Mickey, but he wasn't optimistic. Mickey didn't have a Guardian to locate him, the way I had. And he wasn't just lost, he was taken; it was unlikely that Susannah would simply hand him over, even if Shane did find them. There weren't many other options. Mom had spent most of the night patrolling the streets, watching for any sign of Susannah, but the Cities were unnaturally quiet. Nothing else could be done until Susannah resurfaced.

Esther took one look at my mother and demanded she get some rest. To my surprise, Mom obeyed. She curled up fully clothed on one of the guest beds and didn't stir until dinner.

She was headed back out the door when Mr. Alvarez arrived.

"We need to talk," he said. "I know why Susannah is targeting Guardians."

"Ryan, you should be resting," Mom said.

I had to agree. Mr. Alvarez didn't look good. One of his arms was in a sling, bruises marked his face and neck, and his movements were sluggish. He made his way very carefully into Esther's sitting room and sank into a chair. His eyes were red-rimmed and looked slightly glassy. His hair was matted, and it appeared to have been several days since he'd shaved. I wondered if he'd actually been released from the hospital, or if he'd just taken it upon himself to escape.

Following them into the sitting room, I perched on the edge of one of Esther's plush chairs. Esther herself had left after dinner for a meeting with the elders. Leon lurked behind me like a large, sullen shadow. I looked at Mom, who was aiming a concerned frown at Mr. Alvarez.

"This is important," he said.

"So is your health."

"My health will survive a conversation." He leaned back in the chair, closing his eyes briefly. "The past few days, I've had a lot of time to think. I've been playing it over in my head. The attack."

He fell silent a moment. He wasn't usually easy to read, but now I caught impressions from him, little slivers of Knowing. The blurred vision of a violent struggle. A warning cut off in midsentence. A hoarse cry. The sound of a snap. A long, slow breath emptying into darkness. Peter Winslow's body, motionless on the pavement. "Susannah didn't want any interruptions," he continued. "She sent two of her Harrowers after me, and when Peter tried to call for backup, she killed him. Without any hesitation. Then she stood back and watched. I was the focus. *I* was the target. Peter was just ... collateral damage."

"What happened to Peter wasn't your fault," Mom said.

"This isn't about guilt. Let me finish. The question isn't why did she kill Peter? The question is why *didn't* she kill me? Why didn't she kill any of the other Guardians?"

The two demons that Susannah had sent after him had been weak, he explained. Just like in the other attacks. He'd killed them quickly. And then Susannah had gone after him herself.

"I was certain she meant to kill me. But she didn't. She asked why I was fighting. She seemed ... angry. At the time, I thought she was simply taunting me. It wasn't until tonight that it hit me." He sat forward, gripping the arm of the chair with his uninjured hand. His eyes lost their glassy look. "The pattern. The attacks haven't been random. They've been calculated. Precise. Every Guardian who's been targeted has been between the ages of eighteen and thirty-five, and none of them has been attacked twice."

Mom frowned. "What are you getting at?"

"All of the previous fights—they weren't about killing. They were about observation. Susannah has been monitoring our behavior, seeing how we'd react."

"She's been testing you?" I asked, unnerved.

"Our instincts. When most Guardians are attacked, their first instinct is to defend themselves." His gaze moved past me, to Leon. "But when a Guardian is called to protect a specific person, their first instinct is to defend their charge. Their first *thoughts* are of their charge."

The hairs on the back of my neck stood on end. I was acutely aware of Leon's presence behind me. I thought of that night at the lake, when he'd been attacked. The way the air had changed around us. The sound that broke the stillness, my warning that had come too late. The Harrower that launched itself toward him. How Susannah and Daniel waited and watched.

This Guardian. He's yours? she'd asked. *You're the one he protects?*

And I understood what Mr. Alvarez meant.

"Susannah wants the Remnant," he continued. "We know that. But her identity is hidden. The Kin don't even know who she is. No one has been able to find her. Bleedings don't work; Tigue tried that and failed." He paused, taking a breath. "But there is, in theory, one person who knows who the Remnant is."

My skin prickled. Iris had said the same thing three months ago atop Harlow Tower. "Her Guardian."

Mr. Alvarez's eyes flicked toward me. "Yes. There have only been three other Remnants in the history of the Kin, but each one of them had a Guardian. Susannah must know that."

Or Daniel did. The night he'd escaped from Susannah and tried to speak with me, she'd stated that the plan was his. And his Knowing was strong—much stronger than mine. That must have been why Susannah always brought him with her, I realized: to read the Guardians, to feel where their thoughts led.

"She's hoping to find the Remnant that way," Mr. Alvarez was saying. "Through her Guardian. That's what she's been doing— she's only targeting Guardians who could possibly have been called to protect the Remnant." That was why anyone who had been called prior to the Remnant's birth had been ruled out, he explained. The newest Guardians had been ignored, as well, since it was extremely rare for a Guardian to be younger than their charge.

Mom's frown deepened. "That could be a problem."

He shook his head. "But it isn't going to work," he said. "Because the Remnant's Guardian is dead."

According to Mr. Alvarez, it had happened like this: Lena Gustafson, the Remnant's Guardian, had been killed eight years earlier, during the incident with Tink's father. It had happened quickly, he said. The Guardians had been outnumbered. When the fighting happened, a Harrower had caught Lena from behind. Mr. Alvarez had been with her when she died. She'd held on long enough to utter a few gasping words. That was how he knew.

I watched him as he spoke. His voice was steady, but he'd become closed off again. No hint of Knowing came to me, no images, no sense of anything beyond his words. Just the details as he gave them.

He'd been a teenager back then, I remembered. Not yet a leader. A thin, black-haired youth, still learning to be a Guardian. A boy thrown into a battle that few had survived.

A boy who had been entrusted with a secret.

"This whole time, you've known who the Remnant is?" Mom's voice was incredulous.

"No. That's the problem. I couldn't understand what Lena was trying to say. And now that she's dead, there's no one who *does* know. We have no way of actually finding her."

Mr. Alvarez hadn't been able to make out most of Lena's words. If she'd spoken a name, he hadn't heard it. He knew only that she'd been concerned about her charge. Someone with a great power. A young child, who was either dangerous or in danger; he hadn't been certain which.

It was only later, when he'd discussed the matter with the Kin elders, that he'd realized Lena had been telling him she was the Guardian of a Remnant.

"Then the elders are aware of all this?" Mom asked.

"Yes. At the time, it was decided that it would be safer for the Remnant to remain hidden, so they didn't continue looking."

"They didn't. You did?"

"For a time. I was never able to locate her."

After Lena's death—and against the elders' dictates—Mr. Alvarez had investigated on his own, searching for children that she'd been in regular contact with. That led him nowhere. Lena had taught elementary school, and she'd been well loved. She'd been close with many of her students and had known several of their families. He hadn't found any one child who had received special attention. None of them had had ties to the Kin. Lena herself must have been careful to conceal the connection.

"But my best guess," he said, "is that the Remnant was a student at Grant Elementary at the time of Lena's death. At this point, I'm not certain how that helps us."

I straightened up. The air in the room seemed to thicken. Grant Elementary was the school I'd transferred into when we'd first moved to the Cities. My heart skipped a beat as recognition sparked within me. I'd heard Lena's name before. *Miss Gustafson.*

She'd been Gideon's first-grade teacher. The one who had died in a car accident.

Except, I realized now, it hadn't been a car crash.

My mind sped, thoughts careening. I thought back over what Gideon had told me about her. The entire class had loved Miss Gustafson, he'd said. All of the children had been devastated. After school that day, he and Brooke Oliver had sat together on the curb outside of school, crying; she'd even let him hold her hand. Later, the class had made cards to send to Miss Gustafson's family, notes and well wishes that had been passed along by the elementary staff. On the last day of school they'd released balloons.

Gideon's teacher. The Remnant's Guardian.

Gideon, I thought.

Gideon, who believed he was Kin. Gideon, whose readings were so obscured lately. Who had been troubled by dreams of demons. Who worried that something was wrong, that something was going to happen. And there were those traces of Knowing I'd had, impressions that slid from my understanding. The blank card.

He'd had nightmares before, he'd said. Around the time Miss Gustafson had died.

What part of him are you blind to? Esther had asked.

I turned to Mr. Alvarez. "We're certain the Remnant is a girl? How do we know? They're not always girls, are they?"

He furrowed his brow, but it was Mom who answered.

"Verrick had a vision of her."

And he'd started a Harrowing because of the vision. I knew that much; Elspeth had told me of it. Verrick had Seen the Remnant, she'd said—*a Kin-blooded girl who carries the powers of old.* That's what Iris and Tigue had been seeking; it was why they'd lured girls out into empty twilights, into dark alleys and snow-swirled streets where Harrowers waited. It was why Tink and I had been targeted, attacked, why our ankles had been cut. Verrick's vision.

But visions were often misinterpreted.

Maybe that was why the Remnant had never been located. They hadn't thought to seek a boy.

Gideon's face flashed before me. Not as he was now, but as I'd first seen him. The day we'd met. The day I'd had my first true Knowing. The day that I'd walked into our second-grade classroom and had found him and understood that we would be friends. Gideon had turned and smiled and I'd seen that clear light shining from him. Brilliant. Blinding. A circle spreading outward.

And if he was the Remnant—

The elders meant to seal him. As they had sealed my father.

I took long breaths. I tried to slow the rapid pounding of my heart. I looked at the floor, at Esther's pristine, rose-colored carpet, at my feet. Mom and Mr. Alvarez had moved on. They were talking about Susannah again.

"I compiled a list of all the attacks and all the potential targets," Mr. Alvarez said. "I've done the math. Most of them have already been hit. If I'm correct, there's only one Guardian left who is still a candidate. That gives us an advantage."

Mom was silent a moment, considering. "Which Guardian?"

"Camille."

Her breath came out in a strangled laugh. "You want to lure Susannah into the open by using your own girlfriend as bait."

"She's a target either way."

"Which means she should be protected."

"She will be. We keep the rest of the Guardians near, on standby. The moment Susannah appears, we launch an assault."

"You don't think Susannah will see right through that?"

"I don't see that we have many options," Mr. Alvarez said.

Leon spoke for the first time, stepping around my chair. "Where is Camille now?"

"I spoke to her already. She's with Drew. He has instructions to teleport if there's any sign of trouble."

"He wants to face Susannah himself," Leon said. "Are you certain he'll follow those instructions?"

"He won't compromise Camille's safety."

"We don't have time to be playing games," Mom said. There was an edge to her voice. She turned away, toward the windows at the far end of the room. "We need a real solution. Now. Susannah has taken someone. We need to find a way of getting him back."

"This *is* a solution, Lucy. This entire time, Susannah has been a step ahead. Now we know where she'll strike next. We need to be ready for her."

Mom was silent again, crossing her arms as she faced Mr. Alvarez. The soft glow of Esther's lamps turned to gold in her hair. Her eyes were shadowed. She let out a low sigh. "I hope you aren't intending to lead this assault yourself. You're hardly in any condition to fight."

"I thought I'd leave that to you." He eased himself to his feet, still gripping the arm of the chair. "We don't have time to prepare tonight, but we should begin planning tomorrow. I need to round up the rest of the Guardians."

"What you need is to be in a bed somewhere."

He waved her concern away.

Since Mr. Alvarez's broken arm prevented him from driving—he'd taken a cab to Esther's house—Leon was roped into teleport-taxi service. After they were gone, Mom began preparing to leave for the evening, and I walked upstairs to change into my pajamas. I was spending the night in St. Paul again. How long this arrangement was going to last was something I didn't want to think about. I felt anchorless. I wouldn't feel safe in my own house, but the St. Croix estate lacked the comforting familiarity of home. There were no memories in this place, no spaces that soothed me, no smells I knew. Just long corridors and empty rooms and the faint scent of Esther's rose perfume. Staying here didn't make me feel secure, but adrift.

As I made my way up the staircase, my thoughts returned to Gideon. I tried to tell myself I was being ridiculous. Of course he wasn't the Remnant. It was a coincidence that he'd known Lena Gustafson, nothing more. But the idea wouldn't leave me. My heart drummed in my ears. The blank card had never appeared before. There was something Gideon's readings had been trying to show me, some unknown part of him I couldn't see. Something secret.

And Susannah had reacted to him, I recalled. She'd recognized something within him. If he *was* the Remnant, she hadn't known—but she was searching for a girl, too.

Maybe that had saved him.

Feeling anxious and unsettled, I moved about the guest room slowly, gathering up my pajamas from the floor. I paused near the dresser, where I'd set my Nav cards. I touched them lightly, tracing their edges with my thumb. Gram's warning came back to me. There were places it was best not to look, she'd told me. But I had to know, if only to reassure myself.

Tomorrow, I decided.

I was headed for the shower when I heard a noise nearby and realized that my mother hadn't left yet.

"Mom?" I stepped across the hall and found her in the room Esther had sent her to earlier. She was seated at the edge of the bed, wearing her H&H Security coat instead of her hoodie. Her hands were curled at her sides.

She was crying.

She looked up when she heard me, hastily wiping her face with the back of her hand as she rose to her feet. She straightened her shoulders. "You all right, honey?"

"I was going to ask you that," I said.

Her words came quickly. She sounded a little embarrassed and busied herself putting her hair back into its bun. "I'm fine. You don't need to worry about me."

"You don't seem fine."

"I've just got a lot on my mind right now."

Like Mickey, I thought. I stepped into the room, pulling myself onto the bed and drawing my legs up against me. "Is there anything I can do for you?" I asked, trying to think of something consoling to say, and failing. I felt at a loss. Gram would have known what to do, I thought. What to say—and what not to say.

Mom walked over to me and placed her hand lightly on the top of my head. "You're a good kid."

"Remember how Gram used to sing to me whenever I was sad?" I recalled Gram's warm, lilting voice crooning out the notes to "You Are My Sunshine" and "Bye, Bye, Blackbird." I frowned. "Though, now that I think about it, they weren't very happy songs."

Mom smiled. "She sang to me, too. She sang to me almost the entire time I was in labor with you, did I ever tell you that?" She paused, withdrawing her hand. "You haven't mentioned us running into your father."

"I didn't think you'd want to talk about it, with . . . everything else."

"We can talk about it," she said, and sat down on the bed beside me.

I didn't answer immediately. I turned to look at her. Her eyes were slightly rimmed with red, but she seemed calmer now. She was still smiling slightly. "Did you mind seeing him?" I asked. "I know you didn't want to."

She hesitated. "I wasn't expecting to. It took me by surprise."

I thought of the look on her face when she'd seen my father, of how still she'd gone. I swallowed, looking down at my hands. My next question was quiet. "Do you still love him?"

Another pause. She closed her eyes briefly. I caught the flicker of a memory in her—my father as a young man, grinning broadly. "I'll always love him. But love changes. I gave up all the might-have-beens a long time ago." She let out a shaky breath. "Or I thought I had. But … I'm glad I saw him."

We were silent a moment. When I glanced at her again, her face had shadowed. She was thinking about Mickey again, I guessed.

Seventeen years ago, she'd lost my father to a Harrower.

Now Susannah had taken Mickey.

I bit my lip. "Has Shane found anything? About Mickey?"

"No."

I nodded. I had been trying not to wonder what would happen if Mickey never returned. What explanation would be given, *could* be given. His car was still parked near our house, beside the maple trees. Somewhere, he had an apartment sitting empty, a phone that went unanswered, a bed that went untouched. People would be missing him, were probably missing him already: the police force, his parents, his friends.

And there was no truth that could be given to them. They couldn't be told that he had been taken, that he was trapped in a realm without light or heat, a void where the darkness had claws, where hatred was a living, breathing thing.

The Kin would handle the situation somehow. I knew that much. But that only made it worse—the idea that, even now, someone was crafting a story, working out details. Questions would be asked and answered. A memorial would be held. And then Mickey would simply disappear, as though he'd never been.

My face must have shown my thoughts. Mom pulled me into her arms, stroking my hair. "It'll be okay," she said. "Whatever happens, we'll get through it." I didn't know which of us she was speaking to.

It'll be okay, I told myself, thinking of Mickey and Gideon, of Susannah and Daniel, of the Beneath.

I did my best to believe it.

My plan to do another reading for Gideon was delayed. He and his family had to go up north for some annual Belmonte get-together—which, he told me over the phone, I would have known if I'd bothered to show up to school yesterday. He promised that he'd be free on Sunday. I didn't tell him why I wanted to see him. Worry gnawed at me. I decided to quiet my apprehension by focusing on other things. In the morning, I once again badgered Elspeth into helping me practice my Amplification.

We trained for a couple of hours before Elspeth had to leave. Some of my tension dissipated. I was finally able to hold my Amplification without physical contact for several minutes at a time—though it wasn't entirely consistent.

"Why don't you ask Leon to help?" Elspeth suggested. "You said it was easier with him."

"Leon's pretty pissed at me."

He was no longer hovering around me, but he was checking in now and then to make certain I was still among the living—since, he had told me, he couldn't trust the bond to alert him to trouble.

Go away, I'd told him the third time he'd appeared without warning. *You are making my mom look relaxed. And don't you even think of trying to Hungry Puppy me right now, because it won't work.*

He had left, but he'd showed up again an hour later. I sighed and decided to ignore him.

Because I was growing tired of being cooped up in the St. Croix household, I spent the rest of the afternoon with Tink.

That turned out to be a bad idea. She was once again refusing even to discuss any matters involving the Kin, which meant we were back on the topic of Greg. He'd apparently worked up the nerve to talk her again and had also dumped the freshman.

"I thought you were over Greg," I said.

"Well...he did dump his freshman for me."

"But first he dumped *you* for *her.*"

"I didn't say I was taking him back. But at least I know I can."

I really wasn't in the mood for her boy drama. "And so now only Lars and his discount pizza stand in the way of true happiness," I said.

Tink rolled her eyes. "Hey, you're the one who wanted to hang out."

She drove me back to St. Paul in the early evening, then informed me she was inviting herself in to snoop. That meant wandering through the house and opening doors Esther usually kept shut. I was in the process of shooing her back out the door when Mr. Alvarez arrived. He was headed for Esther's sitting room when Tink and I came down the stairs.

Tink went pale, stopping at the bottom of the steps. "Oh, my God. He looks *awful*," she whispered.

Before I could reply, Mr. Alvarez saw us and changed directions. "Brewster," he called, quickening his stride, as though he expected her to make a mad dash for the door. Which he probably did. He was giving her the no-texting-in-class look again.

I didn't want to get caught in the middle of their dispute, so I started to walk away. She grabbed my arm. "If you leave me here with him," she hissed, "that is *the end* of our friendship."

Since our friendship had survived my putting superglue in her hair—not to mention the time she'd stolen my boyfriend in sixth grade—I didn't believe her, but I stayed.

"I'm told you didn't finish your training," Mr. Alvarez said.

"Two weeks. That was the deal. You teach math, so let's see if you can figure this one out. What does seven plus seven equal?"

"This isn't going to go away. You need to accept that."

"Last time I checked, you weren't my father. And if you think showing up looking like you've been hit by a bus is going to convince me to be a Guardian, you are not nearly as smart as you think you are."

She had a point there, I thought. He was sort of a walking

billboard for the dangers of being a Guardian. Not that he could help it. And he did look marginally better than he had last night.

His gaze was steady. "There's a discussion we need to have. But right now, I don't have the time."

"Wonderful," Tink muttered. She made a hasty exit, telling me she'd give me a call later. Mr. Alvarez frowned after her.

"She's not being stubborn," I said once she was gone. When he gave me a skeptical look, I added, "I mean, she's not *just* being stubborn. She's scared."

"I know." His expression softened.

"She thinks she was called by mistake. And she thinks the Kin hate her because of her father." I doubted she'd appreciate my telling him that, but I knew Mr. Alvarez was right. Sooner or later, Tink was going to have to accept the fact that she'd been called.

His forehead knit, but he didn't answer.

Mom arrived at the house a short time later. She and Mr. Alvarez headed for Esther's sitting room, and since Mom hadn't forbidden me to join them, I followed.

Esther was already seated in one of the plush chairs, holding a teacup, which she raised slowly to her lips. She saw me lingering in the doorway and set the teacup aside. "Don't lurk, Audrey. Either come in or go out."

I went in.

Leon was there as well, standing near the window. I knew he was still angry at me, and I wasn't feeling very happy with him, either, but I crossed the room and stood beside him. Though he didn't look at me, after a moment his hand found mine.

"The Guardians have agreed to go forward with Ryan's plan," Mom was telling Esther.

"They'll be putting it into action tonight," Mr. Alvarez said. "Camille will take her usual patrol. The rest of the Guardians will wait nearby. If Susannah appears, Lucy will lead the strike."

Esther's gaze moved to Mom. "I've never known Lucy to lead."

Mom snorted. "If you mean I'd rather take Susannah on myself, you're right."

Ignoring them, Mr. Alvarez said, "The rest of the Kin will need to take additional precautions. We can't be certain our plan will succeed, and Camille is Susannah's last viable target. There's no telling what she'll do once she realizes she needs another way to find the Remnant. She may go into hiding in order to plot her next move, or she may simply decide on an all-out attack."

I shivered at his words. Leon's fingers tightened on mine.

There were a few more details of the attack to go over, and then Mom had to leave to meet up with the rest of the Guardians. She hugged me quickly before she departed. Mr. Alvarez and Esther left to alert the rest of the Kin to the possibility of an attack. Leon remained behind. The St. Croix estate was even farther from the center of the Circle than my house was, but he wasn't taking any chances, he said. He didn't want me winding up alone if Susannah escaped and retaliated again. I didn't argue with him.

I spent most of the night half awake. I lay on my side in the big guest-room bed, listening for voices in the hall beyond, wondering when the fighting would occur, *if* the fighting would occur. Waiting for some indication that the plan had gone well. I heard nothing. No signal that Mom had returned, no footsteps or whispers or ringing phone. Scenarios played out before me in frightening detail: Susannah's face, a patchwork of scales and skin; my mother on a dark street, surrounded by Harrowers; Guardians lying dead. I shook the images away, replaced them. I saw bright lights and twisting colors, my mother's sure strikes, Susannah falling Beneath. I held to that idea.

Eventually, I slept.

When I woke on Sunday, it was to the news that the evening had been uneventful. The Guardians had waited all night, but Susannah hadn't shown herself. Camille's patrol had gone undisturbed.

"Now what?" I asked, following Mom into the room Esther had given over to her use.

She sighed softly. "We wait. And try again."

In the meantime, the Guardians had been instructed to rest, which was what she intended to do—though only for a few hours. She'd agreed to meet Drew later that afternoon to discuss some concerns he had with Mr. Alvarez's plan. I told her to sleep well, then headed for Gideon's.

Leon had to work, which meant he couldn't spend his time lurking and brooding—at least not in my immediate vicinity—but he did agree to drop me off at Gideon's house on the way to the bakery.

I climbed up behind him on his motorcycle, wrapping my arms around his waist. We still weren't exactly speaking to each other, but at least during the drive the silence felt natural. I was able to just lean against him, feel the rise and fall of his breath, and pretend everything was fine. The highways blurred by around us, eventually becoming familiar neighborhood streets. We passed by our house. I saw Mickey's car still parked there, windshield gleaming with melted frost.

When we reached Gideon's, I slid off the motorcycle and stood for a moment steadying myself. Then, instead of walking into the house, I turned to Leon.

"How long are you going to be angry at me?" I asked.

He faced me, but he wouldn't meet my gaze. "I can't shut off my feelings any more than you can."

I swallowed, closing my eyes briefly. We were at an impasse. No middle ground to meet on. "Then what are we going to do?" I asked, hating the fact that my voice wavered.

"I don't know." He lifted a hand toward me and touched my cheek, then turned away again. "I'll see you after work," he said.

With a sinking feeling, I watched him ride away.

Gideon's house was nearly empty when I entered, most of the

rooms quiet and dark, save for the glow of cat eyes peering at me. His father was running errands, Gideon said, and his mother and sisters were at the mall. Granny Belmonte appeared to have fallen asleep at the computer while playing solitaire.

"They left Granny home?" I asked, tiptoeing past her. She was snoring into the keyboard.

Gideon shrugged. "Mom's still mad at her for spiking the Christmas punch."

I stifled a laugh and followed him down the stairs to the basement. When we reached his room, I said, "I brought my Nav cards. I thought we'd do a reading."

"You came over here just for that?"

"I had an idea," I said.

We sat cross-legged on the floor, a length of blue carpet between us. I'd brought both decks with me—if I couldn't learn anything with one, I figured it might be worth trying the other— but I began with Gram's cards. She had always instructed me to focus upon the familiar when trying something new with my abilities, to remove other variables. When I was little and first learning to use the cards, we'd done countless readings on a single subject, searching for nuance within the known. I followed the same principle now. Since seeking some connection to the Kin had failed in the previous readings, this time I wouldn't seek. I wouldn't search for a link to the Kin, or for the Remnant. I would simply concentrate on Gideon himself. Gideon was known to me:

the shape of his face, the way he spoke and moved. Eight years of memories had built up between us. Then I would move past that.

To whatever part of him I was blind to.

I took my time shuffling—longer than I normally did. I didn't let my thoughts stray. I moved deliberately through our shared memories, going back across years of baseball games and bicycle rides, summers we'd spent swimming in the lake at my family's cabin, our bodies sunburned and covered in mosquito bites. The day we'd been left behind at the zoo and had spent an hour in front of the monkey enclosure before the school came back to fetch us. The day Gideon had learned of Mom's powers, the surprise and excitement on his face. The day that we'd met.

Keeping my concentration, I set down the first two cards. Inverted Crescent and The Prisoner. My card and his. They were simple and expected, telling me that my focus was working, my frequencies clear. I moved slowly, tracing my fingers along the designs. They brought more memories to mind, small moments I had almost forgotten. I smiled and dealt the third card.

Forty. The Siren.

My hand hovered over it, not quite touching the surface. The card brought with it another recollection, this one much more recent, of the night in the parking ramp. My smile died as I saw Susannah. She sauntered toward Gideon. I caught the metallic gleam of her dress, the flame of her hair. She bared her teeth when he gave her his name.

There, she told him. *Now we're friends.*

The impression faded. I withdrew my hand, dealt the next two cards.

Sign of Sickle. Sign of Swords.

More memories came to me, but these weren't my own. I saw two children seated on a curb. One head bowed, bright with blond curls. The second child facing the first, brown hair bronzed with sun. Fingers twined together. Gideon and Brooke. Crying for Lena Gustafson.

Over this lay another image. A blank sky at twilight. Blue horizon turning gray, bleeding into black. A red star shining. The far off sound of laughter. And then a face I couldn't quite see, a figure standing just beyond my vision. *We are bound*, a low voice said.

"Audrey?" Gideon asked. The image snapped.

"Hold on," I said. "Sorry. Just let me concentrate a minute."

I set down the cross cards next. They were the same as the first two readings. Card twenty-six. The Triple Knot.

I saw Iris's face, turned away. The flash of her throat; the fall of her hair. She whispered a name, but I couldn't hear it.

Card twenty-one. Year of Famine.

Harlow Tower flickered before me, gold letters and dark windows. Snow on the rooftop. A soundless night.

Card fifty-one. Inverted Compass.

I saw my mother.

I paused. Compass was the card that I associated with Mom, not its inversion—and that was usually only in my own readings. I tried to puzzle through the card's meaning. A compass indicated direction. Alignment. A way to orient oneself. The inversion signified the opposite. And Gideon himself had told me he was troubled.

But I frowned. The image of my mother flashed again. She wasn't wearing her Morning Star hoodie. Her hair was down about her shoulders, longer than she usually kept it. Her eyes were sad. She looked—young.

I pushed the image away, telling myself to focus, to concentrate on Gideon, to look for nuance within the known.

"Two left," I said. I reached for the next card.

Stopped.

My hand touched the deck, stayed there. A sudden sense of foreboding crawled up my skin, goose bumps along my arms and the back of my neck. I felt abruptly vulnerable, exposed, watched. As though Gideon and I weren't alone in the room. As though some other presence lingered here, eager and expectant. I had felt this before, the sense of something searching as I searched, something sly and full of hate. Something that was waiting, willing me to find it.

It was the same sense I'd gotten when Iris and I had used my Nav cards to seek the Remnant.

There are some places it's best not to look, I heard Gram say. But it was too late. I was already looking.

I flipped the card.

Seven. The Beast.

Knowing shot through me, sudden and relentless, fragments and perceptions that sent my thoughts reeling. Harlow Tower rose before me, impressions from the night of Tigue's defeat. There was the dusting of snow. There was Iris, falling to her knees. There was the blood at my wrists, oozing down my ankles and throat. There was the Astral Circle's blazing light, screaming hot within me. And there was Gideon. His eyes began to open.

More images blinked through me: a deserted street; a sidewalk; Susannah, dressed in green; the night Daniel had escaped. *You set something in motion . . .* she'd told me.

Next. The children on the curb again. Tears streamed down Brooke's face. The sunlight caught in her hair. Gideon inched toward her. They clasped hands.

His fingernails were red.

Time sped backward. I saw Harlow Tower once more, but now my mother stood atop it, her feet touching the ledge, just as she had stood seventeen years ago. A man's voice called from behind her. *You think you're clever, do you?*

A voice I knew.

The images moved forward again. Now it was Susannah, smiling as she said, *The beast within them sleeps.*

That isn't possible, I thought.

With trembling hands, I set down the final card.

And this time it wasn't blank.

Gram had often told me that she didn't believe in coincidence. She believed in connection. She'd believed in patterns, in action and reaction, in cause and effect, one event shaping the next. That wasn't fate, she'd claimed. It was more akin to gravity: the pull one object has upon another.

This felt a lot like fate.

It felt like something inevitable, something that could not be controlled or changed. A course I could not diverge from. A moment that had been determined before my birth, one cold, starless night seventeen years ago.

I stared at the card, unable to move. Barely able to breathe or think.

"Blank again," Gideon said.

He could see nothing in it. But I could.

I saw a face. His face, and not his face. I saw the boy I knew: the dark hair, the slight bump on the bridge of his nose. Features as familiar to me as my own. And I saw the blank, loveless eyes of a man my mother had once known. A man who wasn't a man beneath. I saw them both. Like a coin spinning in the air.

One side Gideon.

The other side Verrick.

For an instant, I was back on Harlow Tower with my mother. It was a vision, but more than a vision. The chill of the wind burned against me. I heard the sounds of traffic far below. The light of the Astral Circle bled into the air around us. I stood silent as my mother battled Verrick. I watched them stagger across the roof. I watched them fight and fall.

I'm bound to you, Verrick told her. *Bound to the daughter that sleeps beneath your heart.*

Kill me and we'll meet again.

And they had.

Now, as I looked at Gideon, I noticed that light again, the aura about him that I'd seen the day we met. The shine that had seemed so clear, so clean. The Knowing that had told me we would be friends.

I didn't understand, didn't want to understand. My thoughts were in chaos. My stomach churned. I wanted to scream out denials. This was impossible, I told myself. This was *Gideon.* I'd known him half my life. I knew everything about him—his favorite color, his stupid jokes, his fear of heights. He cried during *Bambi* and made up nonsense songs for his sisters. He was human. He couldn't be a Harrower.

Iris had done something to him, I decided. The night she'd taken him hostage—that was when this had all started, when he'd begun to have nightmares, when he'd begun to suspect he was Kin. Maybe Iris had needed a vessel, a body to contain Verrick within. Maybe some part of him had crept into Gideon and had become trapped there when I started the unsealing. And maybe it could be removed, like an exorcism, or poison drawn from a wound.

But that wasn't correct. I realized that, even as I fought against it. I sensed it in a way that went beyond Knowing or intuition, a truth I felt in my bones. Gideon *was* Verrick. He always had been.

And Iris had been aware all along. She must have been.

Even as I thought that, understanding struck me, sudden and violent. The final piece of the puzzle, the other secret the reading had been trying to show me.

Two children crying. The gleam of blond hair.

Verrick had known who the Remnant was. He had Seen her. He knew where she would be born, and when. He still knew. Something inside of Gideon recognized her, who she was. And what she was. She was the sole focus of his hope, of his longing. She was his heartache. She was his obsession.

The Remnant was Brooke Oliver.

I felt like throwing up.

Gideon must have seen the alarm on my face. "Are you okay, Audrey? What's going on?"

He touched my arm. I jerked away, staring at him. I saw confusion in his eyes, hesitation. He was waiting for me to speak, but speech was beyond my abilities. The very basis of reality seemed to have shifted. I'd spent my life believing the earth was round, and now I'd fallen off the edge of the map. There was no ground below, no one to catch me.

"Are you sick?" Gideon asked. "Should I call your mom? Do you want me to bring you home?"

I shook my head. I reached toward my Nav cards, scattering them, trying to erase any evidence of the reading. Then a numb calm began to spread through me. Slowly, carefully, I gathered the cards again, returning each one to the deck. I was beginning to process, and to arrange the disorder of my thoughts.

"Audrey?" Gideon said.

I looked at him, really looked. I saw only Gideon.

He didn't know what he was, that much was certain.

But Iris had. And Susannah had at least recognized him as a Harrower that night. Perhaps Harrowers were drawn to Harrowers, just as Kin were drawn to Kin.

"I'm sorry," I said, my voice shaky. "You're right—I'm not feeling well. It just hit me suddenly. Do you mind if we finish this later?"

He offered to drive me back to St. Paul, or at least to my house, but I told him I needed fresh air. I hurried up the stairs and stepped outside, following the path toward the sidewalk. When I looked back, I saw him in the doorway, waving, his brow knotted with concern. I resisted the urge to run.

Gideon didn't know what he was, my mind echoed.

The Kin didn't know.

Mom didn't know.

If I wanted information, I'd have to ask a Harrower.

I took the bus downtown. I hunkered down in the seat, hiding myself in the back corner and praying that no one would sit beside me. The low buzz of chatter rose and fell as passengers entered and exited. The early afternoon was sunny and clear, the road wet with the last of the snowmelt, but someone nearby was talking about rain in the forecast. I rested my head against the window, taking steadying breaths. Streets slid past. We crossed the river, and I saw Harlow Tower standing among the other skyscrapers. My eyes skimmed over the tall, dark windows, the gold lettering, the edge of the roof far above. With a shiver, I turned away.

I exited the bus on Nicollet Avenue and hurried the few blocks to the Drought and Deluge. I wasn't certain what I would do if Shane wasn't there. Wait, maybe. Sit outside and try to escape notice. I didn't have much of a plan beyond finding him and asking him what he knew about Verrick—and hoping that he would tell me.

The club wasn't open, so I stood outside and knocked, peering in through the windows. I didn't see Shane. I saw bare tables, the empty dance floor, the rim of the bar. Near the back, I could just make out the faint, blurred red and gray of the mural he'd painted. I knocked again. When I didn't receive an answer, I walked around the side of the building and moved into the alley. Then I hesitated. I pressed my hand to the wall of the club, feeling the rough brick beneath my fingertips as I inched forward. I had been in this alley twice before. Once, on the night Tink had been attacked, when I'd stepped out of the club and found her unconscious in Shane's arms, blood oozing from her ankles. And once when I'd gone seeking Iris and found a Harrower instead.

Now, I looked down the alley to the club's back door, swallowed, and stepped toward it.

"It's locked. While I'm certain your intentions are honest, I'm afraid the same can't be said for most of this city's inhabitants."

I turned. Shane stood a few feet away, a lazy half smile on his face. He was dressed simply, in a white T-shirt and gray jeans, and his hair once again had that perfect windblown effect, even though there was hardly any breeze. "I was looking for you," I said.

His smile widened. "I'm flattered."

"I need your help."

"Naturally you do. I've been thinking of setting up a new business. Shane Keane, Harrower for Hire. Though that would, of course, seem to imply that I'm being paid."

"Please."

He took a moment to look me over critically, his smile vanishing. When he spoke, his voice was soft. "I warned you not to involve yourself. I said you wouldn't like where it led."

My throat felt tight. "You know about Gideon, don't you?"

"Let's do this inside, shall we?"

I nodded, following him back around the side of the building and into the Drought and Deluge. Once we'd entered the club, Shane pulled a chair from near one of the tables and gestured toward it. I remained standing. He shrugged, then leaned back against the table, folded his arms, and watched me.

"Why don't you tell me what it is you think you know, and we'll go from there?" he asked.

My hands clenched. We stood in semidarkness. Shane hadn't bothered to turn on the overhead lights, and the only illumination came from the sun streaming through the windows. I looked down at the shadows that fell between us. There was a gum wrapper on the floor.

When I didn't speak, Shane said, "All right. I'll start. You have sadly discovered that this friend of yours isn't quite who he believes he is."

"He's Verrick. The Harrower my mother fought seventeen years ago. I just don't know how that's possible."

"Here we're on equal footing, I'm afraid. I don't know how it's possible, either—only that it is."

I felt the sting of tears and blinked them away. Part of me had still been hoping to be told I was mistaken. My voice sounded small, far away. "But he's human."

"Is he?" Shane straightened, holding his left arm out toward me. Then, slowly, he raised his right hand. His fingers turned to talons. I recoiled, moving backward until I was pressed against the window, but Shane didn't seem to notice. He scraped one talon across the flesh of his left arm, letting a thin trail of blood well up under it. Then his hand became human again. Carefully, he traced the line of blood with his thumb. "This body of mine isn't merely an illusion, angel. It's what I am when I wear this skin. Just as your friend wears his. But the trouble is we're incomplete. Imperfect. The Beneath lives inside us. We breathe it. We carry it with us. We never leave." Finally, he looked at me. "And so we're all damaged, you see. All tainted. All corrupted by the Beneath. Though some of us are less corrupted than others."

"Is that what makes you neutral?"

He smiled but didn't answer my question. Instead, he asked, "How much do you know of Verrick?"

"He wanted to end the world," I said. "And was going to use the Remnant to do it."

"Not the world. Just everyone in it."

I started to speak, but Shane interrupted me.

"One moment, if you will. Let me tell you what I know of it," he said. "Verrick hated the Kin, that's true enough. But he hated other Harrowers even more. He reviled what we are. And he coveted your people. He wanted what was stolen from us when your kind crossed over: peace."

"He decided to destroy everyone because he wanted *peace*?"

"Not peace for others. For himself. He wanted to heal the corruption inside him, to leave the Beneath behind forever, just as your ancestors had done. He wanted to become Kin." Shane shrugged lightly, leaning against the table again. "Or, that failing, he wanted your people to suffer as he did."

By opening up the Beneath, I thought. Letting every Harrower in existence loose upon the earth. And killing everyone who had tried to stop him. Including Leon's parents. "But my mother defeated him. She nearly killed him. How is it he became Gideon?"

"I couldn't say. I wasn't there, you understand. The best I can offer you is guesswork."

"Then guess," I said. "Please."

"If I cared to speculate . . . I would suggest that it was the Astral Circle that did it. The Circles were made from the blood of the Old Race. They hold the last traces of your ancestors' power—the power that your people used to cross over and become the Kin. Perhaps that is what altered him. When your mother defeated him, instead of dying, he was—transformed."

That made sense. Verrick had accessed the energy of the Circle that night on Harlow Tower. He had been draining it, drawing its light into him. Trying to take its power for himself.

And there was Gideon's aura. The warm shine that surrounded him.

"So . . . it made him into a human baby?" I said, thinking of how Gideon had been found, a naked infant crying in an alley. That was why he'd never been able to find his birth parents.

He didn't have any.

"That would be my assumption," Shane said.

I frowned. But if the light of the Circle *had* altered Verrick, turning him human, it hadn't finished the job. Some part of him was still Harrower. Still seeking the Remnant. Sleeping. Waiting to awaken.

When I mentioned this to Shane, he suggested that it had something to do with the sealing. Verrick's powers had been sealed along with my father's—and while the powers of the Kin were linked to their humanity, Harrower powers were linked to their corruption. Sealing one meant sealing the other.

"So as long as his powers remain sealed, he'll stay Gideon?"

"Who can say? This is only a theory, angel. To my knowledge, nothing of the sort has ever occurred before. I don't know even what he *is*. He's not human or Harrower, precisely. And yet he's both. He's something different. Something new." Shane shrugged. "But you could be correct. Perhaps he will simply live out his human life, never the wiser. The rest of us would certainly be happier for it. All the same, I would personally prefer to keep my distance. What will *you* do, now that you've stumbled upon his terrible secret?"

"I don't know. I'm still trying to adjust to this." Gideon's face flashed before me. The laughter in his eyes, the slight gap in his front teeth. The dimple that sometimes appeared when he grinned.

He wanted to heal the corruption inside him, I thought.

He wanted to be Kin.

"It isn't his fault," I said.

"He's not your friend, angel. Not really. You would do well to remember that."

I shook my head, searching for a conviction I didn't feel. "That's not true. Verrick is who he *was*. Gideon is who he *is*." Brooke was proof of that, I thought. Even as Verrick hunted for the Remnant, Gideon had always maintained his distance. He could barely even speak in her presence.

I can't talk to her, he'd said.

I don't want to ruin things.

"I doubt your mum would agree with you. But that's hardly my business, is it? And I'm afraid we both have more pressing matters to deal with."

Something in his tone put my senses on alert. "You've Seen something?"

"Yes, but not in the manner you mean. Your mum has had me searching the Beneath."

"For Mickey," I said. "You found him?"

"I found him. I couldn't reach him. It appears that Susannah is amassing an army. And as soon as she has the Remnant, she plans to unleash it."

The air in the Drought and Deluge felt suddenly very chilled. The light through the windows had shifted as the sun moved across the sky, leaving Shane half in shadow. My gaze moved past him, to the mural on the far wall. The Beneath stared back at me. Shane had painted it empty: just the stark gray skyline, with stars overhead. It did not seem empty any longer. Now it teemed with Harrower bodies, restless and waiting. I could almost see the blank white of their eyes, could almost hear the click of talons on concrete.

I blinked the image away and turned back to Shane, who was still leaning against the table. "Explain *army*."

"Are you certain you wish me to?"

"It can't be worse than what I'm imagining."

"I wouldn't be so sure," he said.

My chill deepened. I rubbed my arms, looking at the shadows along the floor, the dark corners beyond the bar. "Would you turn on the lights?"

His eyes glinted with amusement, but he complied, walking across the room to flip each of the switches. After a moment, a soft yellow glow filled the club, revealing the familiar arrangement of tables and chairs, illuminating the booths along the wall. I shifted slightly. I let my gaze travel over the club's decor, carefully keeping the mural from my vision. Shane returned and lifted his eyebrows at me. "Better?"

I nodded. "Are you going to tell me what you meant now, or are you planning to go back to being cryptic?"

He slid into his customary relaxed posture. "Here I thought *army* was a very specific sort of term. Rather illustrative. But since details are what you crave: it appears that Susannah has not been idle these past few weeks. She's been gathering Harrowers to her."

"Drew said that she would do that." He'd killed most of her followers before leaving San Diego, I recalled. He'd told us she would need to replenish her ranks.

"Did he? I suspect he meant those Harrowers she holds under her sway, just as she keeps that unfortunate boy and the good detective. This is much more than that. Susannah's persuasive abilities are impressive, but even she has limitations. I'm not referring to a few unwitting pawns here, angel. Or even a few dozen. Susannah has hundreds of my kind gathered to her, perhaps thousands. She's not controlling them, as far as I've been able to ascertain. They are simply . . . lying in wait."

"For her to find the Remnant." I lowered my gaze, picturing Brooke and trying desperately not to.

"Find her and rip open the fabric that divides our realms. Not a terribly pleasant notion, is it?"

"No." I shut my eyes. Hundreds of demons, I thought, perhaps thousands. Hordes of them clawing their way out from Beneath. And that would be only the beginning, if the Beneath were permanently opened. It wouldn't just be a Harrowing. It would mean the end of the Kin, exactly as Valerie had foreseen. "Is this what you were talking about? That night in Loring Park, when you told me to warn my mom?"

He hesitated. "I hadn't Seen this. Merely—sensed it. At the time, I was still very much hoping not to be drawn into this spot of trouble. It appears I was overly optimistic."

"Have you told Mom about it?"

"I haven't had the opportunity. This is something of a recent development, you understand. And I'm telling *you* because I feel it might be in everyone's best interests if you went away from the Circle for a spell."

"What do you mean?"

His expression turned serious. He leaned toward me, speaking softly. "It's written all over your face, pet. The other dark secret you've unearthed. You know who the Remnant is."

I flinched. I started to respond, but Shane stopped me.

"Don't speak it," he said.

"I wasn't going to. I was going to ask if *you* knew."

"Don't know, and don't care to. And if you want a bit of advice, you'll—"

But I didn't learn what his advice was. The door opened behind me, and my mother strode in.

She must have been hoping for an update on Mickey. She took a few quick steps toward the table where Shane was leaning, her face grim. He waved. I swallowed nervously as I glanced at her. Her hair was up, but she was dressed casually, and didn't have her H&H Security coat on. With her focus on Shane, she hadn't immediately noticed me—though that also might have been due to her exhaustion. She couldn't have gotten more than an hour or two of sleep, I thought. I edged backward, away from the window and toward one of the booths, but it was a useless effort. Mom halted as soon as she saw me. I registered surprise on her face, and then her expression hardened. She approached Shane, eyes narrowed. "What in God's name is my daughter doing here?"

He glanced sideways at me. "You may wish to ask her that."

"I'm asking you."

I moved to her side, touching her sleeve. "Mom. Shane saw something. Beneath."

She stilled. Her face went pale; her body tensed. She thought I meant Mickey.

"He says Susannah has an army," I told her quickly.

"The missing Harrowers." She let out a breath.

Shane shook his head. "If you mean the neutral denizens of the Cities—yes. Some of them. Some have simply fled to places a bit more hospitable than our current locale. But Susannah has plenty of Harrowers to choose from. The Beneath is positively brimming with the mindless monstrosities who hate your Kin." He paused, tapping his fingers against the tabletop as he looked at us. He smiled, but there was an edge in his voice. There was that icy, distant look in his eyes, reminding me once again that he was a Harrower, too. I took a step back.

Mom was silent, her expression unreadable. She closed her eyes for a moment, sighing again. Finally, she said, "All right. Thank you, Shane."

"I am here to serve. Apparently." This time the smile reached his eyes.

Mom turned her attention to me. "I thought you were with Gideon."

"I was." I heard the tremor in my voice and hoped that she didn't. "I needed to ask Shane something."

"I thought we'd agreed to keep your meetings with Harrowers to *nonexistent.*"

Before I could explain—or even come up with something resembling an explanation—Mom lifted her hand and announced that we'd discuss it later. She was in a hurry at the moment, she said. She was supposed to meet with Drew, and I would have to accompany her. She told me she'd have him bring me back to St. Paul before they joined the rest of the Guardians. I only nodded.

But we didn't leave. Abruptly, Shane's indolent stance disappeared. He darted from his position at the table and caught my arm, pulling me backward.

"What are you doing?" I demanded, trying to jerk free.

His voice was low in my ear. "We're about to have a visitor."

I felt it then.

The chill up my spine, along the back of my neck. The way the air itself altered, thickening, filling with the scents of blood and decay. The cold that crept into my lungs. The sudden hush.

Mom sensed it, too. Guardian lights raced up her arms and glowed at her throat.

The space around us seemed to shiver. For an instant, I saw the Beneath: the endless gray, the world twisted and rotting, the mass of Harrowers waiting just beyond the veil of the Circle. Then it was gone. But the Drought and Deluge was no longer empty. Susannah stood before us.

She wasn't alone.

Susannah had brought four Harrowers with her. They weren't bothering to attempt human form. Maybe they weren't strong enough; maybe they simply didn't care. I wasn't sure. One of the demons had positioned itself near the door, barring the exit. The other three were grouped in front of Susannah. They bared crimson teeth. Blank eyes stared.

Susannah herself appeared to have recovered from her wounds.

She looked fully human once more, though the dress she wore was as silver as the skin of the Harrowers ahead of her. She hung on to Daniel, one arm looped about his waist, the other gripping his hand.

Mickey stood beside them.

He still wore his old Twins sweatshirt, but now there was a small red stain crusting the collar. Blood had dried on his neck, where Susannah's talons had pierced his flesh. Two days' growth of beard covered his jaw. I got no sense of Knowing from him, none of the familiar memories or thoughts he held. Nothing but empty space. His face was devoid of expression. He didn't seem to see us.

Mom stood frozen. "Mickey," she said.

He didn't react.

Susannah smiled. "Keep your distance, Morning Star. I can reach him before you can reach me. He might find it difficult to speak without a throat."

Shane had dragged me backward, toward one of the booths. His grip was tight on my arm. I tried to pull myself loose, but he wouldn't release me. Turning to Mom and Susannah, he said, "If you're planning to battle to the death, might I suggest a change of venue?"

"Get my daughter out of here," Mom said.

Susannah's gaze flicked to Shane. "I have a better idea," she murmured. "Why don't you join me instead?"

"I'm obliged to you for the offer," he replied, "but I don't think we'd get on."

"You'd rather go against your brethren? That's a shame. Do you know what the punishment for traitors is?"

He let out a low chuckle. "Execution is such a human tradition. If you're so bent on ridding the world of its excess of humanity, why follow their customs? That shows a considerable lapse in judgment."

Her eyes narrowed. "You will be dealt with later."

"I tremble."

Three of the Harrowers began to slink toward Mom, their talons dragging across the floor, their scaled faces showing gruesome smiles. She didn't pay them any heed. Her gaze was locked on Susannah. "What is it you think to accomplish here, exactly? We both know you're not strong enough to defeat me."

Susannah leaned her head against Daniel. He didn't move. He gazed steadily forward, his eyes as vacant as Mickey's. "Maybe not," Susannah said. "But I don't appreciate traps being laid for me. It's impolite. I've decided to strike first, to face you on my own terms. You see, after our last encounter, it became clear to me that I couldn't take you on. So I'll have to take you out."

My mother snorted. The lights beneath her skin shone in dizzying colors. "And you really think four Harrowers are enough to do the job?"

"That's what your present is for," Susannah said. She turned her head, looking at Mickey. "He's very fond of you, you know. I had him tell me all about it."

Mom's voice came out in a growl. "I don't normally enjoy killing. I believe you'll be the exception."

Susannah didn't react to the words. She was still watching Mickey, a slow grin spreading over her face. "He's annoyingly strong-willed for someone so . . . human. Far more trouble than I anticipated, in fact. But I think it will be worth it. Let's test that." She turned toward Mom once more. Her flat blue eyes were dark with menace.

The demons launched themselves at Mom.

I cried out, once more trying to break free from Shane. He held me firmly, his other arm wrapping my waist, holding me struggling against him.

"I'm not planning to jump into the fray," he said, "and I would advise you not to, either."

"I can help her," I said.

"I hardly think she needs it."

He was right, of course. Mom was handling the demons with what appeared to be little effort. She'd dispatched one before Shane and I had spoken more than two sentences, snapping its neck and tossing it quickly aside. Its body slid across the floor, colliding with tables and knocking a chair to the ground.

But I couldn't just stand there, watching, hoping that Mom would be okay. My insides were knotted. The blood pounded in my ears. I stopped fighting Shane and went slack in his arms. At the same time, my hand caught his wrist. I pressed my fingertips against his skin. If I couldn't free myself with my own powers, I'd have to use his.

Before I could begin to amplify, his voice hissed in my ear. "Unless you want an all-expenses paid trip Beneath, I wouldn't try it."

I went still.

Ahead of us, Susannah had detached herself from Daniel. She was observing the fight with that same broad smile, her arms folded. Mom had killed the second Harrower and was concentrating on the third. This one wasn't quite as weak as the others; it was taking longer.

"I realized something, the last time we met," Susannah said. "You're a *legend. The* Morning Star. Feared by all. The Guardian no Harrower can hope to defeat. But then, we're an old-fashioned lot. Very hands-on. We like to touch death, to feel it within our grip—without the benefit of weapons. Satisfying, true, but it means we're not nearly as adept at killing as humans are. You've really made an art of it."

Foreboding surged through me. I looked at my mother, saw the flash of light at her wrists and throat, the grace of her movements as she dodged a swipe of talons. She met the Harrower's strike, and struck back. The demon fell beneath her blow, writhing and gasping, but the fourth Harrower had moved from the door and had joined the fight. Mom caught it by the throat. Its spine went red. It thrashed against her.

I looked at Susannah. Her expression was sly.

"Lucy," Mickey said. He took a halting step forward. Another.

Mom turned, throwing the Harrower aside.

"And you're correct, of course," Susannah was saying. "On my own, I'm not nearly strong enough to kill you. In order to survive, I'll have to adapt."

Mom wasn't paying attention to her. She was looking at Mickey. She stepped toward him. He seemed to be struggling against Susannah's control. Resisting.

"Lucy, you have to—" He stopped. Raised his hand toward her.

"And that's when it occurred to me," Susannah said.

In Mickey's hand was a gun.

"Why don't I just *shoot* her?"

He fired.

It happened quickly, taking no more than a few seconds. But those seconds would live forever in my memory, burned there, as though I had stared too long into the sun. I saw everything in precise, vivid detail: the empty tables and booths of the Drought and Deluge, the chairs that had clattered to the ground. The hardwood floor stained crimson where a Harrower had fallen, bleeding, before the Beneath claimed its corpse. Susannah in her silver dress, smiling, letting her teeth go red. My mother whipping about. The flow of light around her. The way her eyes widened. Mickey's blank, unseeing gaze. The kick of the gun in his hands.

The first shot caught my mother in the shoulder. The second grazed her arm.

It was the third shot that felled her.

A scream tore from my throat. With a burst of desperate

energy, I broke free from Shane. There was no thought within me. No plan. I was pure adrenaline. Nothing but instinct, raw and relentless. I ran to where my mother had fallen, distantly aware of Susannah's laughter, of Shane calling to me, urging me to stop. I didn't heed either of them. They meant nothing to me. I was conscious only of my mother, of her crumpled form, of the light under her skin that began to lessen, the shining colors that started to ebb. I dropped to the floor beside her, covering her wounds with my hands, as though I could hold the blood in.

I couldn't tell how badly she was injured. One of the bullets had struck her chest, and blood soaked the front of her shirt, but she was breathing, moving sluggishly, trying to rise. She was looking at me. Seeing me. Our eyes met.

Then her gaze shifted out of focus. A moan escaped her, a murmur through closed teeth. The sound of my name. Her eyelids moved rapidly. She reached for my face, but her arm dropped. She went slack.

My own chest felt tight, my own breaths labored, my vision blurry. Dimly, my mind registered the fact that the heat on my face was tears, that I was gulping in air. My hand groped for hers. She was unconscious, but the light at her wrists hadn't completely faded. It throbbed with her pulse, a faint, uneven glow.

I released her hand. Focus on helping her, I told myself. I thought back to my first-aid training. Her airway was clear. She was breathing on her own. But I needed to control the bleeding. I began to apply pressure to the wound in her chest, fighting back the sharp edge of panic that had clawed its way into me. I tried to steel myself against the little voice whispering that this was it, this was how we would end. I shook my head. No, I thought. *No.*

My mother was strong. I knew that. Stronger than any other Guardian. She healed quickly. She would survive this. She wouldn't die.

She couldn't.

From nearby, Susannah's voice intruded, finally breaking into my awareness.

"This is very moving," she said. "And so very familiar. Don't you agree, Daniel? Just like the day I killed your sister."

I glanced up, continuing to apply pressure. Susannah was standing a few feet away, her head tilted toward Daniel's shoulder. He didn't react to her words. She laughed again. Mickey stood immobile beside them, his gun still drawn.

Shane had vanished.

Stepping away from Daniel, Susannah switched her attention to Mickey. "You can stand down now, Detective. You've played your part and I'm done with you. Though it should be interesting to see just how long you can live with yourself."

He lowered the gun. A muscle in his cheek twitched. I had a flicker of Knowing from him—the barest flash, a fleeting impression of horror, the weight of regret. Then it was gone. His eyes remained vacant. Lifeless.

Susannah turned toward me. Her gaze settled on my mother. Her lips flattened. "He didn't kill her? How disappointing. I had hoped he'd take off her head. Even now, he resists. I suppose I needed a bit more time with him. But no matter. I can finish it."

I scrambled to my feet, positioning myself between Mom and Susannah.

Amusement spread across her face. "What do you think you can do? You have no more hidden power to unleash, little dark star. All that fire burned right out of you. And this time I'm prepared for your other parlor trick."

She meant my Amplification. I didn't care. I wasn't close enough to share her powers yet, but I held myself ready, watching, waiting. Blood filled my senses. The color, the scent. My hands were sticky with it. Red as a Harrower's teeth. Redder than Susannah's hair.

She took a step forward.

"Wait," Daniel said. His voice was sharp, loud in my ears.

"I must say, I'm growing very tired of the attention you pay this girl."

"She knows."

Susannah froze. At her sides, her hands curled into talons, then uncurled. "What does she know, Danny?"

"She knows who the Remnant is."

"Well, then. That's different." She retreated, moving to Daniel. She caught his arm and held it. Slowly, smiling, she let her fingers trail down his skin. Then she raised herself up on her tiptoes and pressed her lips to his cheek. Her voice was low, her words soft, but I heard them. "Get it from her."

Dread coiled inside me. I knew I should flee, but I couldn't, not with my mother lying injured at my feet, not with Susannah watching my movements, ready for any attempt at flight. Instead, I tried to will the information from me, to push it from my mind, from my memory. I emptied myself of thought. Made myself blank. As barren as the Beneath, I told myself. Nothing in me to Know. Nothing but open space.

Daniel strode toward me.

His hand slid into mine.

His skin was cold as a Harrower's.

He mouthed two words: *I'm sorry.*

And then my Knowing met his.

I tried to pull away, but I was locked where I stood. For a moment, we traded memories: I saw him as a young boy, standing on a beach. Valerie beside him, kneeling in the sand. Seashells gathered between them. I watched them turn to the sound of Drew's voice, viewed the smiles that lit their faces. And Daniel saw Gram. I felt him seeing her: one morning, just after dawn, when we had gone walking. *Let me tell you a secret,* Gram said.

It was secrets that Daniel wanted. And secrets that he found.

We moved past memory. Brooke's face formed in the thread of Knowing drawn between us. I tried to hide her, to disguise her, to rearrange her features in my mind, but it was useless. There was the straight, slender line of her nose. There were her gray eyes. There was the glossy shine of blond hair. There was her name.

And there was her home, as well. The tall white stucco house two miles from my own, where Gideon and I had gone trick-or-treating as children. The oak trees in her yard, the dark blue door.

Daniel released my hand. He returned to Susannah.

"Don't," I breathed.

But he didn't listen. I wasn't certain how he conveyed the information to her—if it was some aspect of his Knowing, transmitting as well as receiving, or if it was a part of the connection between them. He didn't speak, but he looked at her. Triumph gleamed in the flat pools of her eyes.

"You were right, after all. She was of use to us," Susannah said. She turned toward me, showing her teeth. *"Was."*

I sensed Drew the second before he appeared. I felt the desolation he carried with him, an ache that lingered in the space around us. Daniel must have perceived it, too: he flinched just slightly and edged backward from Susannah. She frowned at him.

Then Drew was there.

He had come looking for my mother, I guessed—but the moment he saw Susannah, his entire being changed. Rage suffused him. It was burning, blinding. It was stronger than the fury he'd felt in the parking ramp, deeper than the anguish that lived inside him and the grief that haunted him. He didn't exist outside it. He didn't see anything beyond Susannah. His eyes looked feverish, almost feral.

I couldn't close off my Knowing. The intensity of his anger

knocked me to my knees and made my stomach roil. I sucked in breaths, trying to steady myself. Drew didn't speak, but a harsh, guttural sound emerged from his throat. Colors surged in his hand, hot light radiating from him. He attacked.

Susannah was ready. She lashed out as he reached her, talons digging into his shoulder. Drew wrenched out of her grasp and fell back, struck her, teleported behind her, lights arcing toward her neck. She swung about. He teleported again.

With Susannah distracted, I returned my attention to my mother, trying not to feel the way Drew's anger scorched the air. The force of his rage made it difficult to concentrate. Mom hadn't regained consciousness. Blood welled beneath her from the wound the bullet had made in her shoulder. Her hair was dark and matted. I pressed my hands to her, and even as I struggled against the strength of Drew's hate, a new thought struck me.

Accelerated healing was part of a Guardian's powers; her bleeding had already slowed. Maybe my Amplification could speed up the process even further.

The connection was instant. Power raced through my veins, so intense I had to stop applying pressure to Mom's wound or risk crushing her. Power so extreme that it was almost frightening— except that with it came a feeling of warmth, of safety. The turmoil inside me began to lessen. I let the Amplification flow through us both, willing it to heal her. I couldn't be certain it was having any effect. Mom coughed once, but she didn't awaken.

In front of us, Drew continued to grapple with Susannah. I heard the rapid exchange of blows, the sound of chairs crashing to the floor and tables turning over, Drew's hoarse breathing. When I looked up, I saw that his shirt was slashed open across the stomach. I saw the three long gashes turning crimson. He fought on, frenzied and uncaring. Instead of tiring, he attacked faster, becoming a blur of motion, a flash of lights that blinked and reappeared as he teleported again, again.

But Susannah was more powerful. She deflected each of his strikes. Her claws sank into his shoulder, scraped his jaw, grazed his chest. Each time he teleported, she anticipated him, evaded him. And then, finally, she caught him. Her talons found purchase on his arms. She lifted him, whispered something I couldn't hear, and hurled him across the room. He hit the wall behind me. I twisted in time to see him smash against the bar. He tried to rise, and then lay still.

The sudden absence of sound was chilling. Susannah studied Drew's unmoving form. She seemed to have forgotten about me. She turned to Daniel, who stood waiting, his brown eyes once again empty of expression.

"Let's go, Danny," she said. She reached toward him.

Drew teleported between them.

He thrust Daniel away with one hand, sending the boy staggering backward. "Daniel, go! Run!" he shouted. Then, before Susannah had a chance to react, Drew caught her by the neck. He lifted her, squeezing as she struggled. Her talons tore into his arm, but he didn't seem to feel it. Her breath came out in choking rasps. I saw her eyes go white, her spine begin to redden.

"You wanted to teach me hate," Drew said. "Let me show you how well I learned it."

Still holding her, he used his free hand to disengage her talons. He wrenched one of her arms backward at an angle. Susannah kicked against him. There was the sound of a snap. Drew's left hand dug into the hollow beneath her collarbone, Guardian lights burning into her, scorching through her skin. He raked his fingers across her neck, ripping the flesh of her throat. Blood gushed forth, soaking both of them.

And then Susannah broke free. Her talons split Drew's arm open to the bone. His grip on her weakened, and she slashed at him wildly, catching him once more and throwing him from her. He struck the wall again. I heard a crack.

Susannah panted. One of her arms hung useless. She looked half-formed: part of her body human, the other part Harrower, silver scales beneath silver dress. She couldn't speak. The only noise she emitted was a strangled gurgling sound. This time, she didn't wait to see if Drew was dead. She didn't go after Daniel.

She went Beneath.

Nearby, Mickey fell to his knees. I heard Daniel moan. My mother's bleeding seemed to have stopped, and she was breathing easier. Trembling, I rose from her and ran to Drew.

He wasn't dead, but he was dying.

He lay on his side against the far wall, his hands curled against him. He was drenched with blood. I lowered myself to my knees, tentatively reaching for him. I pressed my fingers against his arm, intending to use my Amplification, in the desperate hope that it might actually aid him. But no connection formed. There was no sense of a bond, no slender thread drawn between us.

He opened his eyes and looked at me. For an instant, our gazes met. Knowing was loud within me, insistent, telling me what I was trying not to hear. Drew didn't want my help. This was exactly what he had craved, what had driven him. He was going to die for his charge. His haunting had ended.

His eyes lost their focus. And suddenly, all the rage inside him melted away, fading as though it had never been. Gone were his grief, his agony, the hatred that had eaten at him. There was only calm within. A feeling of ease and rest, of relief—and a strange, quiet sense of hope.

He was no longer seeing me, I realized.

He was seeing Valerie.

I Knew the moment he died; I didn't need to feel his pulse stop or hear his final breath. I felt him leave, felt the last flicker of his consciousness ebb. I wasn't certain there was an afterlife, but if there was, I hoped that he was with Val. Now he wouldn't have to carry her. Here on earth he would lie beside her, just as he'd wished.

Something inside me loosened its grip.

As I rose to my feet, I reached out with my Knowing, with my longing, with the unknown, unseen bond that I had struggled so hard against.

Leon, I thought.

I need you.

28

Leon didn't arrive immediately. I left Drew where he lay and walked back across the room, continuing my silent plea. I didn't know if it had worked, if the Guardian bond between Leon and me had been restored, but I still reached out—with thought and feeling, with hope and need, with my very being. And with the certain, terrible knowledge that Susannah had been wounded, but not defeated. She'd gone Beneath. She'd gone to find the Remnant. To find Brooke.

Leon. Please.

Around me, the Drought and Deluge looked very different than it had only a short time ago. There was blood on the floor and on the walls, dark smears from both humans and Harrowers; the coppery scent was thick in the air. Tables had been overturned. Chairs lay in splintered heaps. The sunlight spilling in through the front window seemed somehow wrong, incongruous. At one end of the club, Daniel had fallen to his hands and knees, racked with huge, gasping sobs. Mickey was on the floor beside my mother. His head was bowed. He was gripping one of her hands with both of his. She was still unconscious.

That was when Shane returned. I wasn't certain if he'd gone Beneath earlier, or merely into another room, but suddenly he was there, taking quick strides across the room until he reached me. "Undamaged, angel?" he asked.

"You *left*."

"And am the more living for it." He shrugged, surveying the room slowly before looking at me once more. "I believed my talents to be of better use elsewhere, and thought it might be prudent to call for an ambulance. And you may be glad to know that I've contacted the leader of your Kin. The Guardians have also been made aware of the somewhat tricky situation we find ourselves in."

"They won't be in time," I said. "Susannah knows who the Remnant is. She's on her way to her."

I closed my eyes. *Leon. Please.*

Then, just as it occurred to me to use my phone and try calling him in a more conventional manner, he appeared. He stood in front of me, his face creased with worry. There was flour on his shirt. His sleeves were rolled up. He caught my shoulders. "Audrey, are you—" He broke off, noticing the scene that surrounded us. "What's happened?"

Words tumbled out of me. Hurried, barely coherent. A torrent. I didn't think, didn't breathe, just spoke, hoping that he would understand me. I told him about the fight with Susannah, about Mom's being shot, about Drew. And I told him about the Remnant.

"We need to go," I said, gripping his arm. I held tight, feeling the tension in his muscles. "We need to go *now*. We have to stop Susannah."

Leon's expression hardened. "Where?"

I didn't answer.

He intended to go alone, to face Susannah by himself. I sensed that without any sort of Knowing. I could see it in the stubborn set of his jaw, in the way his eyes suddenly wouldn't meet mine. I heard it in his voice. He intended to go alone, and he would die. Just as Drew had.

"You can't do it on your own," I said. "She's too powerful. You have to take me with you."

"You said she was wounded."

"She was still strong enough to—" I couldn't say it. I shifted my gaze toward the wall where Drew lay motionless.

"I'm not bringing you into danger," Leon said.

"You *have* to. We don't have time to argue about this."

"What about Lucy?"

I tightened my hands into fists. Mom would be all right. I couldn't allow myself to believe otherwise. Susannah had to be stopped.

"Help will be here shortly," Shane said.

Leon's voice was soft, a pained whisper. "Audrey—I can't."

A strange sort of calm came over me. I removed his hands from my shoulders, held them. For a moment, I looked down at the space where our fingers met, at the scar that trailed down his wrist. Then I looked up at him. He still wouldn't meet my eyes. "Leon, I get it. I get it now, I promise—what you were saying to me. About what it's like being my Guardian. About Drew." I swallowed, took a steadying breath. Leon wasn't Drew. He wouldn't lose himself completely if I died. But he would never be the same, either. My death would wound him in a way that would never heal. "But we have to do this. *We* have to do this. Susannah has Harrowers gathered. Hundreds of them. They're waiting for her to open the Beneath. If you fight her, and you die, then I die, too. We all do."

Finally, his eyes met mine. They were dark, troubled. I sensed the conflict within him. Logic warring against instinct. His Guardian programming screaming at him to fight on his own, to keep me safe.

He said my name again, barely audible.

My gaze didn't waver. "Right now, the best way to protect me is to take me with you."

Something in him shifted, relented. He nodded almost imperceptibly. Then his face took on his serious instructor look, the expression he always wore during our training sessions. "Here's how we're going to do this," he said. "I'll do the fighting. You stay close to me. I may need to teleport us, so if I tell you to stop Amplifying, you stop. Immediately. We don't want to risk ending up a hundred miles away again. If the connection breaks—"

"It won't break. I won't let it."

"If it *does*, we'll pull back until you can reinitiate it. And if you get hurt, I'm taking you to safety and returning alone. No argument. Are you ready?"

"Yes," I said, feeling anything but. I glanced at my mother. Mickey was still on the floor beside her, clutching her hand. Nearby, Daniel had begun to struggle to his feet.

"I would suggest you hurry," Shane said.

I nodded, turning back to Leon. I told him Brooke's address. He looked at me a moment. Didn't speak, just looked. I felt his fingers lace through mine. I felt the warmth of his grip, the beat of his pulse. Then he pulled me against him. I closed my eyes.

The last thing I heard before we teleported was the far-off sound of sirens.

I had been in Brooke Oliver's house before on three separate occasions, not counting the Halloweens when Gideon and I had knocked on her door. The first two times I'd been there were for school projects during elementary school. The third time was last spring, when her mother had hosted a kickoff party for some of Whitman High's fund-raising efforts and Gideon had forced me to attend.

The house didn't appear to have changed much since then. It was tidy—at least, the living room, which we'd teleported into, was. The furniture was cream-colored and immaculate, and though the carpet was slightly worn from years of foot traffic, it was spotless. There were framed photos on the mantel: Brooke smiling in her softball uniform; Brooke on horseback; an older couple leaning against each other; some family picnic. The curtains were closed, pale light filtering through gauzy drapes. We were alone in the room.

"Maybe we beat her here," Leon said.

I shook my head. "No. I feel her."

She was close. I sensed that. It wasn't simply Knowing—it was a physical perception I had, along my nerves. The familiar chill.

That was when we heard the scream.

It was close, only in the next room, but Leon didn't bother to run. He tugged me against him and teleported. I blinked through nothingness into the hall of the house, where Brooke was cornered, sobbing, and a man lay on the floor, dead.

Susannah stood over the man. Her face was distorted. Her eyes were pure white, but it was flesh, not scales, that surrounded them. Though she had a human nose and lips, her teeth were sharp and red. The silver began at her neck, rippling and reptilian, part of it torn away where Drew had split her throat. Blood collected there, congealing. Her hands were in talons. At her feet, claws clicked the floor. She hissed when she saw us, still incapable of speech.

Without warning, she lunged at us.

Leon reacted. His arm rose, shining with colors. He parried her strike and thrust her backward. I touched his shoulder.

Through his shirt, I felt the warmth of his skin, the racing of his heart. The link formed: heat drumming in my veins, power surging through both of us, strength building. The connection solidified. I let it sing between us—a hum of energy, a force that I felt in my limbs and in my bones. I broke physical contact, but the connection remained. Leon stepped forward and I stepped with him. We weren't perfectly in sync, but we were close. I stayed near, maintaining the Amplification, and he attacked.

His first blow caught Susannah directly, knocking her to the ground. Leon dropped to strike again, but she rolled out of reach. She snarled and came up with talons slashing. She swiped at him, grazing his chest. A thin line of crimson welled up, spreading across the clean white of his shirt. He blocked her next hit and shoved her away from him. She staggered, her back meeting the wall with a loud thud. But it took her only a second to orient herself. Then she snarled once more and launched herself forward.

"Stop," Leon told me.

I stopped Amplifying.

He turned swiftly. His arm tightened around my waist, drawing me against him. He pulled us through the quick cold of blank space. We reappeared behind Susannah. I Amplified again, briefly touching his arm before withdrawing my hand. I focused on keeping the connection as Leon attacked. He struck out at her, aiming for the back of her neck. The burn of light from his wrist and fingertips was vibrant, dizzying.

The strike didn't connect. Susannah whirled. She caught Leon with her talons, shredding him down the length of his arm before lifting and hurling him from her. He crashed into the staircase, his head rocking backward. The link between us snapped.

Susannah turned toward me.

And now she spoke. Her words were soft and rasping, but I heard them. "No one here to plead for you now. I think it's time to accommodate your death wish."

She flew at me.

Leon teleported between us. His body took the blow. Just as he had the night he and Mom had fought Tigue. The scene came back to me: Leon sinking in my arms, his blood darkening the snow. History repeating itself, I thought, even as I tried to shut out the image. My stomach plummeted. Leon had his arms about me, pressing me against his chest. Susannah's claws sank into his back. He jerked, twisting us away from her, but she wrenched his right arm behind him. I heard it crack.

Leon didn't cry out, but he released a quivering breath. He spun, using his left arm to hurl Susannah away from us. Then he dragged me to him and teleported.

This time we didn't reappear behind her.

Darkness flashed before me, and then we were in the exact spot we'd been in a second before. Susannah had whirled about, anticipating an attack from the opposite direction. Leon's left arm shot out. He gripped her neck.

But he couldn't hold her one-handed. She broke free, stumbling away.

I pressed my fingers to Leon's wrist. Built the connection between us. Power rushed into me, a fire burning under my skin. I looked at Leon.

"Together," I said.

His eyes met mine. He nodded.

We attacked.

Before Susannah could recover, Leon caught her again. His left hand tightened on her throat. I positioned my own hand just beneath his and squeezed.

Susannah lost all semblance of human form. She was nothing but scales, nothing but claws and teeth and useless struggles. Her skin was cold. Once again, I couldn't block out my Knowing. I felt the Beneath in her, the endless rage she carried, the malice that seemed to seep into the air. The hunger. The hate.

She thrashed against us. Her claws caught my arm, scraping, but I barely felt it. I held on, not relaxing my grip. Her spine went red. I couldn't watch. I turned aside and closed my eyes.

I no longer saw Susannah, but I still sensed her. Her fury was an animal that writhed inside of her, trying to kick its way out. She couldn't speak, but I heard the hiss of the Beneath, the part of it she always carried with her. I caught the last, scattered images that ran through her thoughts.

A city gone gray. The night sky filled with bloodred stars. The

Beneath opening wide. Harrowers surging forth. The sound of sirens in the air.

The end of your Kin, she seemed to tell me.

Then it was gone. Everything went dark. No more Knowing. No more struggling. I heard only the anguish of Brooke's violent weeping—and, finally, the sound of a snapping neck.

I didn't want to open my eyes. Even after I withdrew my arm, even as I felt Leon easing me gently backward, I kept my eyelids firmly shut. There was a sick feeling in the pit of my stomach. A strange sort of twisting. I was covered in blood; I had seen my mother shot; I had sat beside Drew as he released his last slow breath—but now I couldn't bring myself to look at Susannah. I couldn't gaze into the presence of death.

Death that had come, in part, from my own hand.

Death that lingered for a moment in the air, until the Beneath stretched wide to gather Susannah's body back into it. The empty was always ravenous, I thought. It always collected its own.

"It's over, Audrey," Leon said, his voice quiet in my ear. He touched my arm. "It's okay. She's gone."

Finally, I looked. The floor was bare before us, save for a thin trickle of blood that marred the carpet. Nothing else of Susannah remained. There was no sense of her fury left behind, no trace of her hate. She had ended.

Because Leon and I had ended her.

It wasn't guilt that coiled inside of me. Not exactly. Stopping Susannah had been necessary. But necessity had nothing to do with what I felt. Without realizing it, without thought or consideration or even the slightest hesitation, I had crossed the border into some unknown land, and now I could never cross back. It didn't feel *wrong*, precisely, but it felt different. I had killed. And, for the first time, I truly understood that that was what being a Guardian meant.

Deliberately, I let out a breath. I felt my bunched muscles begin to relax. I had still been holding the Amplification, clinging fiercely to the connection, but now I let that fade as well. The strength ebbed out of me. The heat abated. I uncurled the fist I hadn't noticed I'd clenched.

I turned toward Leon, surveying him. He needed to get to a hospital. There were thick gashes on his neck and chest, puncture wounds in his back. Not only was his right arm bleeding from three cuts, but it was also likely broken. His face was very pale against his dark hair.

But he was alive. We both were. And for the smallest second, I felt a rush of heady relief pour through me. We had survived. We were whole. Susannah was defeated. Valerie's vision hadn't come to pass. The Kin wouldn't end.

Then brutal reality crashed back in. Beyond us, I saw the

wrecked, lifeless body of the man I assumed must have been Brooke's father. He lay near the front door, his blond hair stained crimson. My stomach turned again. Nearby, Brooke was still sobbing.

I looked at her wordlessly. She was hunkered down in the far corner of the hall, where she'd been trapped by Susannah when Leon and I first entered the house. Her legs were drawn up against her. She was shaking uncontrollably. Her eyes kept flitting between us and her father's ruined form.

It didn't seem to register to her that we weren't a threat. I didn't blame her. She had just seen her father killed in front of her. She had no experience with demons, with the Kin, with any of this. Susannah must have appeared like a creature spawned from nightmares, from hell—a part of some fevered delirium she couldn't seem to wake up from. Nothing would be the same again. Her security was shattered. And Leon and I were trespassers in her home, blood-soaked and dangerous.

"We won't hurt you," Leon said softly, keeping his distance. "You're safe now."

"Brooke, I'm Audrey Whitticomb. We go to school together. Do you know who I am?"

She nodded jerkily. Her sobs had begun to taper off—she was probably too exhausted or too frightened to continue, I guessed— but it took a moment before she was able to speak.

"Is my dad—" The words stuttered painfully out of her and then stopped.

"I'm so sorry," I said, because I couldn't think of anything else.

She nodded again. Her breath came out in ragged gasps. Eventually, she said, "That—thing—went after me. He tried to stop her. You killed her?"

"She's dead."

"What was she? What are you?"

I took a few slow steps across the room, feeling as though I were moving through thick water. My arm was beginning to sting where Susannah's claws had scraped my flesh. My mother's blood had dried on my hands. My lungs felt heavy. But, strangely, I thought of Gram. I thought of her voice in my ear, soothing me, telling me about the infinite pattern that wasn't fate, but reaction. One moment defining the next. This moment would define Brooke.

I looked at her, her blond hair tucked behind her ears, her face swollen, her eyes rimmed with red. I crouched at her side, careful not to touch her. "We're your Kin," I said. "We're here to help."

Mr. Alvarez and two other Guardians arrived fifteen minutes later. From them, I learned my mother's condition was stable. She was being treated at Hennepin County Medical Center. They didn't know any details beyond that. Leon had been in contact with Esther, who had instructed us to remain where we were and do what we could to assist Brooke. That ended up being very little. Though she had calmed down when I spoke with her, she'd since progressed into a state of seeming numbness. She'd permitted me to help her to her feet and had moved mechanically out of the hall, away from her father's body, but she didn't speak again. She sat on the clean, cream-colored love seat, nodding whenever I spoke to her, her fingernails digging into her arms. She seemed to trust Mr. Alvarez, at least. Once he appeared, she managed to utter a few short sentences and agreed to let him take her from the house. To somewhere safe, he said. To the elders, I assumed.

One of the other Guardians informed me that the Kin had located Brooke's mother, who had been at work when the attack occurred. He said they were bringing her in—whatever that meant. When I asked about Brooke's father, all I received was a grim pronouncement that he would be seen to. The Kin had means of handling these situations, I knew, but that didn't bring any comfort. It didn't make Brooke's father less dead. More funerals, I thought. More white flowers and black shoes.

After Mr. Alvarez departed with Brooke, Leon teleported me to St. Paul. I'd wanted us to leave for the hospital immediately, but he insisted I couldn't go looking as I did. Unfortunately, he had a point. My hands and clothing were stained with blood, and there were already going to be too many questions. But I also didn't want Leon to wait to receive medical care.

I told him I'd have Esther drive me later—which I did, as soon as I'd showered and changed my clothes. My own cuts were minor. I bandaged them and hid them under a sweatshirt.

When I arrived at HCMC, Mom was in surgery to have the bullet that had lodged in her chest removed. I discovered later that she was being regarded as something of a medical miracle. The tissue surrounding her wounds had already begun to regenerate and heal on its own. I had no idea how the Kin were going to explain *that* one away.

Leon was also being treated. The majority of his cuts had required stitches, his right arm was definitely broken, and he had two cracked ribs. Since both he and Mom were being tended to, I spent most of the evening curled up in the waiting room, doing my best not to worry. I listened to the news programs being broadcast over the television and played rummy with an old man whose wife was in surgery. Esther had duties to attend to and couldn't remain with me, but around nightfall, Elspeth showed up. She slipped into the chair beside me and squeezed my hand.

It was Elspeth who told me what had occurred after Leon and I left the Drought and Deluge. The Guardians had arrived as my mother was being loaded into an ambulance, she said. Shane had given them an update on the situation, and they'd begun to follow procedures set in place in the event of a Harrowing. I didn't ask what those procedures were. I was simply grateful they'd proved unnecessary.

Mickey and Daniel were being looked after. Physically, they were both fine; psychologically was another matter. Susannah's control over them had ended even before her death, when she'd fled Beneath, but a few residual effects remained. Though Mickey was expected to recover quickly, there was some question about Daniel's mental state. He'd been living under Susannah's influence for the past two months, and much of that time had been spent Beneath. Drew's death had come as another blow to him. The Kin were doing what they could to help, but with a certain level of wariness. Iris's betrayal was recent in everyone's memory. Daniel would need to be watched.

Leon's injuries weren't severe enough for him to be admitted to the hospital overnight. He joined me in the waiting room once his treatment was finished, giving me a small smile. He looked tired. His face had lost most of its color, and his eyes were a little watery, but he assured me he felt fine. Then he leaned his head back against his chair and promptly fell asleep.

A few hours later, we were finally allowed in to see Mom. She was groggy and disoriented, but still managed to look annoyed at being confined to a hospital bed. I started crying in relief the moment I saw her, so it was Leon who had to inform her, as discreetly as possible, that the situation with Susannah was over. She closed her eyes briefly and let out a breath.

"You killed her?" she whispered.

Leon glanced at me. "We both did."

Mom nodded. Her gaze met mine, but she didn't speak.

Leon and I stayed with Esther in St. Paul while Mom was in the hospital. Though I wasn't entirely pleased with the arrangement, I also wasn't ready to return home just yet. Even with Susannah dead, the memory of her lingered. I could shut my eyes and picture the scene in the living room perfectly: how she had appeared before Mickey and me, the malevolence in her eyes, her talons flashing. The house didn't feel quite safe. I wondered if it ever would again.

In the meantime, Esther had decided it was time to resume my Kin lessons—including formal training in Amplification—and she ignored all of my objections and protestations on the subject. I was a St. Croix by blood, she reminded me; more than ever, the family was a part of me, of my heritage. My powers were proof of that. I'd always assumed my Knowing came from Gram, but Esther was right: I had the exact abilities my father had. Except, of course, that he had been a Guardian and I wasn't. After the fight with Susannah, I was no longer certain I wanted to be.

It wasn't until a few days later, when Mom was released from the hospital and we returned home, that I allowed myself to think about Gideon. At school, I'd been doing my best to act normal around him, but he could tell that something was wrong. I'd explained it away by saying I was concerned about my mother. I didn't know how else to answer. There was no truth I could tell him. No way to alter a past he had no memory of, a history he had no control over.

A part of me knew that he was dangerous. That he was deadly. That the darkness inside of him was merely biding its time, that it was patient and careful and watching, always watching. But when I looked at him, I didn't see Verrick. I didn't see hatred or vengeance or venom. There was no malice in him. The cold of Beneath didn't lurk in his eyes. I saw only Gideon: familiar, friendly Gideon, with that sense of warmth and openness he always carried. Human.

I knew the Kin wouldn't see him that way if they learned the truth. They would see a Harrower. And they would kill him.

Eventually, I made a decision.

The night after I returned to my house, I took out my Nav cards—both decks. I looked at their designs, at the triple knot on their backs, at the blank card that had held Verrick's face within it. Then I put the decks away. For the first time since Gram had given them to me, I didn't place my cards in my bag or my desk or one of my bedroom shelves. I went into my closet and pulled out the shoebox where I kept old postcards and collections of notes Tink had written me. I set the cards inside and shut the lid.

Gram had been right. There were places I didn't want to look.

Then I went to Gideon's.

I walked slowly, taking the familiar route between our homes, passing the rows of overgrown hedges, the little park wedged between two brick buildings. Above me, the sky was beginning to darken, but the air was warm; spring had finally gained a foothold. The trees were all beginning to bud, turning green.

Gideon met me at the door. He was wearing an old T-shirt with a hole in the collar that he'd gotten one year at summer camp and could not be prevailed upon to throw away. He smiled when he saw me.

"Sorry I've been so weird the past few days," I said. "I've just been really distracted."

"You're weird most days. But I forgive you."

We went downstairs, ignoring his sisters' attempts to gain our attention and his grandmother's talking loudly about something she'd seen on TV. His father called down the steps after us. "Staying for dinner? It's spaghetti!"

"Warning," Gideon whispered. "He's been letting Isobel help cook."

Isobel was Gideon's youngest sister, and her claim to family fame was that she had a strange fondness for eating mustard with a spoon—but since I didn't think there was much a seven-year-old could do to make or break spaghetti, I answered, "Love to!" I followed Gideon into his room.

He scooped up the cat that was weaving between his feet, sat in his computer chair, and gazed at me. I perched on the edge of his bed, taking a deep breath. Gideon tilted his head.

"You're looking very serious," he said.

I hesitated. For just an instant, I saw it again—the faint glow about him, that shining aura I now knew had come from the Astral Circle's stolen light. Then it was gone, and he was only Gideon, a boy in a ragged T-shirt with a dimple in his cheek.

Dear to you, is he? Susannah had taunted the night we'd met her.

It was more than that. Gideon and I were bound to each other. We always had been. But not in the way Verrick had believed.

"Are you still getting that feeling?" I asked. "That something bad is going to happen?"

"Not really," he said, but he glanced away, and I wasn't certain he was telling the truth.

I didn't question him. I was about to lie to him, too.

"You were right," I began. "There *was* something bad that was going to happen. To the Kin. The Harrower from the parking ramp was planning it, but we stopped it. She's dead. So you don't need to worry anymore. Nothing bad is going to happen, I swear."

Gideon was frowning. "I've been sensing something about the Kin."

"That's right," I said. "I need to tell you something. About the reading I did for you."

I heard his intake of breath. I could almost feel the speeding of his heart. Some part of him knew, I guessed. Some part of him that had almost awoken three months ago atop Harlow Tower and now filtered into his dreams.

But that wasn't who he was. It wasn't who he wanted to be.

Part of him knew. The rest of him never would. I promised myself that.

I reached forward and caught his hand.

"You're Kin," I whispered. "You're Kin, like me."

30

In the week that followed, life began to settle back into routine and gain some level of normalcy. The threat had passed, and the Guardians were able to relax their patrols—to an extent. Mr. Alvarez wanted to maintain vigilance for the time being, in case any of the Harrowers that Susannah had gathered were able to break through the Circle. Shane stated that the majority of the demons had scattered, but Mr. Alvarez didn't want to take any chances. There had already been too much death, he said. The other Guardians agreed.

Brooke and her mother had been brought in to speak with Esther and the Kin elders. I didn't know how much had been explained to them—about demons, about the Kin—but I knew that Brooke had agreed to have her powers sealed. Since her abilities hadn't yet manifested, or at least not been triggered, her blood was tested to confirm that she was the Remnant. Mom didn't tell me when the sealing would take place, and I didn't ask. But she did tell me that the dormancy of Brooke's abilities, along with the fact that her connection to the Kin was so remote, had led the elders to believe the sealing wouldn't have a severe effect upon her. I thought of my father's expressionless face and the puzzlement I'd felt within him. His heart slept; I hoped that the elders were right, and Brooke's heart wouldn't.

She and her mother were convinced to relocate as an added precaution. I didn't see her again. I was uncertain what her disappearance would mean for Gideon, but I hoped that the absence of the Remnant might mean that the part of him that was Verrick would finally let go.

Drew's body had been sent back to San Diego for burial, so that he could rest beside Val. I imagined twin headstones on a quiet green hill, the far-off roll of the sea. I knew it was what Drew had wanted. I'd understood that as I sat beside him, as I'd watched his eyes lose their focus and felt his rage finally fade—but when I thought of him, sadness welled up within me. A weight settled in my heart and lungs, like a stone I couldn't seem to dislodge. I couldn't stop remembering the way he had sat in the darkness of our kitchen, his head in his hands. The desolate, bewildered look in his eyes. He'd wanted to die. I just wished he could have found some way to live.

It was Daniel who showed me that, in some sense, Drew *had*.

"He saved me," Daniel said, when he came looking for me about a week after Susannah was killed. We were seated in the living room, where the broken photo frame had been replaced and the pale afternoon light streamed in. His hands clenched and unclenched reflexively, reminding me of Drew. "He died in order to help me. I know he did."

I thought of the fight in the Drought and Deluge. Aside from the vivid, indelible memory of my mother's being shot—those few seconds that would stay with me, so that I would always hear the gun, always see her fall—my recollections of the night were somewhat scattered. Slivers of sound and image, fragments that didn't quite align. But Daniel was right, I realized. Drew had prevented Susannah from taking him with her. He'd teleported between them and pushed Daniel aside, to safety, shouting for him to run. And if Drew hadn't wounded Susannah, Leon and I would never have been able to defeat her. I held on to that.

Daniel himself was staying in the Twin Cities for the time being. He didn't want to go back to San Diego yet. He wasn't ready, he said. An aunt, his only living relative, was flying in to stay with him. And to watch over him, since the Kin elders weren't yet certain he could be trusted.

He was still recovering from his time with Susannah. Some aspect of the Beneath remained inside of him, inked deeper than the tattoo he was planning to have removed. The emptiness lingered in his thoughts and chased through his dreams. I saw it in his eyes, in his movements, in the Knowing that was thick between us. It wasn't something he wanted to talk about—at least not to me—but he told me there was a matter we needed to discuss.

"I need to thank you," he said. "And I need to apologize. I'm sorry—I can't tell you how sorry I am. But . . . there's a reason I was trying to contact you. Why I was looking for you when I escaped from Susannah that night. It's about Val. About what she saw."

I frowned. "But the Remnant's powers are being sealed. And Val's vision never happened."

He shook his head. "You don't understand. Val figured it out. The night she died—before Susannah killed her—Val figured out what her vision meant. At least, she thought she did. She never had the chance to tell anyone but me." He looked at me with those rich brown eyes that still carried a trace of the Beneath and probably always would. "Val didn't see *the* future. She saw two of them. Two futures. One leads to the death of the Kin. She wasn't certain where the other led. But she did see the girl who would determine it. She saw her face. The Remnant isn't the one who decides it. You are."

I tried to speak but couldn't.

Daniel's voice was low, almost a whisper. "I kept it from Susannah. That was as far as I was able to resist. I told her everything else—I helped her find the Guardians—but I never told her this. I never told her about you."

"Val was positive about this?"

"No . . . not entirely. She wanted to find out more. But she didn't get the chance." He lowered his eyes. "And she didn't know when it would happen. It could be soon, or never. Or it could've already happened. You killed Susannah. Maybe that was what Val saw."

He apologized for not being able to tell me more. He hadn't shared his sister's Seeing ability, he said. He only knew what she'd been able to tell him. But even under Susannah's control, he had known I was the one from Val's vision. He'd felt it important that I live.

After he left, I puzzled over his revelations. I told myself that the future wasn't fixed, and that there was no way to know if Val had correctly interpreted her vision. And even if she had, that didn't make it a certainty; what she'd Seen might never come to pass. Or maybe it had already occurred, as Daniel suggested. Susannah was defeated, and Brooke's powers were being sealed. The Beneath would not be opened. The Harrowing had been prevented. Perhaps that was all the second vision had been.

I didn't have much opportunity to dwell on the subject. Later that afternoon, Tink showed up at my house, invited herself inside, and planted herself on my bed.

"Am I in for another thrilling installment of the Chronicles of Tink and Greg?" I asked, seating myself in my computer chair and turning to face her.

"I'm considering giving him another chance. Lars is sweet, but he's a little boring. But that is not actually the reason I'm gracing you with my presence." She flopped backward onto the bed and lay there a moment, staring up at the ceiling. Then she let out a long breath. "I thought I should tell you. I've agreed to continue Guardian training."

"Okay. Now are you going to tell me what you've done with the real Tink?"

She propped herself up on her elbows. "What? I changed my mind."

"Just like that?"

"Mr. Alvarez talked to me," she said, shrugging.

I snorted. "I can guess how *that* went."

But apparently he'd actually managed to get her to listen. Instead of threatening to sic the elders on her again, he'd told her about the night her father had been killed. Howard Brewster hadn't been to blame, he'd said.

"He said my dad died trying to help the Guardians. He said my dad saved his life. That he was a hero," Tink said. She looked skeptical.

"You don't believe him?"

"I don't know. But it was nice of him to say."

He'd also apologized for the way the Kin had treated her—and told her it would be different now.

"Not that I plan to have much to do with the rest of the Kin," she said. "But he made a good point. He said the best way for me to defend myself was to know how to use my powers." She paused, wrinkling her nose. "That sounds so weird. My *powers*."

"You'll get used to it."

"Anyway, I agreed to training. But that's it. I'm still not going on patrols, or whatever else it is that Guardians do."

I doubted that Mr. Alvarez would let the matter rest there very long, but decided not to mention it. "Are you still going to work with Camille?"

"For now. He promised not to have her nag me. Did you know he actually tried to use her as Harrower bait? If I were her, I would dump him."

I laughed, but I sensed that Tink was more worried than she was letting on. "Are you sure this is what you want to do?"

She hesitated. "I'm still scared. But I'm ... less scared. And I didn't promise to do this training thing indefinitely. I'm just giving it a shot." Which meant she was still on track for her tragic love affair and her lottery win.

"I'll help you," I said. "However I can."

She smiled. "I know you will."

That night, Mom decided to talk to me about Susannah.

She'd already been told the details. She knew what had occurred in the Drought and Deluge, and that Leon and I had gone to help Brooke. She was aware that we had killed Susannah together. What she *didn't* know, she said, was how I felt about it.

I bit my lip. We were seated on the front steps, watching the sky darken and the first stars appear through the veil of city lights. The air smelled of rain. Mom was still bandaged, and not yet up to her full strength, but she already looked much better than she had in the last days before Susannah's defeat. She watched me, waiting for my answer.

"I'm...adjusting," I said.

She reached toward me and tucked a stray lock of hair behind my ear. "It wasn't what I wanted for you."

"I know."

"But I'm proud of you."

My superhero mother, proud of me for killing a Harrower. Somehow, that made me laugh. "Does this mean I get a merit badge?"

She rolled her eyes—then revealed her other reason for wanting to talk with me: she needed backup again.

"We're having dinner with the Wyles this Saturday," she informed me.

I gave her a dubious look. "Are you sure you wouldn't rather meet Mickey's parents alone?" The fact that she was having dinner with them at all came as a surprise to me: the last I'd heard of the situation, Mickey had been determinedly avoiding her. He was racked with guilt, and since there really wasn't a gift that said *Sorry I got mind-controlled and shot you*, I wasn't certain how he was going to get past it.

But apparently the way to Mom's heart was through a bullet, because she was now the one pursuing him.

"Are you kidding?" she said. "I want to make a good impression. And you, kiddo, are the best chance I have."

I couldn't exactly say no after that, so I narrowed my eyes at her. "They'd better have really good food."

She squeezed my hand. "Thanks."

"Does this mean Mickey's stopped blaming himself for what happened?"

Mom sighed. "I'm still working on that one. It's going to take some time."

Not to mention that Mickey now had membership in the very exclusive club of humans who had gone Beneath and lived to tell about it, I thought. He had a lot to deal with. "But I guess you guys are official now," I said.

"Official what?"

"Dating. Seeing each other. Whatever."

She looked at me a moment before answering. "Maybe. Does that bother you?"

"Of course not!" I said. "I like Mickey. And I bet Gram would've liked him."

She laughed, putting her arm around my shoulders. "I think so, too."

I was glad Mom and Mickey seemed to be working things out, but I had my own relationship to worry about. Though the Guardian bond between Leon and me had been restored—and Mom hadn't renewed her threat to kick him out of the house—we hadn't really discussed where things stood between us. Then, Friday evening, he took me to his lake again.

"Are you sure we want to be here?" I asked, looking at the empty park and remembering the night Susannah had appeared. Now, everything was hushed and still. The snow had melted, and ice no longer hung from the grills. The lake had thawed; its surface was calm and gray beneath the overcast sky. The area felt peaceful, but I was hesitant. I turned toward Leon.

He shrugged. "I think we're safe."

"It's going to rain," I pointed out.

"Are you going to melt?"

I narrowed my eyes. "You only bring me out here to annoy me, admit it."

Now he grinned.

"How did you know where I was, anyway?" I asked. He'd pretty much abducted me from Esther's, where I'd been finishing up an Amplification lesson.

"I always know where you are. At least, as long as the bond is working."

"That's . . . a little weird."

He looked sheepish. "I can't help it. And that's actually what I wanted to talk to you about."

"The fact that I'm a fixed point on your teleportation radar?"

"The fact that we can't change it."

Because he was my Guardian. And always would be.

Those bonds are messy, Mom had said. Complicated. I understood now what she'd meant by that. Leon's feelings might not have stemmed from his need to protect me—but they were tied to it. He was bound to me forever, as Drew had been bound to Val.

I took a deep breath. "I don't like you getting hurt for me. I won't ever like it," I said. "I can't promise I'll ever accept it. And I'm not going to allow you to die for me just because some cosmic calling says you should. But I meant what I said when we went to fight Susannah. I do understand. And I'll let you protect me. As long as you let me protect you."

He frowned. "The Guardian bond doesn't really work that way."

"This time it does."

Leon didn't answer. He looked at me a long moment, long enough that I began to feel uneasy and lowered my gaze, expecting another argument. But instead of speaking, he placed a hand beneath my chin, tipped my face up, and kissed me.

It was a slow kiss, soft at first, just the barest touching of lips. Then I eased toward him. His arms slid around me, drawing me tightly against him, and he kissed me harder. A light rain had started. I ran my hands through his damp hair, making it stick up haphazardly, then trailed my fingers down his spine.

Abruptly, he broke away, releasing me and taking a step backward. I gazed at him questioningly.

His serious expression had returned. "This won't be easy."

He meant our relationship, I supposed. "Our favorite sport is arguing," I said. "Was it ever going to be easy?"

Now he grinned again. "*Your* favorite sport, maybe." I moved to hit him, but he caught my arm and held it. "What I meant to say is—we're going to figure it out. This thing between us."

A giddy thrill shot through me. It was difficult not to match his grin. But all I said was, "Okay, but we're seriously going to have to progress past *thing* here. And we still need to have a real first date."

"We can go tomorrow."

I grimaced, remembering my promise to have dinner with the Wyles. "Um, I'm kind of busy tomorrow."

He gave me a stern look. "You're making this somewhat challenging."

"You could try kissing me again," I suggested.

"I was getting there."

"Get there faster."

He picked me up, then set me on one of the picnic tables. I sat facing him, only the smallest sliver of space between us. For a moment, neither of us spoke. I looked up at him. The rain had made little spikes of his lashes. His dark hair was wet, beginning to curl at the ends. He was fighting another smile. I leaned forward to loop my arms around his neck.

"And you'd better not be planning to laugh again," I said.

Before he could respond, I lifted my mouth to his.

Acknowledgments

Let me be honest here: this book wasn't easy! If you'll forgive a bit of writerly hyperbole, there were times when I wasn't certain I was going to survive it. The fact that *Burn Bright* didn't end with me setting my laptop afire and hurling it out a window—but instead turned into something I truly love and had fun with—is thanks to the support of a number of people. In particular: my terrific agent, Caitlin Blasdell, and the fantastic team at Hyperion, especially Christian Trimmer, Abby Ranger, and Laura Schreiber.

Thanks also to the usual suspects: Sarah Bauer, Leah Raeder, Brinson Thieme, and Laura Castine, for their constant encouragement . . . and their willingness to put up with a barrage of frantic e-mails about "emotional transitions." (I wish I were making that up.) And not even complaining about it. To my face, anyway.

And of course, my parents (you count here, too, Linda and Bob!), who are endlessly supportive. Even though my mother has the strangest ideas about fancasting. (And no, I'm *not* sharing.)